pauker.

W0376971

Abschluss2023

Realschule Bayern

Name:

Schule:

Klasse:

hutt lernhilfen
hutt.lernhilfen ist eine Marke der
Bergmoser + Höller Verlag AG
Karl-Friedrich-Straße 76
52072 Aachen

T 0241 93888123
F 0241 93888188
kontakt@buhv.de

Umsatzsteuer-Id.Nr.: DE 123600266
Verkehrsnummer: 10508
Handelsregister Aachen HRB 8580

Vorstand:
Andreas Bergmoser
Peter Tiarks

Aufsichtsratsvorsitz:
Holger Knapp

Autorinnen/Autoren:
Peter Brysch, Christa Duppel, Joachim Krick, Annika Leal Mayer

Lektorat:
Peter Brysch, Annika Leal Mayer

Gestaltung: Hanne Hutt

Umschlag:
Konzeption + Gestaltung
Hanne Hutt
Fotografie:
Anna Leippe

Audioproduktion:
Paul Harriman, Oliver Utzt, dropD GmbH, Waiblingen
Sprecher/-innen: Fraser Cameron, Paul Harriman, Mark Hay,
Lucy Hickey, Josee Hurlock, Harry Neusser, Ann Noisternig,
Sara Pohl

Ausgabe 2022/2023

ISBN: 978-3-88997-867-7

klimaneutral Printprodukt
natureOffice.com | DE-077-178633

KEINE MACHT DEN DROGEN

Über diese Lernhilfe

Liebe Schülerin, lieber Schüler,

Englischkenntnisse werden heute nahezu überall vorausgesetzt. Deshalb ist es wichtig, sich eine fundierte Basis zu verschaffen und dazu gehört auch ein guter Abschluss. Unsere Lernhilfe unterstützt Sie, dieses Ziel optimal vorbereitet zu erreichen. Mit dem Trainingsteil können Sie noch vorhandene Lücken schließen und dann mithilfe der Originalprüfungen der Jahre 2018 bis 2022 gezielt die Inhalte der Prüfung trainieren. Die Lösungen sind in diesem Band inklusive, jedoch herausnehmbar.

Farbleitsystem Training | Prüfung

Training
- Alle wichtigen Themenbereiche der Klasse 10
- Erklärungen
- Typische Aufgabenstellungen mit ausführlichen Musterlösungen
- Übungsaufgaben zu jedem Themenbereich
- Verschiedene Schwierigkeitsgrade

Prüfungen
- Originalprüfungen der letzten fünf Jahre
- Original-Punkteverteilung

Downloads
- Alle LCT-Texte als Audiotracks zum Download und per QR-Code abrufbar
- Zahlreiche zusätzliche Übungsaufgaben zu Grammatik und Wortschatz inklusive Lösungen
- Übungsaufgaben zum Speaking Test

Lösungen
Alle Lösungen finden Sie im herausnehmbaren Lösungsteil.

Das Themenverzeichnis
Dieses Verzeichnis ab Seite 7 dient zum schnellen Auffinden bestimmter Englischinhalte (Grammatik, Vokabeln etc.). Zudem sind dort alle Audiotracks zu den LCT-Texten zusammengestellt.

Prüfungsinfos und nützliche Tipps
Ab Seite 9 sind alle wichtigen Prüfungsinfos für Sie zusammengestellt. Sie finden hier außerdem den gültigen Notenschlüssel.

- Sollten sich nach Drucklegung noch Änderungen ergeben, finden Sie aktuelle Informationen unter www.pauker.de/info-aktuell

Inhaltsverzeichnis

Allgemein

Themenverzeichnis 7
QR-Codes 8
Prüfungsinfos 9

Training

A. Listening Test 11

B. Written Test

Part I: Reading 15
Part II: Use of English 22
Part III: Guided Writing 30
LCT-Texte 34

Prüfungen

Prüfung 2018 37
Prüfung 2019 48
Prüfung 2020 60
Prüfung 2021 72
Prüfung 2022 82
LCT-Texte 93

Extra

„Schule – und dann?" A1

Themenverzeichnis

Mit dem Themenverzeichnis lassen sich einzelne Aufgabentypen schnell und einfach finden. Der Buchstabe P bezeichnet den jeweiligen Part, der durch römische und arabische Zahlen bzw. durch A oder B weiter unterteilt wird.

Vocabulary

Vocabulary									
2018		2019		2020		2021		2022	
Seite	Nr.	Seite	Nr.	Seite	Nr.	Seite	Nr.	Seite	Nr.
46	PII/4	58	PII/4	69	PII/4	80	PII/4	90	PII/4

Explanations/Definitions									
2018		2019		2020		2021		2022	
Seite	Nr.	Seite	Nr.	Seite	Nr.	Seite	Nr.	Seite	Nr.
45	PII/2	57	PII/2	68	PII/2	79	PII/2	89	PII/2

Synonyms									
2018		2019		2020		2021		2022	
Seite	Nr.	Seite	Nr.	Seite	Nr.	Seite	Nr.	Seite	Nr.
45	PII/1	56	PII/1	68	PII/1	79	PII/1	89	PII/1

Word family									
2018		2019		2020		2021		2022	
Seite	Nr.	Seite	Nr.	Seite	Nr.	Seite	Nr.	Seite	Nr.
45	PII/3	57	PII/3	69	PII/3	79	PII/3	90	PII/3

Grammar

Verb forms / Tenses									
2018		2019		2020		2021		2022	
Seite	Nr.	Seite	Nr.	Seite	Nr.	Seite	Nr.	Seite	Nr.
46	PII/5	58	PII/5	70	PII/5	80	PII/5	91	PII/5

Reading

Find answers in the text									
2018		2019		2020		2021		2022	
Seite	Nr.	Seite	Nr.	Seite	Nr.	Seite	Nr.	Seite	Nr.
42	PI/1	54	PI/2	65	PI/1	76	PI/1	86	PI/1

Match information									
2018		2019		2020		2021		2022	
Seite	Nr.	Seite	Nr.	Seite	Nr.	Seite	Nr.	Seite	Nr.
42	PI/2	53	PI/1	65	PI/2	76	PI/2	86	PI/2
43	PI/3	54	PI/3	66	PI/3	77	PI/3	87	PI/3

Mediation									
2018		2019		2020		2021		2022	
Seite	Nr.	Seite	Nr.	Seite	Nr.	Seite	Nr.	Seite	Nr.
44	PI/4	55	PI/4	67	PI/4	78	PI/4	88	PI/4

Writing

Writing an e-mail/report/letter etc.									
2018		2019		2020		2021		2022	
Seite	Nr.	Seite	Nr.	Seite	Nr.	Seite	Nr.	Seite	Nr.
47	PIII/A	59	PIII/A	70	PIII//A	81	PIII/A	91	PIII/A
47	PIII/B	59	PIII/B	71	PIII/B	81	PIII/B	92	PIII/B

Listening Comprehension

Titel	Jahrgang	Aufgaben	QR-Code	Text
Task 1: Reasons for Visiting Hawaii	2018	Seite 37		Seite 93
Task 2: At Hawaii Volcanoes National Park	2018	Seite 37		Seite 93
Task 3: Kamakawiwo'ole Israel	2018	Seite 38		Seite 94
Task 4: Corals of Hawaii	2018	Seite 39		Seite 94
Task 5: The Hawaiian Language	2018	Seite 40		Seite 95
Task 1: Why are the Oceans Important?	2019	Seite 48		Seite 96
Task 2: Surprising Facts about the Oceans	2019	Seite 48		Seite 96
Task 3: The Great Pacific Garbage Patch	2019	Seite 49		Seite 97
Task 4: Oceans' Health	2019	Seite 50		Seite 97
Task 5: Saving the Seas	2019	Seite 51		Seite 98
Task 1: Tips for your Internship	2020	Seite 60		Seite 99
Task 2: Young Businessman	2020	Seite 60		Seite 99
Task 3: Unusual Jobs	2020	Seite 61		Seite 100
Task 4: At a Job Fair	2020	Seite 62		Seite 100
Task 5: Learning a Job – What it Takes	2020	Seite 63		Seite 101
Task 1: Weather Apps	2021	Seite 72		Seite 102
Task 2: An Interview with a Weather Forecaster	2021	Seite 72		Seite 102
Task 3: Weather Report	2021	Seite 73		Seite 103
Task 4: Calling the Weather Service	2021	Seite 74		Seite 103
Task 5: Floods and Droughts	2021	Seite 74		Seite 104
Task 1: Specialised Bike Shops	2022	Seite 82		Seite 105
Task 2: An E-Bike Trip through California	2022	Seite 82		Seite 105
Task 3: Who invented the Bicycle?	2022	Seite 83		Seite 106
Task 4: Bike Rental	2022	Seite 84		Seite 106
Task 5: Go Cycle	2022	Seite 84		Seite 107

Alle Hördateien auch zum Download unter:
www.buhv.de/Schule/hutt.lernhilfen/Pauker/rsbay-e/audiotracks/

QR-Codes im Trainingsteil sowie für alle Hörtexte

Dem QR-Code (Quick Response) sind Informationen, Bilder, Videos oder Hördateien hinterlegt. Alle Inhalte sind lediglich zur Auflockerung des Lernalltags gedacht und verschaffen keinem Schüler und keiner Schülerin einen Vorteil.

In diesem Buch sind alle QR-Codes außer der Audiofiles nummeriert. Für alle, die kein Smartphone besitzen, haben wir im Folgenden hinter jeder QR-Code-Nummer die entsprechende Internetadresse aufgeführt, unter der die jeweiligen Inhalte abrufbar sind.

(1) www.buhv.de/download/Pauker/Dolphins.pdf
(2) www.buhv.de/download/Pauker/School_Uniforms.pdf
(3) www.buhv.de/download/Pauker/Hollywood.pdf

Audiofiles: www.buhv.de/Schule/hutt.lernhilfen/Pauker/rsbay-e/audiotracks/

Prüfungsinfos

Schriftliche Prüfung

Die Verwendung eines Wörterbuchs ist in der schriftlichen Prüfung nicht erlaubt.

Ablauf

Listening Test
Pause
Written Test

Listening Test	Aufgaben zu gehörten Texten	30 Minuten	30 Punkte
Written Test	Part I: Reading	105 Minuten	90 Punkte
	Part II: Use of English		
	Part III: Guided Writing		

Listening Test

In diesem Teil geht es darum, Ihr Hörverständnis zu überprüfen. Zu Beginn haben Sie eine kurze Einlesezeit, in der Sie sich die Aufgaben und das Thema anschauen können. Die Aufgaben beziehen sich meistens auf vier bis fünf verschiedene Hörtexte und beinhalten *matching, multiple choice, error spotting* oder *note taking*. Die letzte Aufgabe ist oft etwas anspruchsvoller und umfangreicher. Insgesamt hören Sie die Texte jeweils zweimal hintereinander.

Written Test

- **Reading:** In diesem Abschnitt wird die Fähigkeit getestet, Informationen aus einem vorher gelesenen Text herauszuziehen. Mögliche Aufgaben sind *multiple choice, true, false or not in the text, matching, answering questions, sentence completion* oder *error spotting*. Zudem gibt es eine Aufgabe zur Sprachmittlung. Das bedeutet, Sie lesen einen englischen Text und beantworten dazu Fragen auf Deutsch.
- **Use of English:** Anhand von mehreren Aufgaben werden Ihre sprachlichen und grammatikalischen Kenntnisse sowie Ihr Wortschatz überprüft. Mögliche Aufgaben können *dictionary, synonyms/opposites, definitions/paraphrasing* oder *filling gaps* sein.
- **Guided Writing:** In diesem Teil wird Ihre Fähigkeit zur Produktion eigener Texte geprüft. Sie haben die Wahl zwischen zwei Aufgaben, wobei die Aufgabenstellungen unterschiedlich sein können, z. B. *Write a report / letter of application or an e-mail*. Bevor Sie sich entscheiden, lesen Sie beide Aufgaben durch. Der Umfang sollte ungefähr 200 Wörter betragen.

Mündliche Prüfung

Speaking	General Conversation	ca. 15 Minuten	30 Punkte
	Responding to visual prompts		
	Simulated situation		

Die mündliche Prüfung dauert 15 Minuten und ist im Gegensatz zur schriftlichen Prüfung dezentral, d. h. sie wird durch die Schule gestellt. Die Prüfung besteht aus insgesamt drei Teilen:

- **General Conversation:** Im ersten Prüfungsteil geht es darum, über eine Person, die Sie nicht kennen, möglichst viel zu erfahren, beispielsweise ihren Namen, die Hobbys, die Lieblingsfächer usw. Auch über sich selbst sollten Sie im Gespräch Auskunft geben. Während der Prüfung ist diese „unbekannte" Person natürlich einer/eine Ihrer Mitschüler/-innen. Neben der Unterhaltung müssen Sie in diesem Teil auch einen Namen, Wohnort oder Ähnliches buchstabieren.
- **Responding to visual prompts:** Im zweiten Prüfungsteil erhalten Sie ein farbiges Bild, das Sie Ihrem Gegenüber möglichst genau beschreiben sollen. Außerdem sollen Sie die darauf zu sehende Stimmung interpretieren. Im Anschluss erhält Ihr Mitschüler oder Ihre Mitschülerin ein Bild und tut dasselbe. Sie haben jeweils ca. eine Minute Zeit. Diese beiden Bildbeschreibungen bilden dann die Grundlage für die weitere Diskussion.
- **Simulated situation:** Ausgehend von einem Blatt mit mehreren Bildern sollen Sie im dritten Prüfungsteil Ihrem Gegenüber Vorschläge zu einem bestimmten Thema machen und auch auf seine Ideen reagieren, ihm zustimmen oder widersprechen und schließlich zu einer Einigung kommen. Ihre Diskussion basiert beispielsweise auf dem Thema „Geschenk für einen Geburtstag". Sie tauschen Vorschläge aus, stellen die Vor- und Nachteile des Geschenks dar, und nach einer ausführlichen Diskussion kommen Sie und Ihr Partner oder Ihre Partnerin dann zu einem gemeinsamen Ergebnis.

Die Punkte aus der schriftlichen und mündlichen Prüfung werden zu einer Gesamtpunktzahl addiert.

Notenschlüssel

Punkte	Note
150 – 130	1
129 – 109	2
108 – 88	3
87 – 67	4
66 – 46	5
45 – 0	6

Die Abschlussprüfung

Die schriftliche Abschlussprüfung in Englisch ist stets ähnlich aufgebaut. Die Prüfung ist in zwei Bereiche aufgeteilt:

Listening Test
Im Listening-Teil wird Ihr Hörverstehen getestet. Hier sollen Sie zeigen, dass Sie gesprochene Texte verstehen und gezielt Fragen dazu beantworten können.

Written Test
Dieser Bereich ist wiederum in die folgenden Teile unterteilt:

- Part I: Reading
  Hier geht es darum, einen unbekannten Text zu verstehen und Fragen zum Inhalt selbstständig beantworten zu können. Es wird von Ihnen auch verlangt, dass Sie Kernaussagen eines Textes auf Deutsch wiedergeben – dies ist die sogenannte *Mediation* (Sprachmittlung).
- Part II: Use of English
  In diesem Teil werden Ihre Grammatik- und Wortschatzkenntnisse geprüft.
- Part III: Guided Writing
  Hier gilt es, selbst einen Text zu verfassen. Sie können zwischen verschiedenen Aufgabenvorschlägen wählen.

Für Ihre Vorbereitung ist es wichtig, dass Sie sich mit den typischen Aufgabenarten der einzelnen Prüfungsteile vertraut machen und immer wieder üben. In unserem Trainingsteil finden Sie hierzu viele Aufgaben.

A. Listening Test

Erklärung

Die Vorbereitung
Die beste Vorbereitung auf diese Prüfung erreichen Sie durch intensives und wiederholtes Hören von englischen Texten. Sie können zum Beispiel englische Fernsehprogramme anschauen oder beim Anhören Ihrer Lieblingssongs einmal versuchen, den Text wirklich zu verstehen. Oder schalten Sie doch einfach mal beim nächsten Film die Originalsprache ein. Zusätzlich können Sie sich auch die Untertitel auf Englisch zeigen lassen. So können Sie das Gehörte durch Lesen noch besser nachvollziehen.

In der Prüfung
Die Hörtexte der Prüfung variieren in Länge und Art. Die Fragen dürfen Sie sich vorab schon durchlesen. Hierbei sollten Sie darauf achten, dass Sie auch die Fragestellung genau lesen, damit Sie wissen, was zu tun ist. Keine Angst, wenn Sie beim ersten Hören nicht alle Wörter erfassen, meist können Sie den Sinn der Aussage trotzdem verstehen. Zwischen dem ersten und zweiten Anhören bekommen Sie Zeit, die Aufgaben zu bearbeiten. Lösen Sie hier erst mal nur das, was Sie genau wissen. Beim zweiten Hören können Sie sich dann ausschließlich auf die noch nicht gelösten Aufgaben konzentrieren. Sie sollten auf jeden Fall versuchen, alle Aufgaben zu lösen, auch wenn Sie nicht ganz sicher sind. Wenn Sie alles beantwortet haben und noch etwas Zeit übrig ist, lesen Sie auf jeden Fall noch einmal alle Ihre Antworten in Ruhe durch.

Typische Aufgabenstellung

You will hear a phone call. Listen carefully and fill out the grid.

Hörtext

Mark: Hi, is that Ted? This is Mark.
Ted's dad: Hi Mark. Ted isn't here. Can I give him a message? I'm his dad.
Mark: Oh yes, thanks. Well, can you tell him please that football training is an hour later on Thursday?
Ted's dad: Football, one hour later. You mean at 3, not at 2?
Mark: That's right. Thanks. I'll see him there. Bye.

Erläuterung

Bei diesem Aufgabentyp müssen Sie in eine Tabelle die Antwort zu vorgegebenen Fragen eintragen. Da Sie die Fragen vorab durchlesen dürfen, wissen Sie bereits, welche Informationen für die Antwort wichtig sind.

Who is calling?	**Mark**
Who is answering?	**Ted's dad**
What day is the football training?	**Thursday**
When does the training start?	**One hour later as usual / at 3**

Übungsaufgaben

Task 1

Various Announcements

(Audiotrack: QR-Code rechts / Hörtext S. 34)

You will hear four announcements. What is each announcement about?
Write the correct numbers (1 – 4) in the boxes next to the categories (A – H).
Be careful: Use each number only once.

A ☐ Special bargain
B ☐ Opening times
C ☐ Swimming course
D ☐ Priority boarding
E ☐ Weekend opening times
F ☐ Lost child
G ☐ Delayed plane
H ☐ Member's only course

Task 2

Conversation

(Audiotrack: QR-Code oben / Hörtext S. 34)

You will hear a radio show about "Your favourite sport".
One ending to each of the following sentences (1 – 4) is correct. Tick (✓) A, B, C or D.

1. Patrick's favourite sport is ...
A ☐ football.
B ☐ basketball.
C ☐ volleyball.
D ☐ beach volleyball.

2. In his teens Patrick found himself ...
A ☐ at a summer camp.
B ☐ on a trip through the US.
C ☐ on a trip to Spain.
D ☐ camping with his parents.

3. On the beach they …

- **A** ☐ lounged in the sun.
- **B** ☐ played with Spaniards.
- **C** ☐ swam a lot.
- **D** ☐ sat at the beach bar.

4. Patrick likes about beach volleyball that …

- **A** ☐ it requires a lot of strength.
- **B** ☐ you can play it solo.
- **C** ☐ you need to be a team player.
- **D** ☐ it involves a lot of physical contact.

Task 3

Voicemail message

(Audiotrack: QR-Code S. 12 / Hörtext S. 35)

You will hear a message on an answering machine of a dental practice.
Underline the wrong words in the text and write the correct version in the space provided.

"You have reached the voicemail box of Dr. Miller's dental practice.	______________
Finally, this week our practice is closed because Dr. Miller	______________
has fallen ill. Next week our practice will be closed as usual, that is	______________
on Monday, Tuesday and Thursday from 8am to 5pm, on Wednesday	______________
from 8am to 2pm and on Friday from 8am to 12 midnight. In case of an	______________
emergency please contact the university skin clinic in Henry Street.	______________
The clinic's phone number is 1122887. If you would like to make an	______________
appointment with Dr. Miller for next week, please leave your name,	______________
your phone number and your preferred time for the appointment before	______________
the beep. Thank you."	______________

Task 4

TV Interview

(Audiotrack: QR-Code S. 12 / Hörtext S. 35)

You will hear a section of the quiz show "What's my job?".
Listen and take notes. You do not have to write complete sentences but one word is not enough.

Name	What they do
Betty	
Catherine	gives
Tom	
Holly	
Jack	▶ collects information ▶
Bill	

Task 5

Dinner conversation

(Audiotrack: QR-Code S. 12 / Hörtext S. 36)

You will hear a dinner conversation between Jenny and her parents.
Listen to the conversation and take notes. Be careful, one word is not enough.

1. Jenny and her classmates were away for a ______________________________

   ____
2. Robben Island used to be a prison where Nelson Mandela ______________________________
3. On the second day ______________________________

   ____
4. Jenny's favourite were the Botanical Gardens and the Aquarium with ______________________________

   ____
5. Table Mountain has its name because ______________________________

   ____
6. On the way up, their ______________________________

   ____
7. The Maths teacher started trembling and told them ______________________________
8. Jenny enjoyed the break because ______________________________

   ____

B. Written Test

Part I: Reading

Erklärung

Die Vorbereitung
Um das Lesen englischer Texte zu trainieren, können Sie Zeitschriften wie „Spotlight" oder „Read On" lesen. Diese sind zum Üben gut geeignet, da sie viele Artikel enthalten und für einzelne schwierige Wörter auch gleich die Übersetzung anbieten. Sie finden diese am Kiosk oder auch in einer gut sortierten Bücherei.

In der Prüfung
Lesen Sie den Text zuerst genau durch und unterstreichen Sie dabei Wörter, die Sie nicht kennen. Meist können Sie deren Bedeutung aus dem Zusammenhang heraus erschließen. Beim zweiten Lesen können Sie die Wörter nachschlagen, deren Bedeutung Sie selbst dann noch nicht kennen.
Achten Sie genau auf die Arbeitsanweisung. Denn hier steht zum Beispiel manchmal, dass Sie gar nicht in ganzen Sätzen antworten müssen *(give short answers)*. Oder, dass Sie ganze Sätze schreiben sollen *(write complete sentences)*.
Auf jeden Fall sollten Sie alle Fragen beantworten, auch wenn manche vielleicht erst einmal schwierig erscheinen. Lösen Sie erst die für Sie leichten Fragen und bearbeiten Sie dann in aller Ruhe die schwereren. Achten Sie vor allem auf Ihre Rechtschreibung. Fehler können hier zu Punktabzug führen. Berücksichtigen Sie auch, dass Sie in der gleichen Zeitform antworten, in der die Frage gestellt wurde, zum Beispiel in der Vergangenheit.

Typische Aufgabenstellung

Erläuterung
Sie bekommen einen längeren Text und dazugehörige Fragen. Es geht darum, zu zeigen, dass Sie den Inhalt auch im Detail verstehen. Sie haben zum Beispiel eine Aufgabenstellung, bei der Sie herauslesen müssen, ob die angegebenen Aussagen richtig, falsch oder nicht im Text sind.

(1)

Never annoy a dolphin, he'll remember what you did twenty years later

MARINE LIFE

A study of male bottlenose dolphins shows they are more cooperative with dolphins that have been nice to them in the past.

BY JOHN BILSTEIN

A DOLPHINS have the highest brain to body ratio[1] of any animal. Only humans have more brain per pound of body size. This means dolphins are really smart. They're excellent at playing all sorts of games, and experiments have shown that, much like dogs, they can understand complex commands.

B Each dolphin has its own signature whistle, similar to the way each person has a name. Dolphins seem to have individual personalities like humans do. And they are very sociable animals. They even make friends with large whales, especially humpbacks, who often help protect dolphin calves from shark attacks. [...] And now a study has shown that, like most of us, dolphins pick their buddies[2] from among those that have been nice to them.

C A team of researches from the University of Bristol under Dr Stephanie King found that male bottlenose dolphins in Shark Bay, Western Australia, responded strongly to calls from old friends. However, the study also showed that male dolphins will only work together with other animals that have helped them in the past. Dolphins that didn't help them earlier in life will be ignored.

D Dr King says that dolphins know exactly which relationships are useful to them and which are not. After all, they make great team players [...]. Why would they want to team up with a guy who doesn't play along!

E But, as Dr King's team found, there's a downside to all that so-called intelligence: dolphins have good memories and don't forgive easily if they've been treated badly in the past. Earlier findings published by Jason Bruck of Chicago University in 2013 showed that they will remember former tank mates for at least twenty years.

F So, it's best to be nice to dolphins in case you meet them again in the future. These amazing animals have saved drowning sailors in the past, but who knows if they would bother to save a drowning whaler!

[1] ratio: Verhältnis(wert) [2] buddy: Kamerad, Kumpel, Spezi

Adapted from: Read On, July 2021, Nr. 7, 68. Jahrgang, Carl Ed. Schünemann AG

		true	false	not in the text
1.	Experiments have shown that dolphins can't understand complex commands.		✓	
2.	Dolphins like to be together with other animals and even make friends.	✓		
3.	Many bottlenose dolphins have been killed in shark attacks.			✓
4.	The intelligent animals don't like to play in teams.		✓	
5.	Male dolphins only cooperate with helpful dolphins.	✓		

Übungsaufgaben

Text 1

Digital superstars

Many YouTubers now have as many fans as pop stars. Their audience is very attractive to companies. That is why companies are happy to use YouTubers for their advertising.

Johannes Steger, Handelsblatt Düsseldorf

Vienna, October 2016: Thousands of girls are screaming, jostling – wanting to get as close as possible to the stage. Twenty police officers are not enough to keep the youth under control. As a result, the officials decide to end the event. What was going on? YouTuber Bibi came to distribute autographs. It was not the first experience of this kind for the beauty blogger. Back in 2014, the 24-year-old had to end a fan event that she was holding together with her colleague Dagi Bee (22) in Cologne after a mass hysteria.

Bibi and Dagi Bee are YouTube stars and therefore celebrities in a world that is mainly of interest for young people. 67 percent of 10 to 19-year-olds use YouTube daily according to the Youth Insight Panel 2016 conducted by the Bauer Media Group. Whether gaming, beauty or comedy – each field has its own heroes. They are product testers, life coaches and entertainers. Dagi Bee has about 1.5 million Facebook fans and about 4.5 million on Instagram. For comparison: The supermodel Heidi Klum has 3.5 million followers on Instagram.

Companies are very interested in these digital fan bases. They want to tap into this huge target group. On the one hand, they do this via YouTube itself. The video platform, a subsidiary of Google, is mainly financed by advertising revenue. Companies can pay YouTube to play their commercials before or during videos. They try to create ads that are frequently clicked on and fit the target group of the respective brand. The Google subsidiary keeps a share of this money and gives the rest to the video producers – to people like Dagi Bee and Co.

On the other hand, companies also collaborate directly with YouTubers. These might involve showing products in their films or working with the company as prominent advertising figures. This is a second source of income for the YouTubers. Dagi Bee has worked with the biscuit manufacturer Oreo and mobile operator Vodafone in the past. Unge, DNER and Julien Bam worked with the Techniker Krankenkasse as part of its #wireinander campaign. The YouTubers shot films relating to health issues for the campaign portal.

Critics point out that the campaign was not clearly identified as advertising for the TK. In Germany, advertising must be identified as such. If, for example, the same product is shown frequently in a broadcast, a notice must be displayed that the respective TV or web show is supported by product placement. This also applies to YouTubers. This is necessary because many fans trust their celebrities. If they are excited about a product in a film, this is perceived as a recommendation to buy that product. It is no surprise, then, that YouTubers are often suspected of engaging in surreptitious advertising. And this can get them into real trouble. Lifestyle blogger Sami Slimani learned this lesson when the Broadcasting Authority of Baden-Württemberg threatened to fine him. He now has a disclaimer indicating his cooperation with companies.

For particularly successful YouTubers, the video platform is just the launch pad for entering other marketing channels. In 2015 for instance, Bianca Heinicke, or Bibi as she is known on YouTube, presented her own cosmetic line "bilou" that was initially available only at the drugstore chain dm. The products temporarily sold out on the first day. By contrast, Sami Slimani has been a moderator on Viva since 2014, wrote a book with his sisters and created his own fashion collection in collaboration with REVIEW, a Peek & Cloppenburg brand.

YouTube reports are even becoming an accepted form of journalism: Chancellor Angela Merkel usually only gives interviews to established media outlets. But she made an exception for the YouTuber LeFloid. In 2015, he interviewed the Chancellor – asking questions previously suggested by his followers. To date, his interview video has received around 5.2 million views. […]

Adapted from: Johannes Steger, Handelsblatt GmbH, Düsseldorf, März/April 2017, Ausgabe 43, S. 2 – 3. Übersetzer: John Dalbey
Der Handelsblatt Newcomer ist die Wirtschaftszeitung für Schüler und ein Angebot der Handelsblatt Bildungsinitiativen: https://www.handelsblattmachtschule.de/newcomer

Task 1

Read the text 'Digital superstars'. Are sentences 1 – 8 'true' or 'false'?
If there is not enough information to answer 'true' or 'false', choose 'not in the text'.
Tick (✓) the correct answer.

	true	false	not in the text
1. Bibi had never had something like that in Vienna happen to her before.			
2. More than 50 % of young people use YouTube daily.			
3. Heidi Klum has more followers on YouTube than Dagi Bee.			
4. The fans of digital superstars are important for companies.			
5. YouTubers work closely with brands by showing their products.			
6. On Instagram you have to indicate if you're advertising certain brands.			
7. "bilou" is the name of a YouTuber.			
8. Sami Slimani published a book.			

Task 2

For questions 1 – 4 choose the correct answer (a – c) according to the text.
Tick (✓) the correct answer.

1. The world of YouTubers ...

a) ☐ appeals mostly to younger people.
b) ☐ appeals to everyone.
c) ☐ appeals only to girls.

2. For companies YouTubers ...

a) ☐ are good advertising characters.
b) ☐ are of no interest.
c) ☐ are too expensive to book.

3. In Germany underhanded advertising ...

a) ☐ is no problem.
b) ☐ is regulated by law.
c) ☐ is done by everyone.

4. LeFloid ...

a) ☐ is big on Instagram.
b) ☐ did something no one else did before.
c) ☐ interviewed the president.

Task 3

Verwenden Sie die Informationen aus Text 1.
Fassen Sie anhand der Fragen 1 – 4 die wichtigsten Informationen auf Deutsch zusammen (keine wörtliche Übersetzung nötig, Einzelwörter genügen nicht als Antwort).

1. Was geschah in Wien bei Bibis Auftritt? (2 Details)

____

____

2. Wie sah die Zusammenarbeit zwischen der TK und den YouTubern aus?

____

____

3. Warum müssen YouTuber auf Produktplatzierungen hinweisen? (2 Details))

____

____

4. Was erfährst du über die Kosmetiklinie „bilou"? (2 Details)

____

Text 2

Here is a description of some music festivals in Ireland. Read the descriptions. Match questions 1 – 6 with the correct sites (A – D). Fill in the correct letter in each box. The festivals may be chosen more than once.

A – Soma Festival

The Soma Festival is an annual festival of folk music performances, well-being, languages, food and drink, music workshops and pub sessions. The festival began in 2013 and takes place in Castlewellan, County Down in Northern Ireland.

To celebrate NI Year of Food and Drink 2016, the Soma Festival initiated the now-annual Soma Taste Experience, bringing together artisan food and craft beer producers from County Down and around Ireland.

https://en.wikipedia.org/wiki/Soma_Festival, last accessed February 2018

B – Cork International Choral Festival

The Cork International Choral Festival is held annually in Cork, Ireland and features choirs from all over the world. About 5,000 choristers take part every year; they come from all over Ireland, from Britain, from the European continent, and sometimes from as far away as Africa, America, and Asia.

Since its foundation in 1954, there have been about 3,500 choir entries. The festival will take place April 18th to April 22nd 2018.

https://en.wikipedia.org/wiki/Cork_International_Choral_Festival, last accessed February 2018

C – Electric Picnic

Electric Picnic is an annual arts-and-music festival which has been staged since 2004 at Stradbally Hall in Stradbally, County Laois, Ireland.

The festival incorporates attractions such as the 24-hour cinema tent, the Body and Soul arena (offering an ambient lounge with beanbags, massages and tarot card readings) and the Comedy Tent (curated by Gerry Mallon) and a silent disco.

https://en.wikipedia.org/wiki/Electric_Picnic, last accessed February 2018

D – Pan Celtic Festival

The Pan Celtic Festival is a Celtic-language music festival held annually in the week following Easter, since its inauguration in 1971. The first Pan Celtic Festival took place in Killarney, County Kerry, Ireland. Its aim is to promote the modern Celtic languages and cultures and artists from all six Celtic nations: Brittany, Cornwall, Ireland, Isle of Man, Scotland and Wales.

Each participating nation holds its own national selection event to choose its representatives at the Festival. The most successful Celtic nation is Wales, with fourteen wins, with Cornwall close behind, having won ten times.

https://en.wikipedia.org/wiki/Pan_Celtic_Festival, last accessed February 2018

Which of the festivals …

1. wants to uphold the modern Celtic languages?	
2. is the youngest of the four?	
3. brings together singers from all over the world?	
4. even offers you massages?	
5. has brought lots of success for the Welsh?	
6. was founded in the 1950s?	

Text 3

My Great-Grandmother

My great-grandmother was born in 1914, the year of the beginning of the First World War. She lived in a small village with four brothers and sisters. Her oldest sister died of dysentery[1] at the age of 12. My great-grandmother was seven at the time. Every morning, she had to walk for an hour to get to school and the same again, home in the afternoon.

The winters were very cold at that time, and most people didn't have warm clothes or shoes. ❶ There were 45 girls in her class, all of different ages. The lessons were held by nuns.

Education finished after eight years of school when the students were about fourteen. During the holidays, she was sent to her grandparents to help on the farm. ❷ There was no electric light and the only source of warmth was a big tiled stove in the living room of the farmhouse. After she left school, she stayed with her grandparents for two years helping on the farm.

At 16 she went to work on a big estate about 100 miles away from home. She had to look after two little boys and help in the household. ❸ Then she left and started work in a hotel in a big city about 200 miles away from home. She had long working hours but for the first time in her life she had a tiny little room of her own.

That was the time she met my great-grandfather. ❹ They didn't have their own flat for the first two years of their marriage, but lived with my great grandfather's parents in their flat. In 1939 at the age of 23, my great-grandfather had to join the army. It was the beginning of World War II. My great-grandmother moved back to her parents because she was pregnant. ❺ The baby almost didn't survive because of the bad living conditions. In 1942 my great-grandmother's mum died and she moved back to town. Shortly afterwards she got the news that her brothers and her husband had been killed in the war. She moved out of town to a little farm and helped there, in order to feed herself and the toddler.

After the war was over in 1945, she returned to her flat in town. She found herself a little garden and grew all sorts of vegetables and fruit. Years later she got a job. After retiring in 1974 she travelled around the world a lot. ❻ We all visit her as often as we can. She is 94 years old now and still lives on her own. If we are not fast enough to help her, she still climbs the ladder to take down her curtains!

[1] dysentery = Ruhr (Durchfallerkrankung mit oft tödlichem Ausgang)

Look at the text. Six sentences have been removed from the text. Choose the correct gap (1 – 6) in the text for each of the sentences below (A – F). Write the correct number of the gap behind each sentence.

A She stayed there for three years.	
B I like listening to her stories, and admire and love her.	
C During the summer, children never wore shoes.	
D They got married in 1934.	
E Her grandfather sometimes gave her cake.	
F Her daughter was born in 1940.	

Text 4

Multicultural London

Embracing London is about much more than getting to grips with Britishness: the UK's capital is one of the world's most multicultural cities. Roman soldiers, Huguenot silk weavers, Jamaican airmen, Bangladeshi sailors and a whole host of other people from around the world have helped to shape its history and its future.

"London is a city that has been going for so long that multiculturalism has become a habit," said Georgina Young, a senior curator of contemporary history at the Museum of London. "There are communities here from pretty much everywhere in the world. During the London Olympics we discovered that there were people from every competing country already living here."

The best way to learn about London is to get out and experience it by talking to people, said Young, who spends a lot of time doing just that in her job. Festivals, exhibitions and other events are other entertaining ways to get to know the city's layers.

London hosts an enormous number and variety of festivals. It has the largest Chinese New Year festival outside China and other celebrations include Vaisakhi (Sikh New Year), Diwali (the Hindu Festival of Lights) and the Shubbak festival of Arab culture, as well as many more events.

Walking around East London is a good way to see how different communities have played their part in the city's development. Today Spitalfields and Brick Lane are best known for their Asian connections, with some of the city's most popular curry houses to be found in the area. In the 16th and 17th centuries, however, it was home to Huguenots, Dutch and Flemish refugees fleeing religious persecution on the continent.

The area's history can be seen in buildings such as the Brick Lane Mosque. It was built in 1741 as a Huguenot church, spent much of the 19th century as a Baptist chapel, became a synagogue in 1893 before eventually becoming a mosque in the last quarter of the 20th century. While the mosque is not open to the public, you can go to the Museum of Immigration around the corner: the former silk weaver's home served as a synagogue before reopening as a museum.

London has had Asian and Afro-Caribbean communities since the 18th century. As Britain built an empire, more people came in as part of that from the Asian subcontinent and from Africa and the Caribbean. The slave trade also played its part, with Afro-Caribbean people arriving as slaves or servants of slave traders; a number sought and were granted freedom when they arrived, going on to form a community that agitated against the slave trade in the 1780s.

The next big wave of Afro-Caribbean migration came in the 1940s and 50s. The place to go is Brixton Market. It's the centre of the black British community. It dates back to the 1948 arrival of the ship Empire Windrush and its 492 passengers, mostly ex-servicemen from Jamaica and the West Indies. When they came they were housed in disused bomb shelters below Clapham Common and directed to the nearest labour exchange, which was in Brixton. The area had a large number of boarding houses, so they found accommodation there.

Irish people are the "most unseen community" in London. They have been here since James I. They built London, from the docks through to the canalisation systems and the railways. Later came a group of Anglo-Irish professionals, including authors such as Oscar Wilde and George Bernard Shaw. In the 19th century, neighbourhoods such as Seven Dials, Bermondsey and Whitechapel were all Irish areas.

Other multicultural hotspots worth a visit include Ridley Road Market in Dalston, with a mixture of people from Turkey and West Africa; Green Lanes in Haringey, which has some great Turkish restaurants run by people with Anatolian heritage; the Portuguese and Moroccan shops around Goldborne Road, just off Ladbroke Grove in West London; and Korea-influenced New Malden.

Adapted and simplified from: Carly Chynoweth, "Getting to know Multicultural London", The Times, http://www.thetimes.co.uk/article/getting-to-know-multicultural-london-33d602bwxxs,13.5.2013

Task 1

Read the text. Are sentences 1 – 8 'true' or 'false'?
Tick (✓) the correct answer.

		true	false
1.	In London you find nearly every country of the world represented.		
2.	The largest Chinese Christmas celebrations take place in London.		
3.	Curry houses in the Asian communities are rare.		
4.	Most of London's canals were built by the Irish.		
5.	The Brick Lane Mosque used to be a church.		
6.	In Brixton you find mostly white communities.		
7.	George Bernard Shaw was a Scot.		
8.	There were slaves that were let free.		

Task 2

Verwenden Sie die Informationen aus Text 4.
Fassen Sie anhand der Fragen 1 – 4 die wichtigsten Informationen auf Deutsch zusammen (keine wörtliche Übersetzung nötig, Einzelwörter genügen nicht als Antwort).

1. Was entdeckten die Londoner während der Olympischen Spiele?

____

2. Welche Stadien durchlief das Gebäude der Brick Lane Mosque? (3 – 4 Details)

____

3. Was passierte 1948? (2 – 3 Details)

____

4. Was bauten die Iren in London?

____

Text 5

Read the following letters between Sarah and Mrs Green about a job as a babysitter, then fill in the missing words.

Task 1

Dear Mrs Green,

I ____________ **(1)** read your advertisement for a job as a babysitter. I ____________ **(2)** 16 years old and would like to earn some extra pocket money. First, I ____________ **(3)** a few questions. ____________ **(4)** old are your children, how often do ____________ **(5)** need a babysitter, ____________ **(6)** could I start and how ____________ **(7)** money do you pay per hour? I have a younger brother who is five ____________ **(8)** old. In the last three years I have often ____________ **(9)** after him, which is why I have a lot of ____________ **(10)** as a babysitter.

I am looking forward to hearing from you.

Best regards
Sarah Petersen

1 Green Bow Road
Harlow, Essex
CM19 6EA

Task 2

Dear Sarah,

____________ **(1)** you for your letter. My children ____________ **(2)** three and five years old. So your babysitting experience with your younger brother would suit me just fine. In the morning I take my children ____________ **(3)** kindergarten at 8 o'clock every day from Monday to Friday. They have lunch in kindergarten at 12:30, and I always ____________ **(4)** them up from there at 1pm. Since I work Tuesday and Thursday afternoons, I would ____________ **(5)** a sitter for those times. Would you have ____________ **(6)** on Tuesday and Thursday afternoons from 1pm to about 4pm? Of course, you would ____________ **(7)** to collect my children from kindergarten at 1pm on those two days. In your letter you ask about how much money you would ____________ **(8)** per hour. ____________ **(9)** we discuss money, I would like to meet you, so please ____________ **(10)** me on 0123-456789 so that we can fix a date for a meeting.

Regards
Ann Green

Part II: Use of English

Erklärung

Wortschatzübungen
In diesem Teil sollen Sie zeigen, dass Sie im Laufe Ihrer Schulzeit viele Vokabeln und Redewendungen gelernt haben und dass Sie diese auch anwenden und schreiben können. Ihr Wortschatz wird zum Beispiel mit Lückentexten, Synonymfindungen oder Worterklärungen getestet.

Die Grammatik
Zur Prüfung Ihrer Grammatikkenntnisse müssen Sie beispielsweise Sätze in die richtige Reihenfolge bringen, richtige Formen oder Zeiten in Lückentexte einfügen oder auch Personalpronomen oder Adjektive einsetzen.

In der Prüfung
Am besten fangen Sie immer mit den Aufgaben an, die Ihnen leichtfallen. Lesen Sie die Arbeitsanweisungen sorgfältig durch. Steht ein Beispiel bei den Aufgaben, lesen Sie auch das genau durch, da Ihnen hier gezeigt wird, wie die Aufgabe gelöst wird.
Bei den Wortschatzübungen unterscheiden sich manche Wörter teilweise nur durch einen Buchstaben, zum Beispiel „though" und „through". Sie bekommen dadurch aber eine ganz andere Bedeutung; hier gilt es, besonders aufzupassen. Falls Ihnen ein Wort nicht gleich einfällt, überlegen Sie, ob Sie ein anderes wissen, das fast dasselbe bedeutet. Bei Lückentexten sollten Sie zuerst den ganzen Text lesen, sodass Sie wissen, worum es geht. Dann fällt es Ihnen auch leichter, das entsprechende Wort einzusetzen. Beachten Sie auf jeden Fall die englische Satzstellung von Subjekt – Prädikat – Objekt. Prädikat und Objekt stehen immer zusammen. Wie bei allen Aufgabenteilen der Prüfung sollten Sie auch hier versuchen, alle Aufgaben zu lösen, selbst wenn Sie nicht ganz sicher sind.

Typische Aufgabenstellung

1. **Write the opposites of the underlined words.**

a) The film I saw yesterday was not interesting, it was ______________________.

b) My new jeans weren't cheap, they were ______________________.

c) You enter the cinema through the entrance and leave it through the ______________________.

Erläuterung
Hier müssen Sie zeigen, dass Sie Ihre Vokabeln auch wirklich gelernt haben. Denn es gilt, das Gegenteil des unterstrichenen Wortes zu finden.

Lösung
a) The film I saw yesterday was not interesting, it was boring/dull.
b) My new jeans weren't cheap, they were expensive/costly.
c) You enter the cinema through the entrance and leave it through the exit.

2. Fill in the verbs in the correct tense.

Last winter my family and I ______________ **< go >** on holiday. We ______________ **< fly >** from Frankfurt to Miami. After we arrived at Miami airport, a taxi ______________ **< bring >** us to the hotel. From the first moment we ______________ **< to be >** fascinated by the white beaches. And overall we ______________ **< to have >** a really great time.

Erläuterung
Mit dieser Grammatikaufgabe wird geprüft, ob Sie die angegebenen Wörter in die richtige Zeit bringen können und die Verbformen beherrschen.

Lösung
Last winter my family and I **went** on holiday. We **flew** from Frankfurt to Miami. After we arrived at Miami airport, a taxi **brought** us to the hotel. From the first moment we **were** fascinated by the white beaches. And overall we **had** a really great time.

Übungsaufgaben

Task 1

Look at Text 1 'Digital superstars' (page 16). What do the following words mean? Match the expressions (A – F) with their corresponding definitions (1 – 6). Write the correct numbers in the grid below.

A to distribute (line 5 – 6)
B to tap into sth. (line 21)
C target group (line 26)
D income (line 33)
E to suspect (line 48)
F collaboration (line 62)

1. the group of people that a programme, product, etc. is aimed at
2. to give something out to people or places
3. the activity of working together to create or achieve the same thing, or a product
4. to use part of a large supply of something for your own advantage
5. to think that someone may have done something bad
6. money that you earn by working, producing goods, etc.

A	B	C	D	E	F

Task 2

Find a word or expression in Text 1 'Digital superstars' (page 16) which means the opposite of each of the words (1 – 6) below. The lines where you can find the word or expression are indicated in brackets.

1. nobody ______________________ (line 10 – 15)
2. little ______________________ (line 20 – 24)
3. invisible ______________________ (line 30 – 34)
4. sparsely ______________________ (line 39 – 44)
5. unimportant ______________________ (line 44 – 47)
6. rejected ______________________ (line 64 – 67)

Task 3

Fill in the missing word in the right form.

a) My father ______________ **< to work >** as an engineer in a construction company.

b) I ______________ **< to be >** to London five times.

c) Do not disturb me! I ______________ **< to read >**.

d) It often ______________ **< to snow >** in the mountains in December.

e) Tomorrow I won't have time. I ______________ **< to repair >** my bike.

f) We ______________ **< to meet >** Carol yesterday.

Task 4

Use the word given in brackets to form a word of the same word family that fits in the space.

The procedures for ______________ **< rent >** an apartment can differ widely, and thus knowing what ______________ **< expect >** can help you in your apartment search.

First of all, decide on the type of apartment you want to rent. How big should it be? How much money are you willing to spend? Figure out the exact costs for renting an apartment and determine your budget. Is public ______________ **< transport >** available nearby?

Secondly, many apartments ______________ **< advertisement >** in the local newspaper. These listings ______________ **< general >** describe the size, location, and amenities of the place. Looking over these ads will give you a general idea of the types of apartments ______________ **< availability >**. Also ask people you know if they can ______________ **< recommendation >** any specific place to live.

Finally, be sure to carefully read and understand the terms of the rental agreement. Because once you sign, you will be bound ______________ **< upholding >** the terms of the contract. Ignorance is no excuse. Can you keep pets in the apartment? Is smoking allowed? How much notice do you need to give the landlord before you ______________ **< moving >** out? Better ask questions if you aren't sure.

Task 5

Look at Text 2 'Music festivals in Ireland' (page 18). What do the following words mean? Match the expressions (A – F) with their corresponding definitions (1 – 7). Write the correct numbers in the grid below. The letter and lines in brackets indicate where you can find the words or expressions. Be careful: There is one definition that you do not need.

A artisan (A, l. 8)
B choir (B, l. 2)
C staged (C, l. 2)
D attraction (C, l. 4)
E promote (D, l. 5)
F successful (D, l. 10)

1. to support or encourage something
2. to organize and produce a performance of music or a play, etc.
3. someone who does skilled work with their hands
4. something you can visit that is interesting or enjoyable
5. to do well in a tournament, career, etc.
6. to decide which you want from a number of people or things
7. a group of singers who perform together

A	B	C	D	E	F

Task 6

Find a word or expression in Text 2 'Music festivals in Ireland' (page 18) which means the same as each of the words below. The letter and lines in brackets indicate where you can find the words or expressions.

1. yearly → ____________________ (A, l. 1 – 5)

2. started → ____________________ (A, l. 6 – 9)

3. occasionally → ____________________ (B, l. 1 – 6)

4. includes → ____________________ (C, l. 4 – 8)

5. goal → ____________________ (D, l. 1 – 7)

Task 7

Use the words given in capitals at the end of the lines to form a word of the same word family that fits in the space in the same line.

1. There were ____________________ people in the streets. **< NUMBERS >**

2. People at the party were ____________________ very strangely. **< BEHAVE >**

3. There is no ____________________ for this. **< EXPLAIN >**

4. You have to go through the ____________________ over there. **< ENTER >**

5. His mother got ____________________ when she saw the mess in his room. **< ANGER >**

6. That really isn't ____________________ . **< NECESSITY >**

7. The children were screaming in ____________________ . **< EXCITING >**

Task 8

Fill in the right form of the comparisons.

a) I am ____________________ (good) in English than in Maths.

b) This is the ____________________ (bad) thing I have ever seen!

c) The Mont Blanc is the ____________________ (high) mountain of the Alps.

d) Your bike was ____________________ (expensive) than mine.

e) The more we know about a problem, the ____________________ (great) is the chance to find a solution.

f) The journey to Wales was ____________________ (exciting) of my life so far.

Task 9

Choose the right relative pronoun. Do not use 'that'.

a) On Saturday, I will go to the cinema with my best friend ____________________ really loves science fiction movies.

b) My aunt, ____________________ garden is a little paradise, lives in Chester.

c) During our journey through the Scottish Highlands we saw many deep blue lakes ____________________ are called "loch" there, such as Loch Lomond.

d) There was a helpful old man ____________________ showed us the way to the theatre by accompanying us and explaining many details of the play on our way.

e) This is the recipe ________________ I told you about last week.

f) The most famous feature of the Houses of Parliament, ________________ are also known as the Palace of Westminster, is its clock tower "Big Ben".

Task 10

Look at Text 4 'Multicultural London' (page 19). What do the following words mean? Match the expressions (A – F) with their corresponding definitions (1 – 6). Write the correct numbers in the grid below.

A habit (line 8)
B persecution (line 30)
C eventually (line 35)
D agitated (line 47)
E mixture (line 66)
F worth a visit (line 65)

1. oppression because of political or religious beliefs
2. in the end
3. combination of different things in which the component elements are individually distinct
4. good or interesting to be treated or regarded in the way specified
5. a settled or regular tendency or practice
6. campaigning to arouse public concern about an issue

A	B	C	D	E	F

Task 11

Fill in the right word in the right form, using the words from the box.

to be supposed to • to be used to • to have sth done
to make sb do sth • to let sb do sth

a) Lucy ____________ her friend ____________ (to come) with her to the theatre.

b) You ________________ be back at 11pm.

c) Ben ____________ his homework ____________ before he went to his football training.

d) I ________________ getting up early.

e) Don't ____________ anyone ____________ (to know) that you have told her.

Task 12

One part of the if-clause is missing. Fill in the correct verb form.

a) If I have more time, I ________________ to play the piano.

b) If I ____________ enough money, I would tour the world.

c) If somebody ____________ us back in 2010 that we would win the championship this year, we certainly would not have believed him.

d) My brother will have to repeat the 6th grade, if he ________________ more.

e) If Mr Cooper ____________ her address, he would send her a parcel.

f) I am convinced that more people ________________, if there were more cycle ways in our city.

	A	B	C
a)	had learned	learned	will learn
b)	had	would have	had had
c)	had told	would tell	could tell
d)	won't learn	doesn't learn	don't learn
e)	knew	had known	would know
f)	did cycling	would be cycling	were cycling

Task 13

Find a word or expression in Text 3 'My Great-Grandmother' (page 19) which means the same as each of the words (1 – 7) below. The lines in which you can find the word or expression are indicated in brackets.

1. diverse → ______________________ (l. 8 – 11)

2. Throughout → ______________________ (l. 12 – 18)

3. resource → ______________________ (l. 12 – 18)

4. property → ______________________ (l. 19 – 24)

5. small → ______________________ (l. 19 – 24)

6. apartment → ______________________ (l. 25 – 29)

7. Soon → ______________________ (l. 29 – 36)

Task 14

Find a word or expression in Text 3 'My Great-Grandmother' (page 19) which means the opposite of each of the words (1 – 6) below. The lines in which you can find the word or expression are indicated in brackets.

1. night → ______________________ (l. 1 – 7)

2. warm → ______________________ (l. 8 – 11)

3. last → ______________________ (l. 19 – 24)

4. leave → ______________________ (l. 25 – 31)

5. die → ______________________ (l. 29 – 36)

6. adult → ______________________ (l. 29 – 36)

Task 15

Complete the second sentence so that it has a similar meaning to the first sentence, using the key word given in brackets. Do not change the key word given. You must use between two and five words including the key word.

1. Fitness clubs gain more and more popularity. **< INCREASE >**

Fitness clubs ______________________ popularity.

2. Learning to play the piano is hard work. **< PRACTICE >**

Playing the piano takes a ______________________.

3. Turn down the volume, I can't hear you. **< LOUD >**

The TV ____________________ , I can't hear you.

4. You don't even know who he is, do you? **< HEARD >**

You ____________________ , have you?

Task 16

Fill in the missing prepositions. The box contains more prepositions than you need.

into • in • from • at • with • below • on towards • for • between • after • through

Once we took our cat with us to our holiday home. When I was sitting __________ the train __________ my parents and my sister, suddenly the conductor came and asked: "Excuse me, is the cat __________ the end of the carriage yours?" We looked at each other and denied his question: "No. Our cat is sitting __________ his basket here ________ the bench." The conductor turned away. I had a look __________ the basket – it was empty! I jumped up ________ my seat and walked __________ the end of the carriage. There Garfield sat __________ two big suitcases. He seemed to have been waiting __________ me already.

Task 17

Use the word given in capitals at the end of some of the lines to form a word of the same word family that fits in the space in the same line.

1. Yesterday our class went on a hiking day. It was slightly ____________________ **< RAIN >**

2. and most of us didn't feel like hiking at all. But our teacher ____________________ **< DECIDE >**
to walk up a mountain not far from our school. On top of it there was a restaurant which was our destination. We started at 9 o'clock in the morning and shortly after

3. Mike was not able to walk any more. He complained about a ____________________ **< BAD >**
aching foot. When he took of his shoe, we saw that he had two blisters.
Mrs Davis, our teacher, decided to turn round and walk back to our school as

4. ____________________ Mike was not able to walk to the top of the mountain. **< OBVIOUS >**

5. So poor Mike ____________________ all of us from hiking through the rain for hours. **< SAVIOUR >**

Task 18

Complete the second sentence so that it has a similar meaning to the first sentence, using the key word given in brackets. Do not change the key word given. You must use between two and five words including the key word.

1. We have different musical groups at our school. **< DIVERSE >**

The musical groups at our school ________________________

2. I always eat cereals in the morning. **< USUALLY >**

My breakfast ________________________ cereals.

3. Wales will be this year's destination for our class trip. **< TRAVEL >**

For our class trip________________________ Wales this year.

4. You must show your passport to cross the border of a foreign country. **< ORDER >**

_____________________________ a foreign country, you must show your passport.

Part III: Guided Writing

Erklärung

Die Vorbereitung
Es ist ein Gerücht, dass man das Schreiben von Texten nicht erlernen kann. Zwar kann man es nicht so einfach üben wie Vokabeln oder Grammatik, aber eine langfristige Vorbereitung ist durchaus sinnvoll. In der Prüfung können verschiedene Textsorten auftauchen, mit denen Sie sich zuvor vertraut machen sollten. Sie müssen zum Beispiel einen Bericht, eine Stellungnahme oder einen Tagebucheintrag schreiben oder auch Texte in Form von E-Mails oder Briefen verfassen. Zusätzlich hilft es, wenn Sie englische Bücher oder Zeitschriften lesen.

In der Prüfung
Sie können zwischen zwei Aufgaben auswählen. Lesen Sie sich beide Aufgaben genau durch, bevor Sie sich für eine entscheiden.

Letter/Application/E-Mail
Bei diesen Aufgaben bekommen Sie in der Arbeitsanweisung genau gesagt, an wen Sie warum schreiben oder wem Sie worauf antworten sollen. Es sind auch immer entsprechende Anhaltspunkte gegeben, was Ihr Schreiben oder Ihre Antwort enthalten soll. Daran sollten Sie sich beim Schreiben halten und es hilft Ihnen auch, da Sie sich nicht erst alles selbst ausdenken müssen. Vor allem können Sie sich so auch auf die äußere Form konzentrieren. Denn es ist wichtig, dass Sie sich höflich ausdrücken, die richtige Anrede und einen passenden Schluss finden. Im Unterricht lernen Sie wichtige Redewendungen, die hier immer vorkommen. Lernen Sie diese unbedingt noch einmal gründlich.
Lesen Sie am Schluss noch einmal alles durch und achten Sie darauf, dass Sie alle Punkte bearbeitet sowie Anrede, Schlussformel und Unterschrift nicht vergessen haben.

Report/Blog/Journal/Story
Auch bei diesen Aufgaben bekommen Sie in der Arbeitsanweisung genau gesagt, was Sie schreiben sollen, und Anhaltspunkte, was enthalten sein soll.
Diese Formate sind sehr viel offener gehalten und Sie können kreativer in Ihrem Stil sein. Achten Sie bei allen Arten darauf, dass Ihr Erzählstil lebendig und flüssig ist. Es ist nicht schön, wenn Sie einfach nur Sätze aneinanderreihen. Die Übergänge und der Erzählfluss sollten fließend sein. Wichtig ist auch die Zeitform, denn da Sie sich meist auf etwas Vergangenes beziehen, müssen Sie auch entsprechend in der Vergangenheit schreiben. Achten Sie auf die Zeitform in der Aufgabenstellung.

Formales
Bei beiden Aufgabenformaten ist eine Mindestanzahl an Worten gegeben, die sie erfüllen müssen. Sie erhalten Punkte für den Inhalt, den Aufbau des Textes, grammatikalische Richtigkeit und Ihren Wortschatz. Außerdem wird der Gesamteindruck Ihres Textes bewertet – also ob Sie die Länge beachtet, die Textsorte und den Zweck des Textes berücksichtigt haben und ob Sie einen angemessenen Sprachstil haben.
Lesen Sie also am Schluss noch einmal Ihren gesamten Text gründlich und sorgfältig durch.

Typische Aufgabenstellung

You know that school uniforms are the normal dress for students in many countries. They do have a long tradition. Your pen pal Linda from Nijmegen/Holland, who attends an international school, wrote a letter and she talked about the discussion concerning school uniforms at her school. She asked you to write an article for the next issue of her school's magazine about the situation at your school. Her letter also included the following article about school uniforms.

BLUE or GREEN
"Bright colours and jeans not allowed on these premises." British schools set the trend. An increasing number of schools on the Continent are seeking for ways to reduce tension and violence among students. One topic for discussion are dress codes like the ones in the UK. A growing number of schools introduce the idea of a special school wear and encourage their parents to decide in favour of school uniforms. Head teachers and council officials in Germany and Holland say that fashion has become a battlefield among their students. Those kids whose parents cannot afford the attractive and expensive brands tend to lose out among their fellow classmates. The negative effects of a dramatic increase in prices for energy and food on family budgets lead to unexpected rivalry and tension. School uniforms may be a solution but it remains an open issue.

Write the article for Linda's school magazine and tell her what the situation is like at your school. You may use the information given in the article above.
Write about 200 words.
In your text include the following aspects:

(2)

- What do you think about school uniforms in general?
- How does the majority of your friends feel about them?
- Would it be a good idea to introduce school uniforms at your school as well? Give reasons.

Erläuterung
In dieser Aufgabe sollen Sie einen Artikel verfassen, in dem Sie sich auch auf den zitierten Artikel beziehen können. Achten Sie darauf, dass Sie interessant und ansprechend schreiben und die angegebene Wortzahl einhalten.

Lösung
School uniforms
I think that every teenager likes trendy clothes. It's fun to be dressed in bright colours following the latest fashion. But among students tensions may arise, because not everyone can afford these clothes. So a special school wear can solve this problem, and when the school uniform doesn't resemble a prison uniform but is practical and attractive, I would accept it at once.
The majority of my friends feel the same and when the discussion about school uniforms started, the girls in my class made some pictures showing what their ideal uniform should look like. It was really interesting and sometimes funny to see their imagined uniforms.
With our own school wear, rivalry and tensions in the school could be avoided. And outside school we could make a good impression and improve the image of our school. The perfect school uniform for boys and girls should consist of trousers/skirt, jacket, shirt and tie.

Übungsaufgaben

Task 1

Write a letter.
During your last holidays you rented a scooter to discover the countryside. When you came back there was a letter from your American friend asking about your trip. Send an answering letter to him and tell him everything about it.
Write about 200 words.

Include the following topics:
- Thank him for his letter.
- Where did you go?
- What did you experience?
- Would you do it again?

Task 2

You have read the following job advertisement in the London Telegraph, a local newspaper for London. Write a letter of application of about 200 words.

General Office Clerk 21/08/2022

London Office Inc. is looking for an experienced person for a General Office Clerk position. The candidate will be responsible for answering phones, entering purchase requisitions and general administration support. An excellent knowledge of MS Word and Excel and the ability to be flexible and adapt to changes quickly is absolutely necessary. We offer health insurance benefits, a service bonus and good opportunities for advancement.

Apply in writing to:
London Office Inc.
Clarè McWilliams
24-144 Royal Avenue
London BT1 1EB
Great Britain

Task 3

In a magazine you see this article.

How to make money as a teenager
As a teenager you never have enough money. There are name brand clothes and shoes to buy, new videogames, the newest technology and so on. Most of the teenagers can't just ask their parents for all these things – so they have to find ways to be able to afford more.
Look at this overview to see how other teenagers make money:

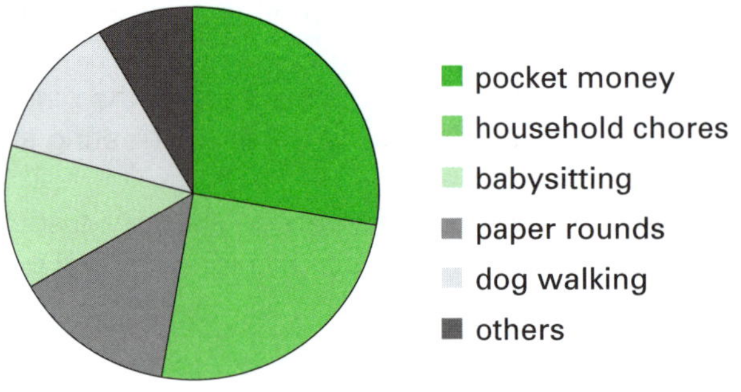

Now tell us how you make money to buy all those pretty things you like.
Send your entry to: info@teenagemoneymaking.com

Write an entry to this survey of about 200 words.

Include the following points:
- How do other teenagers make money? Use the information from the chart.
- What are the advantages of part-time jobs?
- Write about the jobs your friends do.
- What do you do to earn some extra money?

Task 4

Read the following start of a story and continue it. Write about 200 words.

Let me tell you a story about our last school outing. After having arrived at our destination in Gstadt am Chiemsee we were all told that we should under no circumstances walk off alone, we had to keep in small groups. So on our first free afternoon Peter, Anna, Tobias, Marie and I went to town. Once there, we wondered what to do. Suddenly Anna said "Where's Peter? Has anyone seen Peter?" …

Task 5

You have seen this advert for a holiday job in Youth Magazine.

Ideal summer job
Backpackers' Paradise Hostel Edinburgh

- Easy work (in a team of five people)
- Computer skills required
- Good pay
- Free food and accommodation
- Applicants must be 16 or over

For further details write to:
Backpackers' Paradise Hostel
Ian McGowen
107 High St
Edinburgh EH1 1S6
Scotland

You write a letter to the hostel to get more information about the job. Write about 200 words.

You want to find out about
- working hours: hours per day
- kind of work (office, cleaning, working in the kitchen, …)
- payment
- vegetarian food
- shared bedrooms for staff
- start work beginning of July (your 16th birthday is on 15th July)

Task 6

Staying a year in the US as an exchange student you have the opportunity to visit Hollywood. There you see a lot of stars. Write an e-mail to your friend at home telling them all about it. Write about 200 words.

(3)

LCT-Texte

Task 1: Various Announcements

(Audiotracks: QR-Code rechts / Aufgaben S. 12)

Announcement 1: At the department store

May we have your attention please. Five-year-old Anna Smith is looking for her mother. She is wearing blue jeans and a green sweater. Would Anna's mother please go to the information desk on the ground floor where Anna is waiting for her. Thank you.

Announcement 2: At the airport

To all passengers of flight 685 to Paris. The departure gate has been changed to 30B. Also there will be a slight departure delay due to heavy snow fall. The ground crew is deicing the wings in preparation for departure. We should be boarding in about 40 minutes. Thank you for your patience.

Announcement 3: At the swimming pool

Attention, please! The next aqua aerobic course will start in a few minutes. The course is for registered members only. All other visitors are kindly asked to leave the pool. The outdoor pool will be open for everyone during the time of the course. Please leave the pool if you don't want to take part in the course.

Announcement 4: Answering machine

Thank you for calling the public library. This is a recorded message. We are open weekdays from 8 to 12.30, and from 2.30 to 5.30. On Saturdays we are open from 9 to 12 o'clock. If you need any further information please check out our website at www.publiclibrary.com. You can also leave a message after the tone.

Task 2: Conversation

(Audiotracks: QR-Code oben / Aufgabe S. 12)

Radio Host: Good morning everyone. Welcome to my weekly show "Your Favourites". Today's topic is "Your favourite sport". So if you would like to share your ideas about your favourite sport with our listeners, please call 330065. And here we have our first caller already. What's your name?

Patrick: My name's Patrick.

Radio Host: Hello, Patrick. Welcome to the show. Now, what is your favourite sport?

Patrick: My absolute favourite is beach volleyball.

Radio Host: That sounds thrilling indeed. Please tell our listeners when and why you started playing beach volleyball.

Patrick: Well, when I was 10 years old, I did what most young boys do. I started playing football. I was not a bad player, and I even kind of liked football, but it never became my passion. When I turned 17, I asked my best friend Daniel to join me on a two-week summer holiday. At first we wanted to go to Italy, but in the end we decided to go to Southern Spain. And when we went to the beach on the very first day, we saw some teenagers playing beach volleyball. Daniel and I were fascinated right away.

Radio Host: Did you and Daniel just watch or did you join the game?

Patrick: The players invited us to join them, and we were happy to do so. All the players were Spanish, and it was a bit hard to communicate with them because their English was quite poor. Nevertheless Daniel and I learned how to play beach volleyball pretty quickly.

Radio Host: And why exactly do you find beach volleyball so fascinating?

Patrick: First of all, beach volleyball is not a contact sport, and physical contact is what I always disliked about football. Second, beach volleyball is a sport that requires not only extreme physical fitness but also sensitivity and team spirit. Third, the body movements in beach volleyball are beautiful and athletic at the same time. Last but not least, beach volleyball is always associated with the sun, the ocean and a holiday feeling.

Radio Host: I certainly agree with everything you have just said. Patrick, thank you very much for sharing your enthusiasm about your favourite sport with us today.

Task 3: Voicemail message

(Audiotracks: QR-Code S. 34 / Aufgabe S. 13)

"You have reached the voicemail box of Dr. Miller's dental practice. **Unfortunately**, this week our practice is closed because Dr. Miller has fallen ill. Next week our practice will be **open** as usual, that is on Monday, Tuesday and Thursday from 8am to 5pm, on Wednesday from 8am to 2pm and on Friday from 8am to 12 **noon**. In case of an emergency please contact the university **dental** clinic in Henry Street. The clinic's phone number is 1122887. If you would like to make an appointment with Dr. Miller for next week, please leave your name, your phone number and your preferred time for the appointment **after** the beep. Thank you."

Task 4: TV Interview

(Audiotracks: QR-Code S. 34 / Aufgabe S. 13)

Presenter: Welcome to my quiz show "What's my job?". I have invited six people who are going to tell us something about what they do in their jobs. However, none of them will tell us the title of their job. As usual, my in-studio guests will later have to guess what job each of the six people has. Now, let's start with you, Betty. Tell us something about your job.

Betty: I have a lot of contact with young adults who come to the place where I work in order to learn something. These young adults are usually between 18 and 25 years old, which is why I do not usually have to discipline them. After all, it was their own personal decision to come to the place where I work.

Presenter: Thank you, Betty. Let's now give Catherine a chance to tell us something about her job.

Catherine: Well, when people come to the place where I work, they usually need some advice or help. Some people just do not know where they can find the things that they are looking for, so they ask me. Other people just cannot decide what exactly they want to buy, so they ask me for advice about what may be the most suitable product for them.

Presenter: Thank you, Catherine. Now it's Tom's turn. Go ahead, Tom.

Tom: People who come to me also need advice. However, the advice they want relates to where they might spend their next holidays and how much their holiday trip will cost.

Presenter: Thank you so much, Tom. Let's continue with Holly. What is your job all about?

Holly: Well, the people who come to the place where I work are usually ill. My job is to care for them, to bring them food and medicine or to prepare them for treatments and operations.

Presenter: Okay, that was Holly. And now it's Jack's turn.

Jack: I have a workplace with a desk and a computer. But I often have to leave my office to interview people and collect information about things that happen in my home town. Once I'm back at my desk, I write articles about those interviews and events.

Presenter: Thank you very much indeed, Jack. Now it's time for our last candidate, Bill, to tell us about his job. Bill, go ahead, please.

Bill: My job is similar to Betty's. But the people coming to the place where I work are younger. They are usually between 10 and 16 years old. And they come to me because they want to – or maybe I'd better say they have to – learn something.

Presenter: Thank you, Bill. Now let's see if our in-studio guests can tell me what jobs these six people have.

Task 5: Dinner conversation

(Audiotracks: QR-Code S. 34 / Aufgabe S. 14)

15-year-old Jenny comes from a small town located about 250 km north of Cape Town in South Africa. She has just returned from a 3-day school trip to Cape Town and is now having dinner with her parents.

Jenny's mother: Dad and I are really anxious to hear about your trip to Cape Town. You didn't call or text us at all during your trip.

Jenny: Mum, I was away for only three days, and I am 15 already. None of my classmates were in touch with their parents in those three days either.

Jenny's father: But now you might tell us something about your trip. What exactly did you do in Cape Town?

Jenny: Well, on our first day we visited Robben Island Museum. That was a little boring. I mean, what's so interesting about a dark and miserable prison that has been turned into a museum?

Jenny's father: Jenny, I perfectly understand that a museum like that is not really what 15-year-olds would call an exciting tourist attraction. But that's not the point. Robben Island is where Nelson Mandela, the most important and most famous black freedom fighter of South Africa, spent 27 years of his life in prison, just because he wanted black people in South Africa to have the same rights as white people. That's why Robben Island is a sad, but very important part of our South African history.

Jenny: Maybe you're right, but for my classmates and me it was basically a waste of time.

Jenny's mother: What about the second day of your trip then?

Jenny: On our second day we did a hop-on hop-off bus tour around the city. That was quite interesting. What I liked very much was the Kirstenbosch Botanical Gardens with all those exotic flowers and the Two Oceans Aquarium with all the huge fish tanks there.

Jenny's father: And what did you do on the last day of your trip?

Jenny: That was a really thrilling day. We took the cable car to get up to the top of Table Mountain.

Jenny's father: You know why it is called Table Mountain, don't you? It is about 3 km wide and has a very flat top, which is why it actually looks like a table from a distance.

Jenny: Yes, I know. Our teachers explained that to us, too. But what I wanted to tell you about is that our cable car suddenly stopped while we were going up. We didn't know what had happened. But some of the people in our cabin started screaming.

Jenny's father: What about you and your classmates? Were you scared, too?

Jenny: Not really. But Mrs Baker, our Maths teacher, was quite frightened. She started trembling, but Mr Tyson, our Geography teacher, took her hand and tried to calm her. Mrs Baker said that she was afraid of heights and that she hadn't liked the idea of entering a cable car in the first place.

Jenny's mother: How long did it take before your cabin started moving again?

Jenny: It took about 5 minutes. To be honest, I even enjoyed this short break because our cabin was hanging about 100 meters above the steep cliffs, and from up there the view was just breathtaking.

Jenny's father: Obviously, all in all it seems that you had an exciting time in Cape Town. But now it's time to go to bed. You will have to go to school again tomorrow.

Listening Test

ALOHA HAWAII

Task 1: Reasons for Visiting Hawaii
(Audiotrack: QR-Code rechts / Hörtext S. 93)

You will hear five statements why people visit Hawaii. **What reasons** are described?
Write the correct numbers (1 – 5) in the boxes next to the categories (A – H).
Be careful: Use each number only once.
(You will have 5 seconds after the first listening and 5 seconds after the second listening.)

A ☐ Tourist infrastructure
B ☐ Predictable weather
C ☐ Active volcanoes
D ☐ Special food
E ☐ Cultural variety
F ☐ Breathtaking geography
G ☐ Surprising history
H ☐ Friendly people

5 p

Task 2: At Hawaii Volcanoes National Park
(Audiotrack: QR-Code oben / Hörtext S. 93)

You will hear a conversation at the Visitor Center at Hawaii Volcanoes National Park. Look at the points of interest in the park **(1 – 5)**. **Find their position on the map. Write the numbers in the correct boxes.**
Be careful: Use each number only once. There is one example (0) at the beginning.
(You will have 5 seconds after the first listening and 5 seconds after the second listening.)

Points of interest:

(0) Visitor Center (EXAMPLE)
1 Viewing platform
2 Jaggar Museum
3 Closed zone
4 Lava cave
5 Volcano Hotel

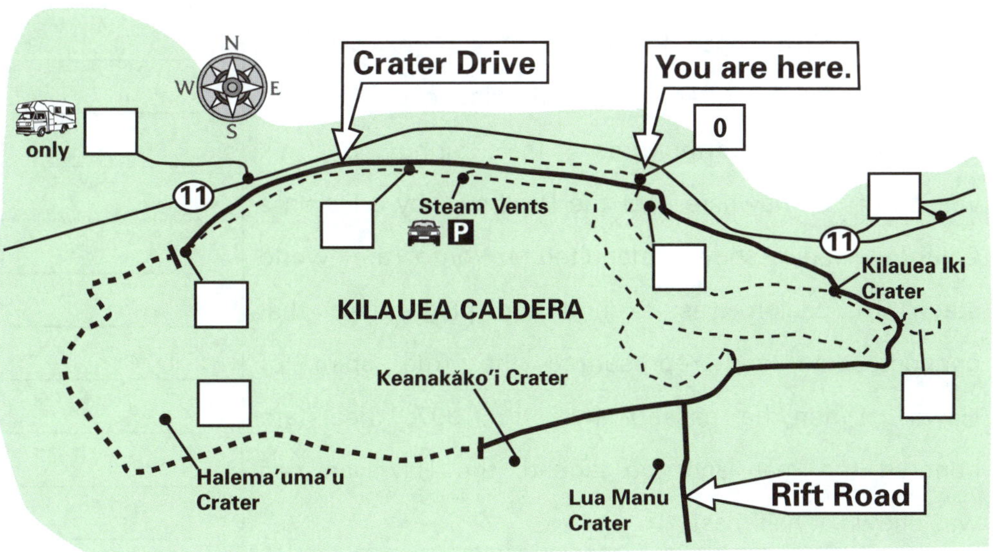

5 p

Task 3: Kamakawiwo'ole Israel

(Audiotrack: QR-Code S. 37 / Hörtext S. 94)

You will hear a radio report about Kamakawiwo'ole Israel, a famous Hawaiian musician.
Find the five wrong words in the text and write the correct version in the space provided.
(You will have 10 seconds after the first listening and 15 seconds after the second listening.)

"Kamakawiwo'ole Israel"

Kamakawiwo'ole Israel, known to his fans as Iz, a singer and a musician as well as a campaigner for Hawaiian culture, sights and way of life, was born in Honolulu, Hawaii, in May 1959. At the age of six, Iz learned to master the ukulele by watching others play. He first performed publicly at around age ten, when he was hauled up to the stage at Steamboats, a popular Waikiki nightclub. In the 1970s Iz dropped out of high school. When his brother Skippy and other aspiring Hawaiian musicians formed a band in 1976, Iz was the band's first choice. In the 1980s, after the death of his beloved older brother, Kamakawiwo'ole began to be the star of the band. In 1993, seventeen years later, he launched a solo career. Shortly afterwards, the airing of his version of "Somewhere over the Rainbow" by a DJ on a California radio show catapulted Iz onto the world stage. His vision was to find and play music that connected to and represented the true spirit of Hawaii. When he passed away in 1997, the state honored the man and the legend: the Hawaiian flag was shown at half-mast.

5 p

Adapted from: Rona L. Holub, Kamakawiwo'ole, Israel Ka'ano'i, http://www.anb.org/view/10.1093/anb/9780198606697.001.0001/anb-9780198606697-e-1803801, Oxford University Press

Task 4: Corals of Hawaii

(Audiotrack: QR-Code S. 37 / Hörtext S. 94)

You will hear a conversation between journalist Ed Young from "Youth & Nature" magazine and Dr. Pearl Oyster, who investigates the coral reefs of Hawaii. Listen and **take notes.**
You do not have to write complete sentences but **one word is not enough**.
(You will have 10 seconds after the first listening and 20 seconds after the second listening.)

	Corals of Hawaii	
1.	**Why people think corals are minerals:**	▶ can't move like land animals ▶ ______________________
2.	**Proportion of endangered corals in Hawaii:**	______________________
3.	**Changes to the sea that cause coral damage (2 details):**	▶ ______________________ ▶ ______________________
4.	**What happens to the corals without the algae:**	▶ ______________________ ▶ turn white and begin to die
5.	**How the "Cliff Cleaner" works:**	______________________ ______________________
6.	**Write to:**	Lynn ______________________

7 p

Task 5: The Hawaiian Language

(Audiotrack: QR-Code S. 37 / Hörtext S. 95)

You will hear an interview about the Hawaiian language. **Listen to the interview and take notes.** Be careful, **one word is not enough**.

(You will have 30 seconds after the first listening and 90 seconds after the second listening.)

1. The name Pauahi means ... ______________________

____

2. Until the mid-1980s the Hawaiian language ... ______________________

3. Pauahi feels truly Hawaiian because her ... ______________________

____

4. A language is in danger of dying out when it is regularly used by ... ______________________

____

5. People stop speaking their own language because of ... ______________________

____

6. A long time ago fishermen used surf boards to ... ______________________

____

7. In order to dance the hula, it is important to ... ______________________

____

8. "A hui hou!" is the Hawaiian expression for the English ... ______________________

______________________ **8 p**

Written Test

Text 1

Lewis Carroll Secondary School search GO

Home ▼ News ▼ Information ▼ Prep School 2-11 ▼ Senior School ▼ Sixth Form ▼ Boarding ▼ Events ▼ Contact ▼

▶ class projects

History Project: Queen Victoria and her Time

Have you seen the film 'Victoria & Abdul'? It tells the true story of an unusual friendship between Queen Victoria and her servant, Abdul Karim. Or maybe you watched the series 'Victoria' on TV? (1) Our students have worked on a history project about this remarkable woman. People all over the world know her name; she's probably the most famous queen in history. Victoria was the ruler of a vast empire as well as of Britain. And a long period of history is named after her – the Victorian Age. Read on to learn more about her ...

On May 24, 1819, Victoria was born at Kensington Palace in London. She lived the life of a young royal and her mother was extremely watchful. This meant that Victoria had little contact with other children, spending most of her days with her friendly German governess and playing with dolls when she was young. She grew up speaking German as well as English. Victoria also enjoyed painting, drawing, and writing in her diary. When she was born, she was fifth in line for the crown of England. (2) However, after several deaths in her family she became heir to the throne of William IV, the king at that time. In 1837, eighteen year-old Victoria was crowned Queen of the United Kingdom. She was determined to be a good queen and to restore the faith of the people of the United Kingdom in the monarchy. (3) This impressed her people, who liked her from the start. Victoria was not familiar with political issues. However, she had a good friend and tutor in Lord Melbourne, the Prime Minister at the time. Melbourne advised Victoria on politics and had considerable influence over her for several years.

On October 10, 1839, her German cousin, Prince Albert of Saxe-Coburg and Gotha came to visit the royal court. Victoria immediately fell in love with him. Five days later, they were engaged to be married. (4) Victoria enjoyed married life. At times their marriage was turbulent with furious confrontations between two extremely strong personalities. However the couple were intensely devoted to each other and had nine children. Albert also helped Victoria find her way around British politics.

When Prince Albert suddenly died on December 14, 1861, Victoria sank into deep depression. (5) The Queen decided to wear black for the rest of her life. Until 1866 she rarely appeared in public. There was a time at which many people questioned her ability to rule. Eventually Victoria recovered and began to take a great interest in the British Empire and the colonies, especially India, and was even given the title "Empress of India".

Many of Victoria's nine children were married off into other royal families of Europe. Her first-born daughter became the wife of the Emperor of Germany. (6) Queen Victoria, the "Grandmother of Europe" as she was called, had thirty-seven great-grandchildren.

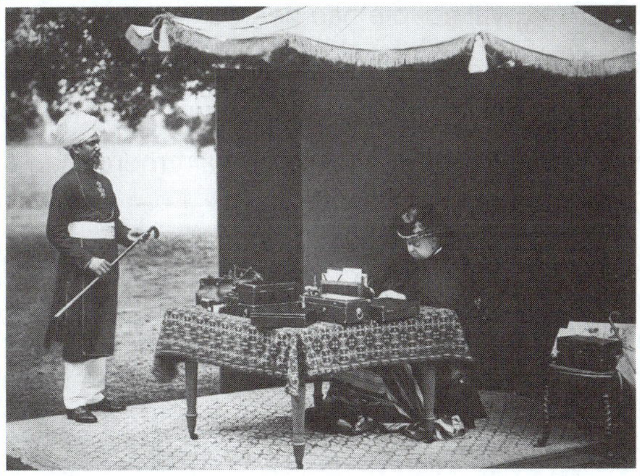

Bild-Quelle: Hills and Saunders, http://www.oldindianphotos.in/2010/01/queen-victoria-and-her-indian-servant.html

Victorian Achievements

The time of Victoria's reign was a period of prosperity and peace for Great Britain. Rapid advances in science and steam technology meant countless inventions, leading to the development of railway engines, bridges and power distribution networks. People had their photos taken for the first time, had electric lights in their homes, made the first phone calls and went on their first car rides. There was incredible wealth but also extreme poverty. (7)

One of the great events of the time was the Great Exhibition of 1851, where Britain's technological achievements and the art of engineering were displayed. Victoria's husband took part in the organisation and it was a huge success. (8)

Interesting facts

- At an advanced age, Queen Victoria started learning Urdu and Hindustani through communicating with her servant Abdul Karim.
- In 1837, Victoria ruled over 16 million subjects in Britain. When she passed away in 1901, there were 41 million.

Adapted from: Biography.com. "Queen Victoria" online available on: https://www.biography.com, BBC. "Primary History – Famous People" [online available on: http://www.bbc.co.uk]

THE VICTORIAN AGE

Part I: Reading

Task 1

Read the text *History Project: Queen Victoria and her Time* (page 41). Are sentences 1 – 8 'True' (T) or 'False' (F)? Choose 'Not in the text' (N) if there is not enough information to answer 'True' or 'False'. **Tick (✓) the correct answer.**

		T	F	N
1.	Young Victoria spoke two languages.			
2.	Victoria knew a lot about politics before she became queen.			
3.	Lord Melbourne introduced Victoria to numerous foreign statesmen.			
4.	It was Victoria who asked Albert to marry her.			
5.	The royal couple had heated arguments.			
6.	The Great Exhibition focused on Victorian paintings and sculptures.			
7.	In later life, Queen Victoria became interested in exotic languages.			
8.	The population of Great Britain more than doubled during her reign.			

8 p

Task 2

Look at the text *History Project: Queen Victoria and her Time* (page 41). Six sentences have been removed from the text. Choose the correct gap (1 – 8) in the text for each of the sentences below **(A – F). Write the correct <u>number</u> of the gap behind each sentence.** Be careful: There are **two gaps** which you do **not need to use**.

A	One of the first things the newly crowned monarch did was to pay off her father's debts.	
B	For socially disadvantaged people, housing conditions in the overcrowded cities were disastrous.	
C	All this shows a renewed interest in the person and times of Queen Victoria.	
D	Other children of hers married royals from all over Europe including Russia.	
E	At that time, it seemed unlikely that Victoria would ever be queen.	
F	She had lost her most trusted adviser in politics.	

6 p

Task 3

Here are four texts about great achievements of the Victorian Age. Read them and **match them with the statements 1 – 6 below**. Choose the correct text **(A – D)** and **write its letter in the box.** The texts may be chosen **more than once**. There is one example (0) at the beginning.

A The opening of the Stockton & Darlington Line in 1825 marked the start of the modern railway age. With its ability to haul a train at over 30 miles per hour, Robert Stephenson's Rocket locomotive set the standard for engine design. By 1845, almost 2,500 miles of railway were open and 30 million passengers were being transported. Short trips to seaside towns with their pleasure piers became a familiar part of social life for Britons of all classes. Queen Victoria made her first train journey on June 13, 1842, and then became a regular passenger. By the end of the 19th century, trains ran at speeds in excess of 70 miles per hour.	**B** The incandescent light bulb, as it was initially called, has become synonymous with Thomas Edison. But actually, a scientist called Joseph Swan was the first to demonstrate a more-or-less workable version of this remarkable creation in 1878. Swan's electric bulb burned out quickly, lasting just about 13½ hours. It was clear that in order to be truly successful the bulb would need to burn longer. This meant the end of Swan's dreams. Then Edison stepped in to improve Swan's creation. From 1879 on, he produced bulbs which lasted 1,500 hours. That – along with a talent for self-promotion – is why Edison became credited with inventing the first light bulb.
C The Crystal Palace was a huge glass and iron structure. It was originally built in 1851 for the Great Exhibition held in London's Hyde Park. The Palace, thought up by Prince Albert and designed by Sir Joseph Paxton, was enormous – 1,848 feet long and 408 feet wide including two huge towers and numerous fountains. The site fascinated two million international visitors a year and was also home to displays, festivals and music shows. However, after being moved to the suburbs of London, the Palace was a financial failure. A huge fire broke out in the night of November 30, 1936, spelling the end of this historic building. By morning the Palace was a burnt-out ruin.	**D** The spread of the railway in Victorian Britain was closely linked to the development of the electric telegraph. In 1837, Cooke and Wheatstone installed the electric telegraph system which linked Euston Train Station and Camden Town Station, and from there it spread all over the railway network. The technology of the telegraph expanded fast, making mass communication possible on both a national and a global scale. A telegraph cable was laid across the Channel in 1851. In 1866, a durable telegraph cable was laid across the Atlantic. Despite many problems, the global network grew rapidly.

Adapted from:
A+D: Atterbury, Paul, Victorian Technology, http://www.bbc.co.uk/history/british/victorians/victorian_technology_01.shtml, BBC London
B: Priya Ganapati, Wired © Conde Nast, Dec. 18, 1878: LET THERE BE LIGHT — ELECTRIC LIGHT, https://www.wired.com/2009/12/1218joseph-swan-electric-bulb, 18.12.2009
C: Crystal Palace: A History,http://news.bbc.co.uk/local/london/hi/people_and_places/history/newsid_8082000/8082928.stm, BBC London

0.	**Travel speed more than doubled within the same century.**	A
1.	It made communication between two railway stations possible.	
2.	The main problem at the beginning was its short life.	
3.	Although it attracted global attention, the project was an economic disaster.	
4.	The ordinary worker as well as the royal family used it.	
5.	It took nearly thirty years to establish intercontinental connections.	
6.	The original invention was only acceptable after an improvement had been made.	

6 p

Task 4

Verwenden Sie die Informationen aus folgendem Text. **Bearbeiten Sie die Aufgaben (1 – 6) stichpunktartig auf Deutsch.** Es ist keine wörtliche Übersetzung nötig, die Aspekte müssen inhaltlich jedoch vollständig erfasst sein. Einzelwörter genügen nicht als Antwort.

Facts you might not know about Buckingham Palace

You have seen it in movies and on postcards, but how much do you actually know about Buckingham Palace? The original building, called Buckingham House, was built by John Sheffield as his London residence in 1703. Sheffield had been made the Duke of Buckingham shortly before, consequently he named the house after his new title. In the 1820s, Buckingham House, which had been purchased by King George Ill, was greatly enlarged into the palace we know today. Three weeks after she came to the throne in 1837, Queen Victoria declared the place her official residence. Queen Victoria's new palace was far from perfect: the bells could not be heard in the servants' rooms and airing the bathrooms was almost impossible. Other weak points of the palace as a family home were revealed when Victoria married Prince Albert in 1840. There was no satisfactory heating in the children's rooms and not enough space suitable for overnight visitors.

Today, Buckingham Palace is Queen Elizabeth's London residence. You can visit it during the absence of the royal family in summer – unless you are lucky enough to be invited to one of the royal receptions that take place throughout the year. People can tell whether the Queen is at home by the flag flying from the mast: if the Royal Standard is flying, it means the Queen is in residence, and at all other times the Union Jack will fly instead.

Adapted from:
Lukas Abrahams, https://theculturetrip.com/europe/united-kingdom/england/london/articles/11-things-we-bet-you-didnt-know-about-buckingham-palace/
https://www.royal.uk/royal-residences-buckingham-palace
https://www.historyextra.com/period/20th-century/9-facts-about-buckingham-palace/

1. Warum nannte Sheffield sein neues Haus „Buckingham House“?

______________________________ **1 p**

2. Wie wurde aus „Buckingham House“ ein königlicher Palast? **(2 Details)**

____

______________________________ **2 p**

3. Welche Probleme mit dem Palast gab es zu Beginn von Victorias Regentschaft? **(2 Details)**

____

______________________________ **2 p**

4. Welche weiteren Schwächen des Palastes zeigten sich nach der Hochzeit? **(2 Details)**

____

______________________________ **2 p**

5. Bei welchen Gelegenheiten kann man den Palast von innen sehen? **(2 Details)**

____

______________________________ **2 p**

6. Was bedeutet es, wenn der Union Jack über dem „Buckingham Palace“ weht?

______________________________ **1 p**

Part II: Use of English

Task 1

Look at **text 1** (page 41). **Find a word or expression which means the same as each of the words (1 – 5) below.** The lines where you can find the words or expressions are indicated in brackets. There is one example **(0)** at the beginning.

0.	**huge**	→	**vast**	**(l. 1 – 5)**
1.	protective	→	________________	(l. 7 – 15)
2.	(to) bring back	→	________________	(l. 16 – 24)
3.	seldom	→	________________	(l. 34 – 44)
4.	(to) get well	→	________________	(l. 34 – 41)
5.	unbelievable	→	________________	(l. 47 – 56)

5 p

Task 2

Look at **text 1** (page 41). What do the following words mean? **Match** the expressions **(A – F) as used in the text** with their corresponding definitions (1 – 7). **Write the correct numbers in the grid below.** Be careful: There are two definitions that you do not need. One definition **(0)** has already been matched correctly.

A **period (l. 4)**
B governess (l. 10)
C heir (l. 15)
D influence (l. 23)
E prosperity (l. 48 – 49)
F distribution (l. 52)

0. **a length of time in the history of a country**
1. success, especially in making money
2. a group of people leading a country
3. the delivery of items to a number of people
4. a person who receives a dead person's money or title
5. the effect someone has on the way a person thinks or acts
6. a woman employed to teach the children of a rich family
7. something that a person owns

A	B	C	D	E	F
0					

5 p

Task 3

Use the word given in capitals at the end of some of the lines to **form a word of the same word family** that fits in the space in the same line. There is one example **(0)** at the beginning.

0. Looking at 19th century English literature, one quickly **(0)** **realizes** that this period **REAL**
1. is inseparably (1) ______________________ to the name of one author: Charles **CONNECTION**
2. Dickens. His many volumes (2) ______________________ works such as **INCLUSIVE**
A Christmas Carol and *Oliver Twist*.
3. Dickens enjoyed great (3) ______________________ during his lifetime. **POPULAR**
4. He was admired for (4) ______________________ criticizing Britain's social system. **STRENGTH**
Finally, in March 1870, three months before his death, Queen Victoria
5. (5) ______________________ him at Buckingham Palace. **RECEIPT**

Adapted from: Sebastian Lehner, https://www.ellopos.net/dickens/lehner-david-copperfield.asp?pg=2

5 p

Task 4

Complete the second sentence so that it has a similar meaning to the first sentence, using the KEY WORD given in brackets. **Do not change the KEY WORD given.** You must use **between two and five words including the KEY WORD**. There is one example **(0)**.

> **Example**
>
> **0.** In Victorian times people dreamed of travelling to the seaside ever year. **(WISHED)**
>
> **(1) (2) (3) (4)**
> In Victorian times people **wished they could travel** to the seaside every year.

1. Victorian girls did not get a proper education if they did not come from a rich home. **(UNLESS)**

_______________________ a rich home, Victorian girls did not get a proper education. **1 p**

2. During the Industrial Revolution, it was possible for the middle classes to invest in the decor of their homes for the first time. **(WERE)**

During the Industrial Revolution, the middle classes _______________________

_______________________ in the decor of their homes for the first time. **1 p**

3. Pollution in the cities was a problem and light dresses turned grey, so that women wore dark colours. **(INSTEAD)**

_______________________ which turned grey, women wore dark clothes, as pollution in the cities was a problem. **1 p**

4. Doctors said they would manage to cure patients by giving them electrical shocks. **(SUCCEED)**

Doctors said they would _______________________

by giving them electrical shocks. **1 p**

5. The royal family published a picture showing them celebrating Christmas the German way, so the Christmas tree was introduced in England. **(HOW)**

The royal family published a picture showing _______________________

_______________________ the German way, so the Christmas tree was introduced in England. **1 p**

Task 5

Complete the following text. Use the correct forms of the words in brackets and find words of your own to replace the question marks. There is one example **(0)**.

Florence Nightingale was a revolutionary figure **(0)** __in__ **(???)** nursing who reformed 19th and 20th century public health care. She is known for her night rounds to aid the wounded, establishing her image as the "Lady with the Lamp". Florence Nightingale, **(1)** _______________ **(???)** work made nursing one of the most regulated and respected professions in the world, was born into an upper-class British family in May 1820. Women of her time and her class **(2)** _______________ **(expect)** to marry and maintain a lovely home. But Nightingale's plans and ambitions were very different from those imagined for her **(3)** _______________ **(???)** her parents. Though nursing was not a valued profession at the time, the 24-year-old woman fought very **(4)** _______________ **(hard)** to become a nurse. She left England for Düsseldorf where she enjoyed **(5)** ______________________ **(do)** her studies at a hospital. Back in London she was soon promoted to head of nursing. Florence Nightingale improved sanitary conditions **(6)** ______________________ **(enormous)**. She insisted on **(7)** ______________________ **(have)** fresh air, water and healthy food for her patients' recovery. And if it **(8)** ______________________ **(not be)** for her, diseases would not have been statistically documented at the time. Nightingale wrote more **(9)** ______________________ **(???)** 60 books. Since that time, her hygienic procedures and lessons for hospital safety **(10)** ______________________ **(influence)** nursing.

10 p

Adapted from: Biography.com. "Florence Nightingale", online available on: https://www.biography.com

Part III: Guided Writing

You only have to do **one** of the following two tasks.
Important: First read both tasks, then decide whether you want to do Task A or Task B.
You can write down your ideas on your extra sheet before you do the task on your exam paper.

Task A

Café Assistant
We offer a part-time job in our Museum Garden Café during the summer season. Some experience in serving guests as well as interest in 19th century literature and Victorian lifestyle are required. We will provide training in hygiene and food safety standards. Your ideas are welcome for this year's youth garden party!
If this sounds like you, please send us your application.

Write a **letter of application** for the job offered above.
Include the following aspects:

- say why you want to work in the café
- explain what job experience you have gained so far
- ask questions about job details not mentioned in the ad
- describe your ideas for the youth garden party

Find a suitable beginning and ending. **Write about 200 words.** You need not write any addresses.

Task B

In Victorian times, more and more people noted down their personal experiences, thoughts and feelings in their diaries. This year, the V&A Museum of Childhood in London has asked young people all over the world to describe online what their daily lives in the 21st century are like. You are taking part in this project.

Adapted from: http://www.vam.ac.uk/moc/exhibitions/the-great-diary-project/ (12/12/17)

Write a **personal text** for the museum's online project, describing your way of life.
Include the following information:

- a description of your social life at present
- an important event in your personal past
- thoughts and wishes about your life in the future
- if you think keeping a diary or writing blogs is important and why (not)

Find a suitable beginning and ending. **Write about 200 words.**

30 p

Listening Test

OCEANS TODAY

Task 1: Why are the Oceans Important?
(Audiotrack: QR-Code rechts / Hörtext S. 96)

You will hear five statements by marine biologists about the oceans. **What reasons for the importance of the oceans** are the people talking about?
Write the correct numbers (1 – 5) in the boxes next to the categories (A – H).
Be careful: Use each number only once.
(You will have 5 seconds after the first listening and 5 seconds after the second listening.)

A ☐ Employment
B ☐ Medicine
C ☐ Marine life
D ☐ Relaxation
E ☐ Climate
F ☐ Shipping traffic
G ☐ Energy production
H ☐ Food supply

5 p

Task 2: Surprising Facts about the Oceans
(Audiotrack: QR-Code oben / Hörtext S. 96)

You will hear an interview with Robert Vaughn, a marine scientist.
One ending to each of the following sentences (1 – 4) is correct. **Tick (✓) A, B, C or D.**
(You will have 5 seconds after the first listening and 5 seconds after the second listening.)

1. The longest mountain range in the ocean ...
- **A** ☐ forms a straight line.
- **B** ☐ is 65,000 kilometres long.
- **C** ☐ is as high as the Alps.
- **D** ☐ is part of the Himalayas.

2. Gold in the oceans ...
- **A** ☐ was mined until 1872.
- **B** ☐ is worth 18 million dollars.
- **C** ☐ cannot be mined cost-effectively.
- **D** ☐ sums up to 4 kg altogether.

3. The ocean floor ...
- **A** ☐ looks like the ground on Mars.
- **B** ☐ is used for chemical tests.
- **C** ☐ glows between rocks.
- **D** ☐ is home to nesting octopuses.

4. The famous "Bloop" was caused by ...
- **A** ☐ unexplainable sources.
- **B** ☐ marine animals.
- **C** ☐ earthquakes.
- **D** ☐ breaking icebergs.

4 p

Task 3: The Great Pacific Garbage Patch

(Audiotrack: QR-Code S. 48 / Hörtext S. 97)

You will hear a radio report about the Great Pacific Garbage Patch.
There are six wrong words in the text. Write their correct versions on the lines provided.
(You will have 10 seconds after the first listening and 15 seconds after the second listening.)

The Great Pacific Garbage Patch

The Great Pacific Garbage Patch – or GPGP for short – is the largest of five huge offshore plastic accumulations flowing in the world's oceans. It is located halfway between Hawaii and California.

The account of the plastic in the GPGP is estimated to weigh approximately 80,000 tons. Experts suppose that a total of 1.8 trillion plastic pieces are drifting in the patch. This is equivalent to 215 pieces of rubbish for every human in the world – an enormous plastic count. Once plastic winds its way into the garbage patch, it falls apart into smaller micro-plastics under the effects of sun and waves.

The vast majority of plastics are made of slick or hard polyethylene or polypropylene, as well as destroyed fishing nets and ropes. In terms of object count, 94 per cent of the total is represented by microplastics smaller than 0.5 cm. Once they become this small, microplastics are very rough to remove. In addition they are often mistaken for food by marine animals.

6 p

Adapted from: The Ocean Cleanup. "The Great Pacific Garbage Patch", online available on: https://www.theoceancleanup.com

Task 4: Oceans' Health

(Audiotrack: QR-Code S. 48 / Hörtext S. 97)

You will hear an interview between a reporter and Mrs Waters, professor for Ocean Science. Listen and **take notes**. You do not have to write complete sentences but **one word is not enough**. *(You will have 10 seconds after the first listening and 20 seconds after the second listening.)*

	NOTES	
1.	**Consequences of overfishing (2 aspects):**	▶ ____________________ ▶ ____________________
2.	**Reason why sharks are killed:**	____________________
3.	**Reason for dead zones:**	____________________
4.	**Mercury pollution:** ▶ **source:** ▶ **health dangers for people (2 aspects):**	____________________ ▶ ____________________ ▶ ____________________

7 p

Task 5: Saving the Seas

(Audiotrack: QR-Code S. 48 / Hörtext S. 98)

You will hear a radio podcast about 'Saving the Seas'. What do the different people say?
Listen to the conversation and complete the grid below. Be careful, **one word is not enough**.
(You will have 30 seconds after the first listening and 90 seconds after the second listening.)

	Mr Brosnan	**Mr Wiener**	**Mrs Earle**
Ideas to save our seas:	______ ______ ______	______ ______ ______	______ ______ ______
Projects and initiatives:	INTERNATIONAL WHALING COMMISSION Situation of the whales today: ______ ______ ______	Foundation for the Protection of Marine Biodiversity Reason for founding: ______ ______ ______	MISSION BLUE Main goal of 'Mission Blue': ______ ______ ______
Further reading:	▶ 'The World is Blue' ▶ ______ ______ ______	*no information given*	'Marine Biology' (by Peter Castro) stresses: ______ ______ ______

Bild-Quellen: International Whaling Commission, Mission Blue

8 p

Written Test

Text 1

Long Walk to Freedom

Nelson Mandela wrote his autobiography in 1994. In it he tells about his life, his years in prison and his career. Here are some extracts from the book describing crucial moments in his life.

A

Apart from life and a strong constitution, the only thing my father bestowed upon me at birth was a name, Rolihlahla. Rolihlahla literally means "pulling the branch of a tree", but its colloquial meaning would be "troublemaker". I was born on the eighteenth of July, 1918, at Mvezo, a tiny village in the Transkei.
My father, Gadla Henry Mphakanyiswa, was a chief by both blood and custom. He had four wives, the third of whom was my mother, Nosekeni Fanny. (...)

B

I was baptized into the Methodist Church and sent to school. No one in my family had ever attended school. I was seven years old, and on the day before I was to begin, my father took me aside and told me that I must be dressed properly for school. Until that time, I had worn only a blanket, which was wrapped around one shoulder and pinned at the waist. My father took a pair of his trousers and cut them at the knee. They were roughly the correct length, although the waist was far too large. My father then took a piece of string and cinched the trousers at the waist. I must have been a comical sight, but I have never possessed a suit I was prouder to put on than my father's cut-off pants. (...)

C

On the first day of school, my teacher, Miss Mdingane, gave each of us an English name. This was the custom among Africans in those days and was undoubtedly due to the British bias of our education. The education I received was a British education, in which British ideas, British culture, British institutions, were automatically assumed to be superior. Miss Mdingane told me that my new name was Nelson. Why she gave this particular name to me I have no idea. Perhaps it had something to do with the famous British sea captain Lord Nelson, but that would be only a guess. (...)

D

I cannot pinpoint a moment when I became politicized. To be an African in South Africa means that one is politicized from the moment of one's birth. An African child is born in an Africans Only hospital, taken home in an Africans Only bus, lives in an Africans Only area, and attends Africans Only schools, if he attends school at all. When he grows up, he can work in Africans Only jobs, rent a house in Africans Only townships, ride Africans Only trains, and be stopped at any time of the day or night and be ordered to produce a pass, failing which he will be arrested and thrown in jail. His life is governed by racist laws and regulations. (...)

E

The day I became President of South Africa, I took some moments to reflect our history. Time and again, I have seen men and women risk and give their lives for an idea. I have seen men stand up to attacks and torture without breaking, showing a strength and resiliency that is beyond imagination. I always knew that deep down in every human heart, there is mercy and generosity. No one is born hating another person because of the colour of his skin, or his background, or his religion. People learn to hate, and if they can learn to hate, they can be taught to love. Even in the grimmest times in prison, I would see a glimmer of humanity in one of the guards in prison, perhaps just for a second, but it was enough to reassure me and keep me going.

For myself, I have never regretted my years of struggle, and I was always prepared to face the hardships that affected me personally. But my family paid a terrible price for my commitment. (…)

F I was born free – free in every way that I could know. But then I slowly saw that not only was I not free, but my brothers and sisters were not free. I saw that it was not just my freedom that was curtailed, but the freedom of everyone who looked as I did. It was during those long and lonely years that my hunger for the freedom of my own people became a hunger for the freedom of all people, white and black. I have walked that long road to freedom. And I have discovered the secret that after ascending a great hill, one only finds that there are many more hills left. My long walk is not yet ended.

NELSON MANDELA: LONG WALK TO FREEDOM

Part I: Reading

Task 1

Read the text *Long Walk to Freedom* (page 52). Which of the headings **(0 – 7)** matches the paragraphs of the text **(A – F)** best? **Write the correct numbers in the boxes.** One heading **(0)** has already been put in the correct place.
Use each number only once. Be careful, there are some headings that you do not need to use.

A lines 1 – 6
B lines 7 – 14
C lines 15 – 21
D lines 22 – 28
E lines 29 – 36
F lines 37 – 46

0. Colonial influence at school
1. Childhood fears
2. A challenge for the future
3. Candidate for presidency
4. Second class citizens
5. Family background
6. A moment of pride
7. Faith and optimism

A	B	C	D	E	F
		0			

5 p

Task 2

Read the text *Long Walk to Freedom* (page 52). Are sentences **1 – 10** 'True' (T) or 'False' (F)? Choose 'Not in the text' (N) if there is not enough information to answer 'True' or 'False'.
Tick (✓) the correct answer.

		T	F	N
1.	The young Rolihlahla was named after his father.			
2.	Mandela was sent to school because he was meant to become a priest.			
3.	Mandela's father bought his son a suit for school.			
4.	Mandela's teacher replaced the pupils' African names.			
5.	Mandela admired Lord Nelson greatly.			
6.	Africans constantly ran the risk of being imprisoned.			
7.	One of the guards in prison tried to protect Mandela from inhumane treatment.			
8.	Mandela was sorry about his frequent conflicts.			
9.	The Mandela family was sent to jail by the government.			
10.	Mandela claimed he had achieved all his political goals.			

10 p

Task 3

The following text is about Kumi Naidoo, the head of Amnesty International. The paragraphs of the text are mixed up. **Put the different parts (A – G) into the correct order (1 – 7). Write your answers in the grid below.** One part **(B)** has already been put in the correct place.

Another South African Success Story

A During this time abroad, he was a Rhodes scholar at Oxford and earned a doctorate in political sociology. After Nelson Mandela's release in 1990, Kumi returned to South Africa to work on the legalization of the African National Congress. Provoked by the fact that South Africa had one of the highest rates of violence against women, Kumi organized the National Men's March Against Violence on Women and Children in 1997.

B A year later he occupied another platform in the Barents Sea in the Russian Arctic. Kumi's most recent role has been as a co-founder of the pan-African organization, *Africans Rising for Justice, Peace and Dignity*. The group, which has forged partnerships across trade unions, religion and civil society, has realized that Africa as a continent has benefited from economic growth.

C As a result of these anti-apartheid activities, he was expelled from high school. Nevertheless Kumi managed to pass the entrance exam at the University of Durban-Westville. In 1986, he was charged with violating the emergency regulations. He went underground for one year before finally deciding to live in exile in England.

D Kumi is now in control of the largest human rights organization with a global presence that includes offices in over 70 countries, 2600 staff and seven million members, volunteers and supporters. The organization, founded in London in 1961, protects individuals wherever justice, fairness, freedom and truth are denied.

E Kumi Naidoo, a human rights activist of Indian origin, who was born in Durban, South Africa in 1965, became politically active at the age of 15. Soon he was deeply involved in neighbourhood organization, youth work in his community, the underground movement, and in the South African liberation struggle.

F Africans themselves, however, have not shared in that increasing wealth and power. This is certainly one reason why Kumi applied for the role as the global head of Amnesty International. As he himself emphasizes, another one was a letter by Mandela to the then newly founded human rights organization in 1962. In this document, Mandela thanked Amnesty International for sending a representative to observe his trial.	G Since this initiative to help the weaker groups in society, Kumi has held multiple leadership roles, but his time as Executive Director of Greenpeace International cemented his reputation as a bold activist who championed civil disobedience, most notably when he was arrested for scaling a Greenlandic oil rig to hand-deliver a petition in protest against drilling in the Arctic in 2011.

Adapted from:
African Success. "Biography of Kumi NAIDOO" [online available on: http://www.africansuccess.org]
TimeSlive. "Kumi Naidoo promises change" [online available on: https://www.timeslive.co.za]
Greenpeace. "Kumi Naidoo" [online available on: https://www.greenpeace.org]
Bild-Quelle: Vesa Moilanen, Lehtikuva, picture alliance/Vesa Moilanen/Lehtikuva/dpa

1	2	3	4	5	6	7
				B		

6 p

Task 4

Verwenden Sie die Informationen über das *Robben Island Museum* und **bearbeiten Sie die Aufgaben (1 – 6) stichpunktartig auf Deutsch**. Es ist keine wörtliche Übersetzung nötig, die Aspekte müssen inhaltlich jedoch vollständig erfasst sein. Einzelwörter genügen nicht als Antwort.

The Robben Island Museum (RIM)

Robben Island is an island near Cape Town, known for its dreaded high-security prison where Nelson Mandela was held captive. On a visit to the island, you will walk past a high wall and buildings which were used for the families' and lawyers' visits to prisoners. You will then be introduced to the site where Mandela spent 18 of his total of 27 years in jail, beginning in 1964. The bus tour passes the limestone quarry where Mandela suffered every day for 13 years, digging up rock. The dust of the rock made breathing difficult, and the reflection of the sunlight on the white stones caused a sort of snow blindness. The prisoners experienced often cruel, though, at times surprisingly kind treatment from the guards.

Many guides on Robben Island Museum are themselves former political prisoners, and they speak openly about their lives inside one of the world's most notorious prison camps. One of them, Itumeleng Makwela, recalls: "Only those who behaved well were allowed to read a newspaper, for example, but it would go to the censorship office first. They cut out every political contribution, you received a paper with holes all over. Letters from our families were treated the same way, so as to leave us hardly any words from home."

The tour route culminates in a viewing of Nelson Mandela's cell. As Mandela noted in *Long Walk to Freedom*, "When I lay down, I could feel the wall with my feet and my head touched the concrete at the other side." In the barely furnished cell, a bulb burned day and night over his head.

Today, the RIM is a must-see for any visitor to South Africa, as it is a testament to courage and strength in the face of inhumanity.

Adapted from:
Robben Island Museum. "The Tour Experience" [online available on: www.robben-island.org]
Johnson, Scott. "A visit to Robben Island" [online available on: https://www.smithsonianmag.com]
Schadomsky, Ludger. "Robben Isalnd. A View into Mandela's Prison Life" [online available on: https://www.dw.com]
Brady, Sean. "Nelson Mandela's inspiring Limestone Quarry Classroom" [online available on: https://prismdecision.com]

1. Welchem Zweck dienten die Gebäude entlang des Fußweges zum Busparkplatz genau?

______________________________ **1 p**

2. Beschreiben Sie zwei körperliche Probleme, die aus der Arbeit im Kalksteinbruch entstanden.

____

______________________________ **2 p**

3. Wie war die Behandlung der Gefangenen durch die Aufseher bei dieser Arbeit?

____

______________________________ **1 p**

4. Was wird über das Lesen von Zeitungen im Gefängnis gesagt? **(2 Details)**

____

______________________________ **2 p**

5. Was sagt Mandela über die Größe seiner Zelle aus?

____

______________________________ **1 p**

6. Welche beiden Angaben zur Zelle werden noch gemacht?

______________________________ **2 p**

Part II: Use of English

Task 1

Look at **text 1** (page 52). **Find a word or expression which means the same as each of the words (1 – 5) below.** The lines where you can find the words or expressions are indicated in brackets. There is one example **(0)** at the beginning.

0.	**to give**	→	**to bestow (upon)**	**(l. 1 – 6)**	
1.	to own	→	______	(l. 7 – 14)	
2.	to believe	→	______	(l. 15 – 21)	
3.	to control	→	______	(l. 22 – 28)	
4.	to think about	→	______	(l. 29 – 36)	
5.	to climb	→	______	(l. 37 – 46)	**5 p**

Task 2

Look at **text 1** (page 52). What do the following words mean? **Match** the expressions **(A – F) as used in the text** with their corresponding definitions (1 – 7). **Write the correct numbers in the grid below.**

Be careful: There are two definitions that you do not need One definition **(0)** has already been matched correctly.

0. the ability to recover readily from misfortune or change etc.

A constitution (l. 1)

B bias (l. 16)

C resiliency (l. 31)

D mercy (l. 32)

E glimmer (l. 35)

F hunger (l. 43)

1. a wish or longing to achieve something

2. a weak sign of something

3. a particular tendency, influence or trend

4. the system of laws according to which a state is ruled

5. the ability to show kindness and compassion

6. physical characteristics, health etc.

7. difficult or unpleasant conditions of life

A	B	C	D	E	F
		0			

5 p

Task 3

Use the word given in capitals at the end of some of the lines to **form a word of the same word family** that fits in the space in the same line. There is one example **(0)** at the beginning.

0. "Nelson Mandela International Day" is celebrated on July 18 in **honour** of the **HONORABLE**

1. political leader who committed himself to promoting __________ **SOCIETY**

2. justice. The day supports Mandela's vision of __________ and **EQUAL**

freedom. It is a time to reflect upon all that one person might accomplish, and

3. emphasizes that everyone has the __________ to take action. **RESPONSIBLE**

4. Therefore, it is meant as an invitation to all of us to __________. **CONTRIBUTION**

5. Its focus is on constant __________. Mandela Day 2018 marked **IMPROVE**

a 100 years since Mandela's birth and was dedicated to "Action Against Poverty".

Adapted from: Longo, Steve. "Nelson Mandela International Day 2018" [online available on: https://www.dailymail.co.uk]

5 p

Task 4

Complete the second sentence so that it has a similar meaning to the first sentence, using the KEY WORD given in brackets. **Do not change the KEY WORD given.** You must use **between two and five words including the KEY WORD**. There is one example **(0)**.

Example

0. On his release from prison Mandela started leading South Africa out of apartheid. **(WHEN)**

(1) (2) (3) (4) (5)
Mandela started leading South Africa out of apartheid **when he was released from** prison.

1. Mandela did not let hatred get the better of him but continued to fight in a non-violent way.
______________________ hatred get the better of **(INSTEAD)**
him, Mandela continued to fight in a non-violent way. **1 p**

2. Mandela became the country's first democratic president. Otherwise, South Africa's path into democracy might have been much harder. **(IF)**
______________________ the country's first democratic president, South Africa's path into democracy might have been much harder. **1 p**

3. In 2009, the UN formally declared July 18 to be "Nelson Mandela International Day". **(WAS)**
In 2009, ______________________ "Nelson Mandela International Day" by the UN. **1 p**

4. Mandela stood up for political issues. Let us all follow his footsteps so the world will be transformed into a better place for all. **(ORDER)**
Mandela stood up for political issues. Let us all follow his footsteps ______________________ the world into a better place for all. **1 p**

5. No matter how small your actions are, they can help change the world for someone.
______________________ small your actions are, **(IMPORTANT)**
they can help change the world for someone. **1 p**

Task 5

Complete the following text. Use the correct forms of the words in brackets and find words of your own to replace the question marks. There is one example **(0)**.

What are human rights? They are the values **(0)** __which__ **(???)** keep society fair, just and equal. Ever since, people **(1)** ______________ **(fight)** for them. Nowadays, our human rights **(2)** ______________ **(protect)** by law. That means we can do something **(3)** ______________ **(oneself)** if our rights are attacked. But for some people human rights are not as important **(4)** ______________ **(???)** they should be. Societies used **(5)** ______________ **(be)** controlled by all-powerful rulers who could be cruel and unjust. Kings only gave rights to people they liked. With every hard won right came new laws that made our lives **(6)** ______________ **(good)** than before. But in the 20th century, dictators came to power. They **(7)** ______________ **(rule)** by fear and terror, like kings of the past, dismantling our rights on an unimaginable scale. After World War II, the leaders of Europe's democracies said 'never again'. They succeeded **(8)** ______________ **(???)** creating a simple document that set out the basic rights which we all need to live a dignified life. The European Convention puts rights, not rulers, at the heart of our society. The aim is to treat all individuals **(9)** ______________ **(respectful),** at work, at home, at school ... anywhere. If we lost these rights, vulnerable people **(10)** ______________ **(pay)** the highest price. **10 p**

Adapted from: Wagner, Adam. Segal, Yoav. Cub Studio. "Human Rights Explained" [online available on: https://rightsinfo.org]

Part III: Guided Writing

You only have to do **one** of the following two tasks.
Important: First read both tasks, then decide whether you want to do Task A or Task B.
You can write down your ideas on your extra sheet before you do the task on your exam paper.

Task A

Here is the beginning of an e-mail you are writing to a friend:

From:

To:

Subject:

Hi .... ,
How are you today? I have found the following statement on the internet:

"It is in your hands to make a better world for all who live in it."
(Nelson Mandela)

Sounds inspiring, doesn't it? Now I would like to do something myself. ...

Continue the e-mail and describe:

- a situation which you would like to improve
- what exactly you want to do
- who could help you and how
- how your idea might be continued in the future

You need not copy the beginning, but find a suitable ending. **Write about 200 words.**

Task B

An international youth organisation is offering an **exchange programme for students from Germany and South Africa**.

Write a **letter of application** for the programme. Include the following aspects:

- reasons for applying
- personal qualifications
- details of your stay in South Africa you would like to know more about
- a special place in your area you plan to show to your exchange partner and why

Find a suitable beginning and ending. **Write about 200 words.** You need not write any addresses. **30 p**

Listening Test

JOB FAIR

Task 1: Tips for your Internship

(Audiotrack: QR-Code rechts / Hörtext S. 99)

You will hear five speakers giving tips for tricky situations during an internship.
What aspects are they talking about? **Write the correct numbers (1 – 5) in the boxes next to the categories (A – H).** Be careful: Use each number only once.
(You will have 5 seconds after the first listening and 5 seconds after the second listening.)

A ☐ Holidays
B ☐ Workload
C ☐ Time pressure
D ☐ Outfit
E ☐ Drinks
F ☐ Feeling alone
G ☐ Being bored
H ☐ Lunch breaks

5 p

Task 2: Young Businessman

(Audiotrack: QR-Code oben / Hörtext S. 99)

You will hear an interview with Mo Bridges, a teenpreneur, who designs fashionable bow ties[1].
One ending to each of the following sentences **(1 – 4)** is correct. **Tick (✓) A, B, C or D.**
(You will have 5 seconds after the first listening and 5 seconds after the second listening.)

[1] bow tie: Fliege

Bild-Quelle: Photo by Scott Webb on Unsplash

1. Mo Bridges' day includes ...
- **A** ☐ working for class.
- **B** ☐ writing e-mails.
- **C** ☐ visiting clients.
- **D** ☐ talking with employees.

2. Mo's father ...
- **A** ☐ worked in fashion.
- **B** ☐ liked wearing ties.
- **C** ☐ was a celebrity on TV.
- **D** ☐ had the business idea.

3. Mo first designed bow ties to ...
- **A** ☐ sell them at school.
- **B** ☐ please his grandmother.
- **C** ☐ follow his passion.
- **D** ☐ make money.

4. Mo is planning ...
- **A** ☐ a game with the NBA.
- **B** ☐ new necktie designs.
- **C** ☐ a fashion show.
- **D** ☐ a charity run.

4 p

Task 3: Unusual Jobs

(Audiotrack: QR-Code S. 60 / Hörtext S. 100)

You will hear a radio report about jobs you may not know about.
There are five wrong words in the text. Write their correct versions on the lines provided.
(You will have 10 seconds after the first listening and 15 seconds after the second listening.)

Unusual Jobs

Bored with your office job? No need for that! Here are three jobs you will never believe exist. ______

Line stander

If you don't like queuing, just order a professional line stander. They queue up for hours to get you a concert ticket or a simple sales item. It's a hard job that can be well paid. ______

Fortune cookie writer

Did you know that your favorite Asian post-meal wisdom comes from a bunch of people writing Chinese fortune cookie quips? Approximately three billion fortune cookies are baked every year. As nobody wants to get the same words over and over again, lots of inspiring one-liners need to be written. ______

Bed tester

Getting paid to lie in a bed? You'd think this job would have an infinite waiting list of lazy applicants, but there's more to it than taking a nap. Your job is not as simple as that: you are to check on a variety of sectors. For example, you must make sure that mattresses and pillows are up to standard for grand hotels. ______

Well, would you want to switch to one of these jobs? ______ **5 p**

Adapted from: BrightSide. The 13 Most Unusual Jobs [online available on: https://brightside.me]

Task 4: At a Job Fair

(Audiotrack: QR-Code S. 60 / Hörtext S. 100)

You will hear an interview between a student and an assistant at a job fair.
Listen and **take notes**. You do not have to write complete sentences but **one word is not enough**.
(You will have 10 seconds after the first listening and 20 seconds after the second listening.)

	File Note	
1.	**Benefits of a foundation apprenticeship:**	▶ combines work and study ▶ equivalent to A-levels ▶ ____________ ▶ ____________
2.	**Possible job sites:**	____________
3.	**Period of time:**	____________
4.	**What an application should include:**	▶ ____________ ▶ CV and school certificates (copies)
5.	**Important for e-mail attachment:**	▶ ____________ ▶ ____________
6.	**Contact person:**	____________

8 p

Task 5: Learning a Job – What it Takes
(Audiotrack: QR-Code S. 60 / Hörtext S. 101)

You will hear a radio podcast with Ellie McCooper, chief recruiter at a software company, and Courtney Rookie, an apprentice, about learning a job. What do these people say?
Listen to the conversation and complete the grid below. Be careful, **one word is not enough**.
(You will have 30 seconds after the first listening and 90 seconds after the second listening.)

Learning a Job – What it Takes

1. Employers firstly try to find out from their applicants ...

____

2. We normally learn soft skills from ...

____

3. People with good **communication skills** give information ...

____

4. Courtney's advice on communication is to ...

____

5. Good **team players** ...

- ______________________________
- ______________________________

6. According to Courtney's boss, **time management** is ...

____

7. Calculating the time for a task is a challenge if ...

____

8 p

Written Test

Text 1

Robots

Will robots change our lives in the future? It is a funny question to ask when they are changing our lives now in so many ways and they have been doing so for years. It was in 1893 when people first saw a toaster pop up by itself. ❶ Long since we have welcomed the idea that machines can be trusted to do things for us. They record our shows, cook our food, play our music, and even run our cars. We just don't name them robots because these machines don't have a face we can talk to or a butt we can kick.

Robots which resemble humans, on the other hand, have gotten a bad reputation from a lot of movies and video games. ❷ However, there are at least some areas in which robots can serve humans right now that will change life for the future, and all in a good way. One is virtual shopping and tourism, another is assistance in the education sector. ❸ In Japan, global leader in robotics, the use of robots for these purposes has already become reality.

Imagine a Saturday morning after a stressful week. You are lying on your sofa with your tablet and guiding a video game character through a small market, except it is not a game, it is a robot shopping for you in Tokyo. Meanwhile you are having a cup of tea in your London flat. ❹ By controlling the human-like robot about your size you get a good sense of what would fit you best. In the future, when the cost and inconvenience of travel will most likely rise, why not "rent-a-rob" for an hour just to make sure the holiday residence you want to book meets your expectations?

Or think of *Elias*, the new language teacher at a Finnish primary school, who has got infinite patience in stressful situations, never makes a pupil feel embarrassed when they ask a question and can even do funky dance moves. *Elias* is also a robot, able to understand and speak 23 languages and is equipped with software that allows it to analyze students' requirements. The robot recognizes each pupil's skill levels and adjusts its questions accordingly. It also gives feedback to teachers about a student's possible problems. ❺ Despite its knowledge of language and mathematics, the robot's inability to maintain discipline among a class of primary school children means that the human teachers' jobs are safe.

Furthermore, robots already support doctors, nurses and hospitals by automating tasks and assisting in patient care. The advantages are obvious. Robots don't have feelings, they can't get tired, and they never have a slip of attention. Scientists at the University of Oxford have already tested a robotic assistant system in complicated eye-surgeries – it turned out to be a success. A healthcare provider in Ontario, Canada, recently received the first robot approved for knee operations and started using it on patients in January 2019. ❻ This robot makes a 3D model of the knee or hip based on the patient's CT scan and provides real-time feedback as the surgeons use special instruments.

All these examples show that robots won't just change our lives in the future. They will expand them. Right now all modern technology is designed to bring the world to you: phone, radio, television, and internet. But if trends continue, robots will soon bring you to the world, everywhere, and at the speed of thought. ❼ We have taken the first steps towards creating robots that interact directly with humans. At this point the most important question to ask is not "What will intelligent robots do?" but "Whom will intelligent robots serve?"

Adapted from: Tilden, Mark. Robotics Can Change our Lives in the Near Future (online available on: https://www.theguardian.com/zurichfuturology/story/0,,1920335,00.html), Copyright Guardian News & Media Ltd 2020 and https://www.roboticsbusinessreview.com/health-medical/5-surgical-robots-2019/

Bildquelle: ©Vladislav Ociacia – stock.adobe.com

ARTIFICIAL INTELLIGENCE

Part I: Reading

Task 1

Read the text *Robots* (page 64). Are sentences **1 – 10** 'True' (T) or 'False' (F)? Choose 'Not in the text' (N) if there is not enough information to answer 'True' or 'False'.
Tick (✓) the correct answer.

	T	F	N
1. Only machines with human features are called "robots".			
2. Media have portrayed human-like robots in a positive way.			
3. Japan has established robots in the travel industry.			
4. Robots might offer new ways of finding suitable clothes.			
5. Travelling will probably become more affordable.			
6. Pupils like *Elias* for his dance moves.			
7. *Elias* finds out what pupils really need.			
8. *Elias* will soon replace teachers in the classroom.			
9. In Canada, a robot carries out operations based on feedback from the doctors.			
10. Robots will mainly serve the people who created them.			

10 p

Task 2

Look at the text *Robots* (page 64). Five sentences have been removed from the text. Choose the correct gap **(1 – 7)** in the text for each of the sentences below **(A – E). Write the correct number of the gap behind each sentence.** Be careful: There are **two gaps** which you do **not need to use**.

A	With a live video and audio feed, you can chat with the sales assistant.	☐
B	They provide you with an extra hand where it is needed while you are safely at home.	☐
C	Today, this device is the most common household appliance although it has only been in existence a little over a century.	☐
D	But it cannot solve every issue.	☐
E	An additional one is use in the medical field.	☐

5 p

Prüfungen

Task 3

Here are four texts about the use of *Artificial Intelligence (AI)*. Read them and **match them with the statements 1 – 6 below**. Choose the correct text **(A – D)** and **write its letter in the box**. The texts may be chosen **more than once**. There is one example **(0)** at the beginning.

A *Artificial Intelligence (AI)* is making important advances in the transport sector. These include self-driving cars, radar devices to detect even the smallest obstacles, intelligent search for free parking spaces and route optimization. These developments have a direct impact on logistics. For example, self-driving cars can be used 24 hours a day without depending on the driver's work hours. So the logistics companies can save time, miles and fuel. This translates into lower costs and higher profitability. While some of these technologies are still in development, analysts expect these solutions to move around $7 billion into the market by 2050.

B Software has replaced people in the travel industry. You may have identified yourself by use of a code or through facial recognition to access rooms and certain services. In addition to such developments in software, *AI* finds its way into business. Currently Chatbots are the most common *AI*-based solutions in use. But more and more, *AI*-software gathers user data like interests, budgets and must-see places, sorts through countless destinations and recommends the most relevant and personalized travel options. Probably 80 per cent of all travel assistants will be *AI*-based robots by 2020, for example at hotel reception.

C We already have several robotic devices that are built to help us with our simple housework. Now some companies are working on humanoids that will perform our daily chores for us in the near future. Regarding health aids, statistics project that *AI* home health aids will grow by 38 per cent over the next ten years. This shows the need for further development. Another area in which *AI* can be really useful is to help elderly people stay in their homes as long as possible. Though there are devices currently on the market, a sustainable humanoid is still in the pipeline.

D One of the greatest applications of *AI* is in space travel and exploration. *AI* can help us reach unknown planets and stars without ever having to risk a human life. In the near future, *AI*-powered humanoids will be smart enough to carry out space missions on their own, finding new resources for humankind. Scientists have predicted that in the future, the behavior of space probes will be governed by *AI* rather than from Earth. For example, both the *Spirit Rover* and the *Opportunity Rover*, which were launched back in 2003, had an *AI* driving system that allowed them to explore the surface of Mars.

Adapted from: Decide Soluciones. How Different Sectors are Using AI 29.10.2018 [online availabe on: https://becominghuman.ai/how-different-sectors-are-using-ai-26470ba334ab]
Schroer, Alyssa: 9 Reasons Why AI is a Traveler`s Best Friend (online available on: https://builtin.com/artificial-intelligence/ai-travel-tech)
Rohilla, Aditya. How AI Will Affect Different Fields of Technology (online available on: https://towardsdatascience.com/how-ai-will-affect-different-fields-of-technology-9977369f3e2b)

0 The best route will be found through *Artificial Intelligence (AI)*.
1 *AI* will be useful for senior citizens.
2 People will not be put into danger thanks to *AI*.
3 Technology can help you enter your accommodation.
4 In this field *AI* helps find the perfect individual deal.
5 *AI* has already proofed its usefulness in two specialized vehicles.
6 In this field *AI* is used to make more money.

0	1	2	3	4	5	6
A						

6 p

Task 4

Aus lizenzrechtlichen Gründen wurden der Text sowie die dazugehörigen Aufgaben durch gleichwertige Muster ersetzt.

Verwenden Sie die Informationen über Londons Verkehrspläne aus dem folgenden Text und **bearbeiten Sie die Aufgaben (1 – 5) stichpunktartig auf Deutsch**. Es ist keine wörtliche Übersetzung nötig, die Aspekte müssen inhaltlich jedoch vollständig erfasst sein. Einzelwörter genügen nicht als Antwort.

Artificial intelligence to tackle[1] London's transport challenges

Transport for London (TfL) are continually improving their services in various projects in order to create better living and travelling conditions in Britain's capital. This includes helping everyone to use cars less and to walk, cycle or use public transport more.

Recently TfL has worked with Vivacity Labs, an innovative London tech firm, on a UK-first trial of artificial intelligence technology, which could make it much easier to plan and operate new cycle routes in the capital.

Until now, TfL has relied mainly on manual traffic counts to work out how many people are cycling on any given road. This helps assess demand for new cycle routes and helps TfL improve how it operates the road network for the growing numbers of people cycling. Manual traffic counts, which are carried out at limited locations on London's road network, are only able to give a snapshot of road use on the given day or time.

Since 2018, TfL has trialled using Vivacity Labs sensors that use artificial intelligence to detect road users and decide which mode of transport they are using. These sensors proved to be up to 98 per cent accurate.

They gather data around the clock, which provides a significantly more detailed picture of how London's roads are being used by everyone 24/7. All video captured by the sensors is processed and discarded within seconds, meaning that no personal data is ever stored.

Data about the numbers of people cycling is a vital part of TfL's planning for new cycleways across London. As the network continues to grow, TfL will use data from sources such as the sensors to work out where investment in new infrastructure can best be targeted.

Enabling more people to walk and cycle is central to the Mayor's efforts to tackle London's toxic air, ill-health and the climate emergency. The Mayor's Transport Strategy target is for 80 per cent of journeys in London made by walking, cycling and public transport by 2041.

[1] to tackle: etwas in Angriff nehmen, bewältigen, mit etwas fertigwerden

Adapted from: https://tfl.gov.uk/info-for/media/press-releases/2020/january/artificial-intelligence-to-help-fuel-london-s-cycling-boom, Seitenaufruf am 24.08.2020

1. Zu welchem Zweck arbeitet Transport for London an der Verbesserung ihrer Dienste?

______________________________ **1 p**

2. a) Wie wurden bisher Daten bezüglich der Nutzung der Radwege erhoben?

______________________________ **1 p**

b) Nennen Sie die Nachteile dieser Methode.

______________________________ **2 p**

3. a) Was kann über die Zuverlässigkeit der Sensoren, die künstliche Intelligenz verwenden, gesagt werden?

______________________________ **1 p**

b) Worin liegt der Vorteil dieser Datenerhebung im Vergleich zur herkömmlichen Methode?

______________________________ **1 p**

c) Wie wird dem Datenschutz Rechnung getragen?

____ 1 p

4. Wozu werden die ermittelten Daten verwendet?

____ 1 p

5. Welches Ziel strebt der Bürgermeister in Bezug auf die Verkehrssituation in London an?

____ 1 p

Part II: Use of English

Task 1

Look at **text 1** (page 64). **Find a word or expression which means the same as each of the words (1 – 5) below.** The lines where you can find the words or expressions are indicated in brackets. There is one example **(0)** at the beginning.

0.	**(to) accept**	→	**(to) welcome**	**(l. 1 – 9)**
1.	intention	→	______________	(l. 10 – 17)
2.	discomfort	→	______________	(l. 18 – 27)
3.	ashamed	→	______________	(l. 28 – 42)
4.	clear	→	______________	(l. 43 – 58)
5.	(to) widen	→	______________	(l. 59 – 68)

5 p

Task 2

Look at **text 1** (page 64). What do the following words mean? **Match** the expressions **(A – F) as used in the text** with their corresponding definitions **(1 – 7)**. **Write the correct numbers in the grid below.** Be careful: There are two definitions that you do not need. One definition **(0)** has already been matched correctly.

A reputation (l. 11)
B assistance (l. 15)
C character (l. 20)
D patience (l. 29)
E requirement (l. 34)
F skill (l. 34)

0. the ability to do something well
1. the feeling or belief that something good will or should happen
2. the action of helping someone
3. the ability to wait, or to continue doing something despite difficulties
4. a person in a novel, play or film
5. an online method to help customers find products
6. people's opinion of something based on past experience
7. something that is needed or wanted

A	B	C	D	E	F
					0

5 p

Task 3

Aus lizenzrechtlichen Gründen wurden der Text sowie die dazugehörigen Aufgaben durch gleichwertige Muster ersetzt.

Use the word given in capitals at the end of some of the lines to **form a word of the same word family** that fits in the space in the same line. There is one example **(0)** at the beginning.

0. The healthcare **industry** is changed by *Artificial Intelligence (AI)* in several ways. **INDUSTRIAL**

Furthermore, *AI* offers possible uses in sports, where health-relevant issues

1. are of ____________________ importance. **ESSENCE**

The players are obliged to engage in physical tests that use *AI* to

2. ____________________ various different health factors. **EXAMINATION**

3. ____________________ or not can be recognized through this reconstruction **EXHAUSTION**

by *AI*.

4. To ____________________ possible physical problems in advance, *AI* systems **IDENTIFICATION**

deal with a flow of data especially in competitive seasons.

5. This makes it possible for sports teams to keep their most ____________________ **VALUE**

assets, their athletes, in first-class condition. **5 p**

Task 4

Complete the second sentence so that it has a similar meaning to the first sentence, using the KEY WORD given in brackets. **Do not change the KEY WORD given.** You must use **between two and five words including the KEY WORD**. There is one example **(0)**.

Example

0. Deepfakes are among the most threatening developments in the field of media manipulation. **(AS)**

There is hardly anything in the developments of media manipulation which is

(1) (2) (3) (4)

as threatening as deepfakes.

1. Deepfakes show images or videos in which people's faces have been altered with **(CAN)**

the aid of Artificial Intelligence (AI) and, as a result, look deceptively real. In order to

get images or videos which look deceptively real, you ____________________

with the aid of Artificial Intelligence (AI). **1 p**

2. Many experts say deepfakes often have serious consequences for the individuals abused **(SAID)**

in them. Deepfakes ____________________ to often have serious consequences for the individuals abused in them. **1 p**

3. Maybe you haven't heard about how deepfakes are technically created. **(MIGHT)**

____________________ about how deepfakes are

technically created. **1 p**

4. In 2020, a British television network channel published an alternative Christmas speech **(BY)** of the Queen. An alternative Christmas speech of the Queen ______________________ British television network in 2020. **1 p**

5. If the technology to detect deepfakes is not improved, they might cause serious **(UNLESS)** harm to individuals or even societies. ______________________ to detect deepfakes is not improved, deepfakes might cause serious harm to individuals or even societies. **1 p**

Task 5

Complete the following text. Use the correct forms of the words in brackets. There is one example **(0)**.

The *Unimate* **(0)** __**was**__ **(be)** the very first industrial robot, revolutionizing manufacturing all over the world. The world might have developed differently if J. Engelberger **(1)** ______________ **(not meet)** inventor G. Devol in 1956 at a cocktail party. The two talked about Devols's latest invention. Engelberger convinced the CEO of a controlling company **(2)** ______________ **(finance)** the development of Devol's invention. After almost two years, a prototype **(3)** ______________ **(produce)**: the *Unimate*.
A car manufacturing company installed it at an assembly line in Trenton, New Jersey. Today, the *Unimate* **(4)** ______________ **(regard)** as the first mass produced robotic arm for factory automation. It became **(5)** ______________ **(immense)** successful. The American company jumped ahead of its competitors to become the **(6)** ______________ **(progressive)** car plant in the world. European companies quickly followed. More and more companies installed *Unimate* robotic arms, focusing on **(7)** ______________ **(employ)** the robots in tasks harmful or unpleasant to humans. The field of robotics **(8)** ______________ **(affect)** numerous facets of human life ever since. The invention of the *Unimate* will certainly remain **(9)** ______________ **(significant)**, not only for industry, but also for civilization. This will be worth **(10)** ______________ **(remember)** in the years to come. **10 p**

Adapted from: Robotic Industries Association. A Tribute to Joseph Engelberger: Unimate (online available on:https://www.robotics.org/joseph-engelberger/unimate.cfm)

Part III: Guided Writing

You only have to do **one** of the following two tasks.
Important: First read both tasks, then decide whether you want to do Task A or Task B.
You can write down your ideas on an extra sheet before you do the task on your exam paper.

Task A

You have bought an electronic device that does not work the way it should.

Write an online review and describe … ★ ★ ☆ ☆ ☆

- the product and your reasons for buying it
- problem(s) you had with the device
- how you tried to solve the problem(s)
- your advice to the reader

Find a suitable beginning and ending. **Write about 200 words.**

Task B

You are starting a network of young inventors in your hometown.

Write an e-mail to invite the first participants. Include ...

- why networking is a great idea
- the first network meeting: organisational details
- the first network meeting: topics
- how the network could be promoted in the future

Find a suitable beginning and ending. **Write about 200 words.** **30 p**

Listening Test

METEOROLOGY

Task 1: Weather Apps
(Audiotrack: QR-Code rechts / Hörtext S. 102)

You will hear five statements about different weather apps. Why are people using these apps?
Write the correct numbers (1 – 5) in the boxes next to the categories (A – H).
Be careful: Use each number only once.
(You will have 5 seconds after the first listening and 5 seconds after the second listening.)

A ☐ Link to social networks
B ☐ Clear layout
C ☐ Data protection
D ☐ Precise local forecasts
E ☐ Warning messages
F ☐ Human expertise
G ☐ Frequent updates
H ☐ Several measuring instruments

5 p

Task 2: An Interview with a Weather Forecaster
(Audiotrack: QR-Code oben / Hörtext S. 102)

You will hear an interview with the weather forecaster Janice Dean.
One ending to each of the following sentences **(1 – 4)** is correct. **Tick (✓) A, B, C or D.**
(You will have 5 seconds after the first listening and 5 seconds after the second listening.)

1. Janice studied meteorology because of ...
A ☐ Canadian winters.
B ☐ the need to pay the bills.
C ☐ her lack of good opportunities.
D ☐ a job at a TV station.

2. Hurricanes are ...
A ☐ amazing above huge cities.
B ☐ seldom to be seen.
C ☐ as dynamic as a snowstorm.
D ☐ less dangerous over water.

3. Janice was glad when ...
A ☐ she saw the first weather app.
B ☐ the balloon reached the tower.
C ☐ the pilot landed quickly.
D ☐ the wind calmed down.

4. According to Janice, weather can ...
A ☐ wipe away sadness.
B ☐ bring people in need together.
C ☐ reduce people's income.
D ☐ separate communities.

4 p

Task 3: Weather Report

(Audiotrack: QR-Code S. 72 / Hörtext S. 103)

You will hear a weather report for the next week in Britain.
There are six wrong words in the text. Write their correct versions on the lines provided.
(You will have 10 seconds after the first listening and 15 seconds after the second listening.)

Weather Report	
Good afternoon! It's a largely rainy but quite warm day	______________
today. Temperatures have been on the up after a tough	______________
start to the week. It's been rather unsettled with showers	______________
affecting Britain most days of the week. This weekend won't	______________
see any serious change to this pattern. There'll be wild	______________
winds and again some rain almost everywhere throughout	______________
the country. We'll see a deep low pressure system moving	______________
across the north on Monday. It will bring more winds to the	______________
areas it affects in the north. At the same time there will be	______________
less rain. As the low pressure system drifts eastwards,	______________
there'll be a spell of north-westerly winds developing. It'll	______________
become colder, and with the strength of the wind on	______________
Tuesday it'll feel chilly.	______________
Next, we'll see high pressure building to the south-west and	______________
then to the rest of Britain. This will drift overhead on	______________
Wednesday, which should be dry and calm, but still rather	______________
cool. The end of the week looks better. And the outlook for	______________
next week: warmer temperatures can be expected.	______________

Adapted from: BBC. Monthly Outlook. [online available on: https://www.bbc.com]

6 p

Task 4: Calling the Weather Service

(Audiotrack: QR-Code S. 72 / Hörtext S. 103)

You will hear a phone call between a young hiker in Australia and a woman from the Hikers' Hotline. **Listen and take notes**. You do not have to write complete sentences but **one word is not enough**.
(You will have 10 seconds after the first listening and 20 seconds after the second listening.)

	Hikers' Hotline / Notes	
1.	**Reason for loss of internet connection:**	____________________
2.	**Amount of rain expected:**	____________________
3.	**Name of closest hotel:**	____________________
4.	**Necessary equipment:**	▶ ____________________ ▶ ____________________ ▶ ____________________
5.	**Street Name of Lil's Place:**	____________________ Drive

7 p

Task 5: Floods and Droughts

(Audiotrack: QR-Code S. 72 / Hörtext S. 104)

You will hear a radio interview with two meteorologists about floods and droughts.
Listen and complete the sentences. Be careful, **one word is not enough.**
(You will have 30 seconds after the first listening and 90 seconds after the second listening.)

Floods and Droughts

1. A slower hurricane leads to a ____________________
____
2. An average car cannot withstand a level of ____________________
____
3. During floods, drinking water can be polluted by ____________________
____________________ **and** ____________________
4. A useful emergency kit should include a first aid kit as well as ____________________
____________________ **and** ____________________
5. Floods and droughts will be reduced if we ____________________
____
6. Perth in Australia wants to become independent of natural water resources with ____________________
____

8 p

Written Test

Text 1

A Late Tribute to the First Computer Programmer

It was December 10, 1815, and the famous poet Lord George Gordon Byron was expecting the birth of the desired boy. Only a few months later, he decided to divorce his wife and left Britain forever. ❶ The little girl had been called Ada by Lord Byron himself but never saw her father again, who died when she was eight years old.

Ada Lovelace had an unusual upbringing for an aristocratic girl in the 1800s. Her mother made her study mathematics and science. Such challenging subjects were not standard for women at the time. But her mother believed that engaging in rigorous studies would prevent little Ada from developing her father's moody and unpredictable temperament. ❷ Ada developed her mathematical and technical skills despite severe illnesses in her childhood. She received instruction from William Frend, a social reformer; William King, the family's doctor; and Mary Somerville, a Scottish astronomer and mathematician who was one of the first women to be admitted into the Royal Astronomical Society. Lovelace considered Somerville to be her role model.

It was also Somerville who introduced her to the company of Charles Babbage, a mathematician and inventor. Lovelace was often seen in aristocratic society, danced, inspired conversations and met quite a few prominent personalities of the time. ❸ On June 5, 1833, Somerville took Lovelace to a party at Babbage's house and she clearly impressed her host with her skills. 41-year-old Charles and 17-year-old Ada became friends, and Babbage served as a mentor to Lovelace. Thanks to him, Lovelace began studying advanced mathematics with the first professor of mathematics at the University of London, Augustus de Morgan. ❹ She paused her studies only for her wedding and to start a family, becoming the mother of three children.

Lovelace was fascinated by Babbage's ideas. He had invented and constructed the "difference engine" in order to perform mathematical calculations. He also came up with ideas for another device known as the "analytical engine", designed to manage more complex calculations. Between 1842 and 1843, Lovelace translated an article by Luigi Menabrea, an Italian scientist, about Babbage's "analytical engine". Lovelace included her own ideas on the machine and her notes ended up being three times longer than the original article. In her work, Lovelace described how codes could be created. ❺ Her remarks cover, among other things, the first known computer programme – an algorithm designed to be executed by the machine. She claimed that the analytical engine could theoretically calculate whatever the programmer wanted and expressed visions about advanced computer skills which are normal for us today: composing music, drawing pictures, and using technology for individuals and society to work together.

As you might guess, Lovelace's article, which was published in an English science journal in 1843, attracted little attention when she was alive. ❻ Indeed, her contributions to the field of computer science were not discovered until 1953, when they were reintroduced to the world by B. V. Bowden in "Faster Than Thoughts: A Symposium on Digital Computing Machines". However, since then, Lovelace has received many posthumous honours for her work. She is said to have inspired Alan Turing's work on the first modern-day computers, the term "Turing complete language" is partly based on processes that Lovelace described. When the U.S. defense department developed their own programming language in the mid-1970s, they named it "Ada" in her honour. ❼ "Ada" has become an international standard.

Lovelace's story is just one example that women have not always been taken seriously enough for their accomplishments. Therefore, the contributions of women to science, technology and mathematics are celebrated on "Ada Lovelace Day", the second Tuesday in October.

Adapted from: Tesar, Jaromir. Barta, Lukas. The Story of Ada Lovelace [online available on: https://medium.com]
Biography.com Editors. Ada Lovelace Biography [online available on: https://www.biography.com]

WOMEN MAKING HISTORY

Part I: Reading

Task 1

Read the text *A Late Tribute to the First Computer Programmer* (page 75).
Are sentences **1 – 10** 'True' (T) or 'False' (F)? Choose 'Not in the text' (N) if there is not enough information to answer 'True' or 'False'.
Tick (✓) the correct answer.

	T	F	N
1. Lord Byron took good care of his daughter.			
2. In addition to having technical lessons, Lovelace also learnt languages.			
3. Lovelace's mother was worried about her daughter's character.			
4. Babbage influenced Lovelace's further education.			
5. Babbage built two mathematical machines.			
6. Lovelace wrote a summary of Menabrea's work.			
7. Lovelace's visions have become reality.			
8. Bowden drew the attention of the scientific world to Lovelace's work.			
9. Turing showed that modern-day computers are capable of networking.			
10. The US defense department named Lovelace's programme "Ada".			

10 p

Task 2

Look at the text *A Late Tribute to the First Computer Programmer* (page 75). Five sentences have been removed from the text. Choose the correct gap **(1 – 7)** in the text for each of the sentences below **(A – E). Write the correct <u>number</u> of the gap behind each sentence.** Be careful: There are **two gaps** which you do **not need to use**.

A One of them was the famous writer Charles Dickens. ☐

B She also suggested a method for the engine to repeat a series of instructions, a process known as "looping" that computer programmes use today. ☐

C It is still used around the world today in the industries of aviation, health care, transportation, finance, infrastructure, and space. ☐

D From early on, the girl showed a talent for numbers. ☐

E He was disturbed by the fact that the baby's mother, Anne Isabella Noel Byron, had not brought a son into the world. ☐

5 p

Ada Lovelace (1815 – 1852)

Bildquelle: https://datumeight.github.io/Hackathon2020/

Task 3

Here are four texts about extraordinary people. Read them and **match them with the statements 1 – 7 below**. Choose the correct text **(A – D)** and **write its letter in the box**. The texts may be chosen **more than once**.

A Laura Redden Searing was a deaf journalist who reported on the US Civil War. She was also a poet, who had the awkward honour of being friends with both President Lincoln and his future assassin, John Wilkes Booth. At the time, there were no colleges for deaf women, so Redden Searing went to Europe and taught herself German, French, Spanish and Italian. She got a job as the European correspondent for *The New York Times*, and later went on to other renowned publications such as *Harper's* magazine; She published books on politics and poetry collections.	**B** Hedy Lamarr was both a movie star and an inventor. She was known as 'the most attractive girl in the world', and her most important invention was called "frequency-hopping". This technology, which she developed together with a friend, prevents the radio guidance of torpedoes from being jammed and hijacked by enemies. The pair were granted a patent in 1942. Today, frequency hopping is the basis of wireless communications like Wi-Fi and Bluetooth. It was not until shortly before her death in 2000 that Lamarr gained recognition for her patent. She is now remembered as 'Lady Bluetooth'.
C Lotfia Elnadi was born in Cairo in 1907. Her father saw no reason for her to pursue further education. As a young woman, she read about a flying school and knew it was for her. Telling her father that she was attending a study group, Elnadi took flying lessons instead. She completed school in just 67 days, paying her fees by working as a secretary, and received a pilot's licence. Elnadi became a national celebrity. Due to an injury she had to quit flying, but not before winning medals and honours as a renowned lady of the Egyptian skies.	**D** Gabriela Brimmer was born with cerebral palsy and was unable to speak. The only part of her body she could use was her left foot. She learned to use her toe to point to letters on an alphabet board, and to type. Initially, she went to a school for children with disabilities, but her mother convinced the local public school that Brimmer's disability had nothing to do with her intellectual abilities. She not only outdid her classmates in high school, but also attended an elite university. Brimmer built an unforeseen career as a bestselling author and launched a disability rights movement in Mexico.

Adapted from: Jewell, Hanna. 100 Nasty Women of History. Hodder & Stoughton (2017)

1 Both a famous politician and his murderer were close to this person.
2 Because of an unforeseen event, this person had to give up her passion.
3 This person's ideas became appreciated only much later.
4 A parent initially stood in the way of this person's education.
5 As there was no suitable school, this person took her education into her own hands.
6 This person not only wrote books but also fought for people's equal chances.
7 This person was renowned for her appearance and her intellectual abilities.

1	2	3	4	5	6	7

7 p

Task 4

Verwenden Sie die Informationen über *Tawakkol Karman* und **bearbeiten Sie die Aufgaben (1 – 5) stichpunktartig auf Deutsch**. Die Aspekte müssen inhaltlich vollständig erfasst sein. Einzelwörter genügen nicht als Antwort.

Am I dreaming too much ...?

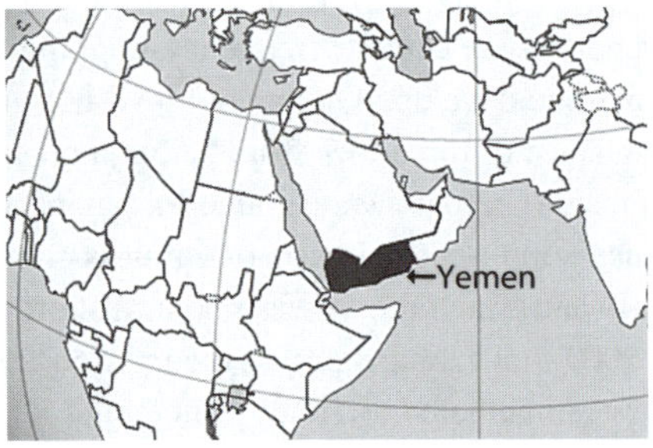

Tawakkol Karman was 32 when she received the Nobel Peace Prize in 2011 for protesting peacefully in her home country, Yemen. In her acceptance speech she emphasized the goal that she and millions of people in the Arab world try to make come true: replacing existing dictatorships with democratic governments that serve their people. Although Karman always protested non-violently, the government continually tried to discourage her with frightening phone calls, and even sent her to prison several times.

Together with seven other female journalists, Karman founded *Women Journalists Without Chains*, an organisation that coaches reporters how to make use of media. It also publishes annual reports on press freedom in Yemen. Unfortunately, the organisation has observed that violence against journalists has increased.

When Karman tried to legally set up an independent broadcasting station for female journalists, her project was rejected by the government. This fact is one of the reasons why Karman and various Arab Spring activists from Egypt, Tunisia, Syria and Libya have asked the democratic world for support.

Karman has stated that the regime itself was the cause of most of Yemen's problems. She has called for international help to take violent rulers to court and to establish a modern democracy with all the institutions that are needed.

Tawakkol Karman is dreaming of a new world which will guarantee basic human rights for all human beings: "Am I dreaming too much … ?"

Adapted from:
Robert F. Kennedy Human Rights. Tawakkol Karman. Speak Truth to Power Curriculum, 2012, Module 17
(online available on: https://rfkhumanrights.org)
Karman, Tawakkol. Nobel Lecture [online available on: https://www.nobelprize.org]

1. Welches Ziel hat Tawakkol Karman für die arabische Welt?

______________________________ **1 p**

2. Wie begegnete die Regierung Jemens dem friedlichen Protest von Karman? **(2 Details)**

▶ ______________________________

▶ ______________________________ **2 p**

3. Nennen Sie zwei Aufgaben der Organisation *Women Journalists Without Chains.*

▶ ______________________________

▶ ______________________________ **2 p**

4. Welches Projekt wurde von der Regierung abgelehnt?

______________________________ **1 p**

5. Wobei bitten Karman und andere arabische Aktivisten demokratische Lander um Hilfe? **(2 Details)**

▶ ______________________________

▶ ______________________________ **2 p**

Part II: Use of English

Task 1

Look at **text 1** (page 75). **Find a word or expression which means the same as each of the words (1 – 5) below.** The lines where you can find the words or expressions are indicated in brackets. There is one example **(0)** at the beginning.

0. to name → to call (l. 1 – 6)
1. to accept → ______________ (l. 7 – 19)
2. to fascinate → ______________ (l. 20 – 32)
3. to interrupt → ______________ (l. 20 – 32)
4. to imagine → ______________ (l. 51 – 65)
5. to motivate → ______________ (l. 51 – 65)

5 p

Task 2

Look at **text 1** (page 75). What do the following words mean? **Match** the expressions **(A – F)** **as used in the text** with their corresponding definitions **(1 – 7)**. **Write the correct numbers in the grid below.** Be careful: There are two definitions that you do not need. One definition **(0)** has already been matched correctly.

A upbringing (l. 7)
B mentor (l. 28)
C algorithm (l. 44)
D journal (l. 52)
E **term** (l. 60)
F accomplishment (l. 67 f.)

0. a word that exactly describes someone or something
1. a number of people united or incorporated for business
2. something which has been achieved or done in an outstanding way
3. a set of rules for solving a problem in a number of steps
4. a daily record of a person's experiences or thoughts
5. a magazine, especially one published for a professional group
6. the treatment and instruction a child receives from its parents
7. a wise and trusted counselor or teacher

A	B	C	D	E	F
				0	

5 p

Task 3

Use the word given in capitals at the end of some of the lines to **form a word of the same word family** that fits in the space in the same line.There is one example **(0)** at the beginning.

0. New parents **anxiously** await their child's Apgar score, which is the gold **ANXIETY**
1. standard for determining the ______________ of a newborn. Virginia Apgar **HEAL**
2. devised that score in 1953, developing the first ______________ tool to **SCIENCE**
3. evaluate a baby's risks. She is said to have created her ______________ **POWER**

checklist in response to a question from a student. The Apgar test has become a

4. ______________ -saving standard. Former U.S. Surgeon General Richmond **LIVE**
5. once said that Apgar had "done more to ______________ the lives of **IMPROVEMENT**

mothers, babies, and unborn infants than anyone else in the 20th century".

5 p

Task 4

Complete the second sentence so that it has a similar meaning to the first sentence, using the KEY WORD given in brackets. **Do not change the KEY WORD given.** You must use **between two and five words including the KEY WORD**. There is one example **(0)**.

Example

0. People say the Godmother of Rock 'n' Roll, Sister Rosetta Tharpe, was a true pioneer. **(SAID)**
The Godmother of Rock 'n' Roll, Sister Rosetta Tharpe **is said to be a** true pioneer.
(1) (2) (3) (4) (5)

1. To understand Tharpe's success, we must look at the musical styles in her songs. **(WANT)**
____
Tharpe's success, we must look at the musical styles in her songs. **1 p**

2. She sang not only gospel songs, but also big band swing jazz. **(AS)**
She sang ______________________________
______________ big band swing jazz. **1 p**

3. Before Rosetta Tharpe toured Europe in 1964 as part of the Blues & Gospel Caravan, she had only played in the US. **(USED)**
______________________________ only in the US,
before she toured Europe in 1964 as part of the Blues & Gospel Caravan. **1 p**

4. It was Tharpe who inspired legends such as Johnny Cash and Little Richard. **(BY)**
Legends such as Johnny Cash and Little Richard ______________________________
______________________________. **1 p**

5. Rosetta Tharpe fans should definitely watch Scorsese's documentary "The Blues". **(WORTH)**
Scorsese's documentary "The Blues" ______________________________
______________________________ for Rosetta Tharpe fans. **1 p**

Adapted from: Liptrott, Josephine. Biography: Sister Rosetta Tharpe – Godmother of Rock'n'Roll [online available on: http://www.theheroinecollective.com]
Elvis Information Network. Spotlight on the King. How Sister Rosetta Tharpe influenced Elvis' Music [online available on: http://www.elvisinfonet.com]
Bildquelle: By James J. Kriegsmann – Scan via James E. Arsenault & Company. Cropped and retouched by uploader; see upload history below for unretouched original. Photograph by James J. Kriegsmann. Published by Tharpe's management. Public Domain, https://commons.wikimedia.org/w/index.php?curid=101564175

Task 5

Complete the following text. Use the correct forms of the words in brackets and find words of your own to replace the question marks. There is one example **(0)**.

Lady Jess, Artistic Director of the *Urban Playground Chamber Orchestra*, New York, introduces herself and the project: "I am a Southern woman **(0)** **whose** **(???)** heart and body has been in New York for over a decade. As a violinist, I **(1)** ______________ **(not, need)** specific types of music to find inspiration. I'd actually prefer it if there **(2)** ____________________ **(be)** no categories, but my first experience was classical music. And today I claim instant cultural equity for black classical music – and for the black composers, singers and instrumentalists who take part **(3)** ____________________ **(???)** our journey. As an ensemble, we try to do this by **(4)** ____________________ **(set)** up unique concert programs and new methods of collaboration. I am **(5)** ____________________ **(true)** honored to lead the orchestra. It **(6)** ____________________ **(found)** to promote the music of African American composers and women, and to explore culturally relevant themes like resistance and existential peace. At the moment, we **(7)** ____________________ **(design)** performances and material in digital format. And not all **(8)** ____________________ **(???)** this will be related to music. Our videos can **(9)** ____________________ **(download)** by our fans from our website. We are looking forward to **(10)** ____________________ **(collaborate)** with you. My name is Lady Jess, Artistic Director of the Urban Playground Chamber Orchestra, and it's my time." **10 p**

Adapted from: Lady Jess. Announcing: Lady Jess, Artistic Director of Urban Playground Chamber Orchestra [video online available on: https://www.upchamberorchestra.org]

Part III: Guided Writing

You only have to do **one** of the following two tasks.
Important: First read both tasks, then decide whether you want to do Task A or Task B.

Task A

You want to start a **democracy club** at your school. In the club, students can talk about and practise their democratic ideas.

Write a **letter to your headmaster** and include the following:

- ▶ why young people should be politically active
- ▶ what project(s) could be interesting at your school
- ▶ how the club should be organized
- ▶ how you plan on getting members

Find a suitable beginning and ending. **Write about 200 words.**

Task B

A radio channel wants to award a prize to **extraordinary women** and to portray them in a special programme. Everyone can suggest a person they admire.
Be careful: you may not use one of the women mentioned elsewhere in this exam.

Write an **e-mail to the radio channel** and include the following:

- ▶ why your candidate is extraordinary
- ▶ how you became interested in this person
- ▶ what prize this person deserves
- ▶ why it is important to have a role model

Find a suitable beginning and ending. **Write about 200 words.** **30 p**

Listening Test

ON YOUR BIKES!

Task 1: Specialised Bike Shops
(Audiotrack: QR-Code rechts / Hörtext S. 105)

You will hear five statements by bike shop owners about the cycling solutions they offer.
What purpose are they talking about?
Write the correct numbers (1 – 5) in the boxes next to the categories (A – H).
Be careful: Use each number only once.
(You will have 5 seconds after the first listening and 5 seconds after the second listening.)

A ☐ Inclusion of disabled people
B ☐ Riding to and from work
C ☐ Refreshed retro look
D ☐ Supreme comfort
E ☐ Fitness workout
F ☐ Individual construction
G ☐ Fast touring
H ☐ Off-road use

5 p

Task 2: An E-Bike Trip through California
(Audiotrack: QR-Code oben / Hörtext S. 105)

You will hear a conversation at an e-bike rentals pick-up in Carson City.
Look at the **locations the tourist wants to use (1 – 5). Find their position on the map.**
Write the numbers in the correct boxes.
Be careful: Use each number only once. There is one example at the beginning.
(You will have 5 seconds after the first listening and 5 seconds after the second listening.)

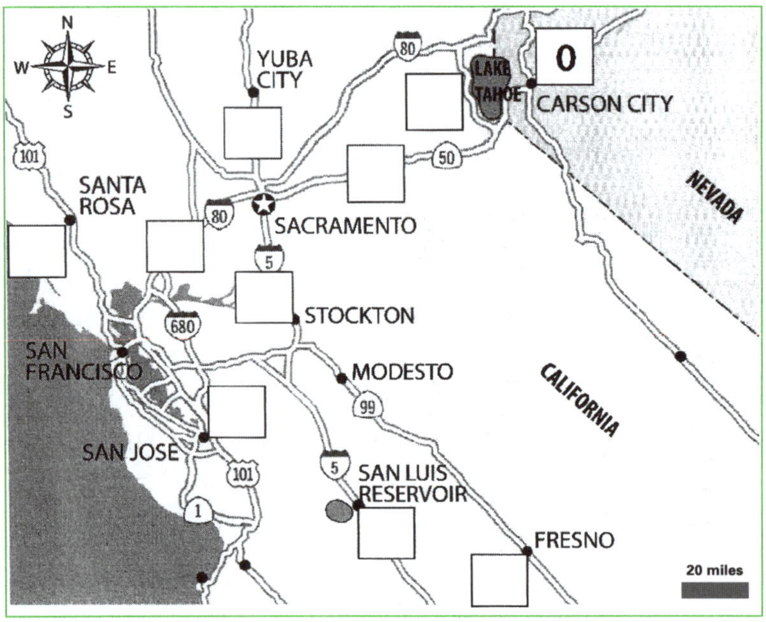

What the tourist <u>wants to use</u>:

(0) e-bike rentals pick-up **(EXAMPLE)**
1 24/7 charging point
2 bike repair
3 bike replacement
4 motel
5 bike drop

5 p

Task 3: Who Invented the Bicycle?

(Audiotrack: QR-Code S. 82 / Hörtext S. 106)

You will hear an extract from a history podcast.
There are five wrong words in the text. Write their correct versions on the lines provided.
(You will have 10 seconds after the first listening and 15 seconds after the second listening.)

Who Invented the Bicycle?	
In 1815, global temperatures dropped because of a natural	______________
disaster; the most powerful volcanic eruption in modern	______________
history rocked present-day Indonesia. This reduced	______________
harvests world-wide and caused working animals like	______________
horses to starve. The German inventor Karl von Drais	______________
realized the need for a mode of transportation that did not	______________
need to be bred like animals, and started working on	______________
designs for a human-powered, two-wheeled device.	______________
Drais's stunning machine had no pedals and no brakes,	______________
and was propelled by the biker's feet. Drais's test run was a	______________
9-mile, one-hour ride. As people began heading out on	______________
"dandy horses", however, it turned out they started to use	______________
sidewalks for their rides. This endangered pedestrians and	______________
led to extensive consequences, such as bans and fines. It	______________
took another 40 years until people developed bikes further	______________
and the public really became interested.	______________

5 p

Adapted from: Earls, Stephanie. A Global Disaster Gave Us The Bike [online available on: https://www.outtherecolorado.com]
Bildquelle: Von Wilhelm Siegrist (1797-1843?) – Drais' 3-page printed description of 1817 (in public libraries), Gemeinfrei, https://commons.wikimedia.org/w/index.php?curid=727702

Task 4: Bike Rental
(Audiotrack: QR-Code S. 82 / Hörtext S. 106)

You are renting a bike at a self-service terminal. **Listen and take notes**. You do not have to write complete sentences but **one word per line is not enough**.
(You will have 10 seconds after the first listening and 20 seconds after the second listening.)

	Bike Rental	
1.	**Jobs of bike staff (2 aspects):**	▶ ____________ ▶ ____________
2.	**One reason for choosing the "explorer bike":**	____________
3.	**Possible problems (3 aspects):**	▶ ____________ ▶ ____________ ▶ ____________
4.	**Verification code:**	_ _ _ _ – _ _ _ _ – _ _ _ _

7 p

Task 5: Go Cycle
(Audiotrack: QR-Code S. 82 / Hörtext S. 107)

You will hear a radio podcast with a cyclist and a bike specialist.
Listen and complete the sentences. Be careful, **one word per answer is not enough.**
(You will have 30 seconds after the first listening and 90 seconds after the second listening.)

Go Cycle

1. The Withers family bought a cargo bike instead of a car for financial reasons and because ____________

2. In the past, cargo bikes were constructed to ____________

3. The Withers can use their bike for ____________ ____________ **and** ____________

4. Mrs Powell decided to develop a new kind of bike because she ____________

5. *Sunny Bikes* are helpful in order to ____________ ____________ **and** ____________

6. You can use a *Sunny Bike* on rainy days, too, because the ____________

8 p

Written Test

Text 1

Just three percent of world's ecosystem remain intact, study suggests.

Bringing back animals to their natural habitat might expand areas of undamaged ecosystems, scientists say.

Just three percent of the world's land remains ecologically intact with healthy populations of all its native animals, plant species and undisturbed territory, a new study suggests. These fragments of wilderness are totally unharmed by human activities. ❶ In some parts of the world such as Australia, however, there are hardly any intact areas left because invasive alien species such as cats, foxes, rabbits, goats and camels have had a negative effect on native populations of wildlife.

Previous analyses identified most wilderness areas by using satellite images that showed whether plants and trees were still intact. Because they only looked at these images, scientists estimated that 20 to 40 percent of the Earth's surface is little affected by humans. However, the scientists behind the new study argue that forests, savannah and tundra can appear healthy on satellite images but that, on the ground, vital animal species are missing. An elephant for instance creates natural clearings in forests and spreads seeds. ❷ Wolves can control populations of deer and elk in the northern hemisphere. "Much of what we regard as intact territory has actually lost species that have been hunted by people, or died because of invasive species or disease," says Dr Andrew Plumptre, the lead author of the study. According to him this is fairly scary, because it shows how unique places like the Serengeti are, which actually have fully functioning ecosystems.

The new study combines maps of human damage to nature with maps showing where animals have disappeared from their original habitats or are too few in number to maintain a balanced ecosystem. The maps for the research featured the homes of 7,000 species both in the year 1500 AD and today. ❸ Most of the data was for mammals, but it also counted in some birds, fish, plants, reptiles and amphibians. The analysis did not include Antarctica.

"We're now in the 2020s, which have been declared *UN Decade of Ecosystem Restoration* by the United Nations, but it all focuses on plants and habitat," Plumptre says. "Let's also think about restoring animal species. ❹" The researchers suggest reintroducing a small number of important species to some damaged areas, e. g. elephants or wolves. "This move could restore up to 20 percent of the world's land to ecological intactness. Of course, we will have to make sure they can survive there". Plumptre mentions the successful reintroduction of wolves into Yellowstone National Park, which helped transform the eco-system.

The new study also points out that many sites with outstanding ecological integrity are located in territories that are managed by native communities. This has been confirmed by a recent UN report saying that indigenous peoples of Latin America are by far the best guardians of the regions' forests. "Their deforestation rates are up to 50 percent lower than elsewhere. ❺" Myrna Cunningham, a native of Nicaragua, explains: "Indigenous peoples have a different concept of forests. ❻ They are seen as a space where we live and that it's given to us to protect for the next generations." The UN report confirmed that supporting these peoples is particularly crucial now. Scientists are warning that the Amazon is nearing a tipping point where it switches from rainforest to savannah, risking the release of billions of tons of carbon into the atmosphere.

In January 2020, more than 50 countries committed to halt the destruction of the natural world by protecting almost a third of the planet by 2030. ❼ In order to reach this goal, suitable measures still need to be discussed and taken. "Putting effort into conserving the remaining intact places is crucial," Plumptre says. "They are so rare and special, and show what the world was like before humans had any major impact, helping us measure how much we've lost."

Adapted from: Carrington, Damian. Areas of Intact Ecosystem May Expand with Animal Reintroductions, Scientists Say;Indigenious Peoples – UN Report [online available on:https://www.theguardian.com/environment/2021/apr/15/just-3-of-worlds-ecosystems-remain-intact-study-suggests]

FORESTS AND THEIR ECOSYSTEMS

Part I: Reading

Task 1

Read the text *Just three percent of world's ecosystem remain intact, study suggests* (page 85). Are sentences **1 – 9** 'True' (T) or 'False' (F)? Choose 'Not in the text' (N) if there is not enough information to answer 'True' or 'False'.
Tick (✓) the correct answer.

		T	F	N
1.	Australia has been able to preserve their original species.			
2.	Satellite images show precisely if an ecosystem is intact.			
3.	In the northern hemisphere, the number of deer increased over the last decades.			
4.	The new study compares data from centuries ago with recent data.			
5.	The study left out a part of the world.			
6.	The UN has dedicated the present decade to re-establishing natural habitats.			
7.	Native species do not fight against each other if reintroduced in small numbers.			
8.	A report proved that native peoples are excellent at protecting forests.			
9.	A number of countries promised to stop the destruction by the end of the century.			

9 p

Task 2

Look at the text *Just three percent of world's ecosystem remain intact, study suggests* (page 85). Five sentences have been removed from the text. Choose the correct gap **(1 – 7)** in the text for each of the sentences below **(A – E). Write the correct <u>number</u> of the gap behind each sentence.** Be careful: There are **two gaps** which you do **not need to use**.

A They are not seen as a place where you take out resources to increase your money. ☐

B That way we can build up these areas where we've got ecologically intact territories. ☐

C They can be mainly found in parts of the Amazon and Congo tropical forests, east Siberian and northern Canadian forests and tundra, and the Sahara. ☐

D They were provided by the *Red List of Threatened Species,* published by the *International Union for Conservation of Nature (IUC).* ☐

E This is why these peoples' voices should be heard in all global initiatives relating to climate change, biodiversity and forestry. ☐

5 p

Task 3

Here are four texts about life in the woods. Read them and **match them with the statements 1 – 9 below**. Choose the correct text **(A – D)** and **write its letter in the box**. The texts may be chosen **more than once**.

A Forty years ago, scientists found out that acacia trees in the African savannah can interact with one another. The giraffes there feed on acacias. When the trees do not want their leaves to be eaten any longer, they pump toxic substances into them and give off a gas that signals to neighbouring trees of the same species that a crisis is at hand. Right away, all the forewarned trees profit from the information and also pump toxins into their leaves. The whole process only takes minutes. The giraffes, too, get the message and move about 100 yards away where they find acacias that have no idea yet that the animals are there.	**B** Bamboo, just like wood, has been closely associated with human wellbeing for thousands of years: this rapidly developing fibre provides a number of critical goods like food, bioenergy, or material for engineering and architecture. Bamboo is economically profitable and also offers a wide range of environmental benefits; it is a crucial part of biological diversity, a source of carbon storage and fresh water provision, as well as a means of soil and flood control. Because bamboo is a grass plant and not a tree, there is little research on how it affects the forests' ecosystems. Consequently, it might play a much bigger role than we think it does.
C During the weekdays in a London office, Stephen Sangster looks out on a "jungle of grey concrete buildings". His weekends, however, are spent in his second home, his very own wood, camping or sometimes just "lying on a blanket, looking at the leaves above". He and his wife bought a neglected plot of woodland because they wanted their kids to grow up aware of the ecosystem they live in with all its natural resources. There are about 40,000 woods in England that are too small to be of commercial benefit to the wood industry. Selling them to private wood-lovers has helped save some tiny ecosystems.	**D** In the 1920s, wolves disappeared from Yellowstone National Park. When they left, the entire ecosystem changed. Elk herds living in the park increased in number and began to make quite a meal of the plants and trees that lined the streams. Vegetation in this area declined and animals that depended on the trees left. When the wolves returned after seventy years, they kept the herds on the move, and the trees flourished again. The roots of the trees reinforced stream banks, which slowed the flow of water down to its original pace. This, in turn, created space for endangered species such as beavers to return, construct their lodges and raise their families.

Adapted from: Wohlleben, Peter. The Hidden Life of Trees [online available on: https://www.themarginalian.org]
INBAR. Understanding Bamboo's Ecosystem Services [online available on: https://www.inbar.int]
Bannerman, Lucy. Families Stump up for Private Woodlands to Escape Rat Race [online avallable on: https://www.thetimes.co.uk]
Farquhar, Brodie. Wolf Reintroduction [...] in Yellowstone [online avalable on: https://www.yellowstonepark.com]

1 Helping the environment and relaxing from work can go hand in hand.
2 People use the fast-growing plants as a resource.
3 The ability of trees to communicate is limited to a certain area.
4 Trees help animals build their homes.
5 Individual landowners have saved natural living environments.
6 In some cases, ecosystems have the ability to repair themselves.
7 The construction industry uses both wood and this natural raw material.
8 Tiny forests are not profitable.
9 Trees get in contact via chemicals in their leaves.

1	2	3	4	5	6	7	8	9

9 p

Task 4

Verwenden Sie den folgenden Text und **bearbeiten Sie die Aufgaben (1 – 6) stichpunktartig auf Deutsch**. Die Aspekte müssen inhaltlich vollständig erfasst sein. Einzelwörter genügen nicht als Antwort.

Ready, steady, grow! – Plant Trees With your School

If you plant trees in your school yard, you will make a real difference to everyone and start a legacy that future students will enjoy. Here is how you can organise your project.

Plan

- Gardeners recommend planting trees between November and March when they grow less rapidly and are therefore less likely to be damaged during planting.
- Purchasing a tree from a certified nursery will make sure your tree does not carry any unwanted insects or disease. These would not only affect the tree itself but could spread to other plants.
- All schools are encouraged to actively engage with official tree planting organisations. This year these organisations have three million saplings in free tree packs, available on a first come first served basis.
- Before you start planting, mark out where each tree will be placed. If your planting area is overgrown, cut the grass short or remove parts of it. This will reduce competition for minerals and water.

Plant

Dig a hole twice the size of the root ball. Do not loosen the ball too much unless the roots are very twisted. Place your tree in the hole, fill it and give the tree a really good feed of water. Cover the area around your tree with compost and plenty of leaves to hold in water.

Protect

- Once your trees are in the ground it is important to care for them to help them grow. When the lawn is mown, people need to know where the tree has been planted. Put a tree guard around the position to avoid accidental cutting. This also prevents animals from eating the branches.
- Where possible use a watering can with a rose attachment on the end or any other method that will distribute the water at a low pressure, imitating rainfall.

Muddy boots. Big smiles. – You'll never forget planting your first tree.

Adapted from: Woodland Trust. Plant Trees with your School [online available on: https://www.woodlandtrust.org.uk]
Queen's Green Canopy. Get Involved [online available on: https://queensgreencanopy.org]

1. Begründen Sie, warum Bäume beim Pflanzen in den Wintermonaten weniger Schaden nehmen.

____ **1 p**

2. Erläutern Sie, was der Kauf in einer zertifizierten Baumschule gewährleisten kann.

____

____ **1 p**

3. Nennen Sie das Prinzip, nach dem die kostenlosen Baumpakete ausgegeben werden.

____ **1 p**

4. Erklären Sie, warum es sinnvoll ist, den Bewuchs um die Pflanzstelle zu entfernen.

____

____ **1 p**

5. Geben Sie die erforderliche Größe des Pflanzlochs an.

____ **1 p**

6. Führen Sie zwei Gründe für die Nutzung eines Baumschutzgitters an.

▶ ____ **1 p**

▶ ____ **1 p**

Part II: Use of English

Task 1

Look at **text 1** (page 85). **Find a word or expression which means <u>the same as</u> each of the words (1 – 5) below.** The lines where you can find the words or expressions are indicated in brackets. There is one example **(0)** at the beginning.

0. original → **native** **(l. 1 – 5)**

1. (to) seem → ________________ (l. 6 – 13)

2. (to) consider → ________________ (l. 6 – 13)

3. (to) concentrate → ________________ (l. 14 – 23)

4. (to) turn → ________________ (l. 24 – 30)

5. influence → ________________ (l. 31 – 34) **5 p**

Task 2

Look at **text 1** (page 85). What do the following words mean? **Match** the expressions **(A – F)** **<u>as used in the text</u>** with their corresponding definitions **(1 – 7)**. **Write the correct numbers in the grid below.** Be careful: There are two definitions that you do not need. One definition **(0)** has already been matched correctly.

A fragment (l. 3)
B alien (l. 4)
C **territory** (l. 11)
D mammals (l. 16)
E reintroducing (l. 20)
F guardians (l. 26)

0. a geographic area
1. the beginning of something that has not been done before
2. the process of bringing something back to its original place
3. a fictional being from another world
4. protectors of an area or idea
5. a special group of animals
6. a small part broken off or separated from something
7. untypical for an area

A	B	C	D	E	F
		0			

5 p

Task 3

Use the word given in capitals at the end of some of the lines to **form a word of the same word family** that fits in the space in the same line. There is one example **(0)** at the beginning.

0. The idea of a **magical** forest is one of the oldest in storytelling. From fairy tales like *Snow White* to modern sagas like *Harry Potter*, the forest has — **MAGICIAN**

1. become an __________ stop on the hero's journey, a place of danger — **ESSENCE**

2. and possibility. In some __________ plays, like *A Midsummer Night's Dream* by Shakespeare, young people flee into the woods. There they — **FAME**

3. seek escape from __________ situations. When they try to find — **CHALLENGE**

4. their way back out, the landscape becomes a __________ of their minds and visions. As forests shrink, writers are more likely to describe them — **REFLECT**

5. as an oasis of __________ from the troubles of civilisation. — **FREE** **5 p**

Adapted from: v. Mullins, Carrie. 12 Unforgettable Forests in Literature [online available on: https://www.electricliterature.com]

Task 4

Complete the second sentence so that it has a similar meaning to the first sentence, using the KEY WORD given in brackets. **Do not change the KEY WORD given.** You must use **between two and five words including the KEY WORD**. There is one example **(0)**.

Example

0. The Chinese invented the process of papermaking. **(WHO)**

(1) (2) (3) (4) (5)

It was the Chinese who invented the process of papermaking.

1. Even if the exact composition of European paper before the 18th century is still a mystery, we know that it was handmade. **(ALTHOUGH)**

We know that European paper before the 18th century was handmade, __________ __________ is still a mystery. **1 p**

2. Studies suggest that in early times, craftsmen made paper from hemp or linen, in particular old rags. **(BY)**

Studies suggest that in early times, paper __________ from hemp or linen, in particular old rags. **1 p**

3. The methods of making handmade paper today haven't changed compared to those used in the middle ages. **(SAME)**

The methods of making handmade paper today __________ __________ used in the middle ages. **1 p**

4. If you want to produce paper by hand, you can mix soaked recycled paper or cooked plant fibre in a kitchen blender. **(INCLUDES)**

The production of paper by hand __________ __________ soaked recycled paper or cooked plant fibre in a kitchen blender. **1 p**

5. Online you can find tutorials as well as images of handmade paper. **(BOTH)**

Online you can find __________ __________ of handmade paper. **1 p**

Adapted from: Silkroad Foundation. The History of Paper [online available on: www.silkroadfoundation.org] and Rogers, Juliet. Paper (Murdoch), Australia, 2006, p. 7/8.

Task 5

Complete the following text. Use the correct forms of the words in brackets and find words of your own to replace the question marks. There is one example **(0)**.

Trees may look **(0)** __**like**__ **(???)** solitary individuals but the ground beneath our feet tells a different story. Trees **(1)** ____________________ **(secret)** talk, trade and wage war on one another. Different kinds of fungi and mushrooms **(2)** ____________________ **(???)** networks grow around and inside their roots help them. The fungi provide the trees with nutrients and they receive sugars in return. This connection runs far deeper **(3)** ____________________ **(???)** biologists first thought. A few years ago, a group of experts **(4)** ____________________ **(find)** out that trees can also share resources with each other by plugging into the network. Since then, the system **(5)** ____________________ **(call)** the "Wood Wide Web". Through the network, older trees, also **(6)** ____________________ **(know)** as "mother trees", help weak seedlings to survive. At the same time dying trees dump their resources into the network for neighbours that are **(7)** ____________________ **(healthy)** in comparison to themselves. If sick or dead trees **(8)** ____________________ **(not be)** there, the forest would not be able to renew itself as easily. In addition, plants use fungi to communicate. If they **(9)** ____________________ **(be)** in danger, trees regularly set free chemical signals through their roots which can warn their neighbours. But the "Wood Wide Web" has its dark side too. Species like the black walnut sabotage their rivals by **(10)** ____________________ **(spread)** toxic chemicals. **10 p**

Adapted from: BBC World Service. "Secret Life of Trees: How They Talk to Each Other" [online available on https://www.youtube.com]

Part III: Guided Writing

You only have to do **one** of the following two tasks.
Important: First read both tasks, then decide whether you want to do Task A or Task B.
You can write down your ideas on an extra sheet before you do the task on your exam paper.

Task A

The Youth Conservation Corps (YCC) is an exciting summer **youth program** that offers team based, paid work experience in US national parks.

Apply for a variety of **projects** on our forest lands: fire prevention, computer-based monitoring, protecting species, visitor education and many more.

Stay with a family or at a hotel room close to the park.

Bildquelle: https://www.fs.usda.gov/working-with-us/opportunities-for-young-people

You have decided to apply for the program. In your **letter of application** include ...

- your reason(s) for applying for the program
- what kind of project you are interested in and why
- your skills and work experience so far
- reasons for your choice of accommodation

Find a suitable beginning and ending.
Write about 200 words.

Task B

You and your best friend are backpacking in the USA and you started a blog for your friends and family at home. Write about your latest **three-day hiking tour in a national park**.

Your blog starts like this:

> *"Hey guys, here's a little catch-up about what happened to us lately. Let's start at the beginning ... "*

In your **blog entry** ...

- ▶ explain why you went on the hiking tour
- ▶ describe where you stayed overnight
- ▶ write about a thrilling moment
- ▶ give advice to future travelers

You need not copy the beginning of the story. Find a suitable ending.
Write about 200 words. **30 p**

LCT 2018

Task 1: Reasons for Visiting Hawaii

(Audiotrack: QR-Code rechts / Aufgabe S. 37)

1. If tourists are looking for paradise on earth, Hawaii is the closest thing. The islands have a drier season and a wetter season, but the temperature remains relatively steady throughout the year.
2. At every vacation destination you can find a number of people who dislike tourists. Hawaii, though, is attractive for tourists because most Hawaiians promote the Aloha spirit of peace and love.
3. In addition to the original Hawaiians, the sunny islands have attracted immigrants from around the world including Chinese, Japanese, Filipinos and many more. That's why the islands are a melting pot which makes for a very different society to most of the US.
4. For most of the last century, tourists had to rely on Asians to get their plates filled. Everything changed in 1991 when twelve chefs established Hawaii Regional Cuisine, a culinary movement that combines international recipes with the islands' diverse ethnic flavors.
5. No Hawaiian island is like any other. Kaua'i is mostly green with amazing sea cliffs, whereas the Big Island has its beautiful volcanic landscapes, stunning waterfalls and the Waipio Valley, where you can experience a tropical rainforest and the Black Sand Beach.

Adapted from: Fischer, John "The Top 10 Reasons to Visit Hawaii", https://www.tripsavvy.com/the-top-reasons-to-visit-hawaii-1533031, 12/01/17

Task 2: At Hawaii Volcanoes National Park

(Audiotrack: QR-Code oben / Aufgabe S. 37)

Receptionist: Welcome to Hawaii Volcanoes National Park. How can I help you?
Tourist: Hello, we have two days to explore the National Park. Could you tell us about the highlights?
Receptionist: Sure. You'll get an overview here at the Visitor Center. You know, our National Park is the most spectacular sight on the island of Hawaii. It offers dramatic volcanic landscapes as well as glimpses of rare flora and fauna.
Tourist: Fantastic. Where should we start?
Receptionist: If you follow Crater Drive westwards, you'll see the large parking area at Steam Vents to your left. Leave your car there and walk about a hundred meters to the viewing platform. From there, you can see the spectacular craters. The view is similar to that found at the Jaggar Museum, which is located at the western end of Crater Drive.
Tourist: Is it worth visiting?
Receptionist: Definitely! The museum offers information on volcanology and working seismographs. It's got a restaurant that gives you a sheltered view of the main crater when the weather is nasty. You know, Kīlauea is one of the world's most active volcanoes.
Tourist: That's awesome! I'd like to take close-ups of the eruptions!
Receptionist: Sure, you can take fantastic snapshots. But be aware that the rest of the road is closed to visitors. It is dangerous to go there due to high levels of toxic gases, such as sulphur dioxide.
They can damage your health. So do not enter the south-west of the park.
Tourist: Ok, we'll keep that in mind. What other interesting places are here?
Receptionist: Well, I can recommend the impressive lava cave. It was formed by solidified streams of lava, and you can explore its fantastic colors and stalactites.
Tourist: Wow! How can we get there?
Receptionist: Follow the Crater Drive in the opposite direction. You'll pass Kīlauea Iki Crater. The cave is the next place of interest. If you drive on, you'll eventually get to Rift Road.
Tourist: Where can we spend the night?
Receptionist: There's a camping ground for mobile homes on Highway 11.
Tourist: We'd rather stay at a hotel, if possible.
Receptionist: Well, there are many inexpensive and nice motels outside the park in nearby Volcano Village along Highway 11.
Tourist: Actually, we'd rather go for a place nearer to the craters.
Receptionist: Sure. There's the Volcano Hotel opposite the Visitor Center. I'm sure they'll have rooms available.
Tourist: Great, thanks a lot.
Receptionist: You're welcome. Enjoy your stay.

Adapted from: National Park Service. "Hawaii Volcanoes, Plan your Visit", online available on: https://nps.gov

Task 3: Kamakawiwo'ole Israel

(Audiotrack: QR-Code S. 93 / Aufgabe S. 38)

Kamakawiwo'ole Israel, known to his fans as Iz, a singer and a musician as well as a campaigner for Hawaiian culture, **rights** and way of life, was born in Honolulu, Hawaii, in May 1959. At the age of six, Iz learned to master the ukulele by watching others play. He first performed publicly at around age ten, when he was **called** up to the stage at Steamboats, a popular Waikiki nightclub. In the 1970s Iz dropped out of high school. When his brother Skippy and other aspiring Hawaiian musicians formed a band in 1976, Iz was the band's first **voice**. In the 1980s, after the death of his beloved older brother, Kamakawiwo'ole began to be the star of the band. In 1993, seventeen years later, he launched a solo career. Shortly afterwards, the airing of his version of "Somewhere over the Rainbow" by a DJ on a California radio show catapulted Iz onto the world stage. His **mission** was to find and play music that connected to and represented the true spirit of Hawaii. When he passed away in 1997, the state honored the man and the legend: the Hawaiian flag was **flown** at half-mast.

Adapted from: Rona L. Holub, Kamakawiwo'ole, Israel Ka'ano'i, http://www.anb.org/view/10.1093/anb/9780198606697.001.0001/anb-9780198606697-e-1803801, Oxford University Press

Task 4: Corals of Hawaii

(Audiotrack: QR-Code S. 93 / Aufgabe S. 39)

Mrs Oyster: Hawaii Oceanic Research Center, how can I help you?
Journalist: Are you Dr. Pearl Oyster, the specialist on Hawaiian wildlife?
Mrs Oyster: Yes, what can I do for you?
Journalist: I'm Ed Young from "Youth & Nature" magazine. We're currently doing a cover story on Hawaii. Can you tell me how climate change affects Hawaiian animals?
Mrs Oyster: Err, yes, above all corals are affected.
Journalist: Corals?
Mrs Oyster: Yes. Most people think corals are minerals. That's because they can't move like land animals and also because they are rock-like structures. But actually, corals are endangered animals.
Journalist: Tell me more.
Mrs Oyster: We estimate that almost half of Hawaii's coral reefs are dying due to changing weather patterns.
Journalist: Terrible, could you explain this in more detail?
Mrs Oyster: One reason for this is the rising sea level because of melting polar ice. The water rises faster than the corals are able to grow, and they can only live close to the water surface.
Journalist: I see.
Mrs Oyster: But this is not the only problem for the corals. The second point is the warming of the sea water. Normally, there are useful algae living inside the corals. They need the algae for many reasons. But when the water temperature rises, these tiny plants start producing poison and turn toxic.
Journalist: Oh.
Mrs Oyster: Now, the corals get rid of the algae because it's the only way they can protect themselves.
Journalist: That sounds serious. And what does that mean for the corals?
Mrs Oyster: When they lose the algae, they don't get enough oxygen. As a consequence, they turn white and begin to die.
Journalist: That's a nightmare.
Mrs Oyster: And unfortunately, around Hawaii, we have a unique problem that makes things even worse. An invasive sea-plant has spread from Asia to Hawaii. It grows incredibly fast, so it further endangers the corals. We developed the "Cliff-Cleaner", a kind of ship-based vacuum cleaner. It collects the sea-plants. This system has proved very valuable.
Journalist: So there is some light at the end of the tunnel. Is there anything our young readers can do to help?
Mrs Oyster: Yes, indeed. They can support the Hawaiian Youth Congress member, Lynn Areccawi. At her official web-site you'll find everything about her projects.
Journalist: That's Lynn who ...?
Mrs Oyster: Let me spell that: A - R - E - double C - A - W - I. Have you got that?
Journalist: Yes, I think so. May I read it back to you ?
Mrs Oyster: Sure .
Journalist: A - R - E - double C - A - W - I.
Mrs Oyster: Perfect.
Journalist: Thank you for your time. You'll find my article in our next issue.
Mrs Oyster: Glad I could help, bye.
Journalist: Bye.

Adapted from:
Ward, Tim. "5 Questions about climate Change and Coral Reefs for Dr. Emily Darling", online available on: https://www.huffingtonpost.com
Pierre-Louis, Kendra. "Hawaii's most popular coral reefs are in big trouble", online available on: https://www.popsci.com

Task 5: The Hawaiian Language

(Audiotrack: QR-Code S. 93 / Aufgabe S. 40)

Presenter: Our topic today is the Hawaiian language, how it almost died out and why it is still spoken today. With me in the studio are Mrs. Palakiko, Professor of Linguistics, and Pauahi, a student from a Hawaiian immersion school at Honolulu. Pauahi, your name sounds typically Hawaiian. Does it have a particular meaning?

Pauahi: Yes, it's the name of a crater located on the Big Island of Hawaii, meaning "fire is over".

Presenter: Wow, that's a cool name! Now, Professor Palakiko, is it correct to say that Hawaiian started to disappear, but was then revived thanks to the efforts of its speakers?

Prof. Palakiko: Absolutely. By the early 1980s, fewer than 50 people under age 18 could speak Hawaiian fluently. Colonialism and its consequences had nearly wiped out the language. Until the mid-1980s, Hawaiian was still forbidden at school. But in the last decades we have been taking great efforts to keep our language alive. Now it is protected by law and promoted in what is known as "Hawaiian immersion schools".

Presenter: Pauahi, you attend one of these immersion schools. In what way is your school different from other American schools?

Pauahi: Well, the classroom language is Hawaiian. Our teachers motivate us to use it in everyday situations. I feel like a true Hawaiian person again, because our traditional language is part of my everyday life.

Presenter: Professor Palakiko, as you said before, a few decades ago Hawaiian was in danger of dying out. When exactly do we speak of endangered languages?

Prof. Palakiko: A language is in danger of dying out when it is spoken by less than 1,000 speakers on a regular basis.

Presenter: But in a large place like Hawaii why would the Hawaiian community stop speaking their native language?

Prof. Palakiko: Imagine your kids at school have to speak the language of a larger group of people. You will soon start to speak this 'larger' language at home because you want your kids to be good at school. So it's the influence of the surrounding 'larger' languages that makes the small languages gradually die out.

Presenter: Pauahi, in addition to the Hawaiian language, what else do you learn about the ways of your ancestors at school?

Pauahi: Well, to continue their traditions, we have optional subjects. My favourite one is surfing. It's one of the oldest sports practised on the planet. The first surfers were fishermen who used the boards to get their catch to the shore. Apart from surfing, I also attend a hula course.

Presenter: What's hula?

Pauahi: It's a dance, you know, movements that go with our traditional songs. These songs are often about important historical events in our culture. In order to dance the hula, it's essential to understand the words of the song.

Presenter: Pauahi, are there some Hawaiian phrases that you could teach our listeners?

Pauahi: I guess most people have heard of "Aloha!" Then there's the simple "Mahalo!" for "Thank you!". And "A hui hou!" can be used to say "See you later!"

Presenter: So, a big "Mahalo" to our guests for being here! And as always you can find a podcast of this broadcast on www ...

Adapted from:
Home, Adele. "Interview: Dr. Peter Ladefoged on Endangered languages", online available on: https://www.pbs.org/pov/tailenders
Love, Bret. "Interview: Keali Reichel on Maui, Hula & Hawaiian Culture", online available on: https://greenglobaltravel.com

LCT 2019

Task 1: Why are the Oceans Important?

(Audiotrack: QR-Code rechts / Aufgabe S. 48)

1. The ocean is home to millions of plants and animals. Most sea animals exist in the top two ocean zones. Sea plants, especially some algae, provide food and shelter to ocean animals. Did you know many of them are invisible to the naked eye?
2. The popularity of fish has increased in recent years because it's seen as being part of modern nutrition. It allows for more variety on menus. Rapid inland transport has made sea fish available in kitchens all over the world.
3. The evaporation of ocean water brings moisture to land areas. Further, ocean currents transport heat from the equator to the poles. The ocean acts as a global control system: it regulates the temperature and the concentration of carbon dioxide in the atmosphere.
4. With its amazing organisms the ocean offers opportunities for scientists to discover and develop new and innovative drugs. It may hold the key to the next cure, which is why we should protect and preserve it.
5. The ocean is subject to the impact of tidal streams, waves, currents or differences in salinity. It therefore works as a natural source for generating power, which is needed for the increasing demands in today's world.

Adapted from: Stickney, Robert R. "Food from the Sea" [online available on: https://www.waterencyclopedia.com]
Weedmark, David. "Ocean Ecosystem for Kids" [online available on: https://sciencing.com]
American Museum of Natural History. "The Ocean: Climate Control" [online available on: https://amnh.org]

Task 2: Surprising Facts about the Oceans

(Audiotrack: QR-Code oben / Aufgabe S. 48)

Interviewer: The oceans may make up 70 per cent of the Earth's surface, but we know very little about them. My guest today is Robert Vaughn, a marine scientist. Welcome, Professor Vaughn.

R. Vaughn: Hello, thank you for having me. And yes, you're right, when you're sitting on the beach you may not be aware what a complex thing the Earth's oceans actually are. ... We made it all the way to the moon a full four years before we saw the longest mountain range on Earth, lying deep down at the bottom of the ocean.

Interviewer: That's the Mid-Oceanic Ridge, isn't it?

R. Vaughn: Correct. The global Mid-Oceanic Ridge system snakes across the Earth's surface, like the zigzag stitches on a baseball, covering an impressive 65,000 kilometres. It has peaks higher than those in the Alps and it makes up almost a quarter of the Earth's total surface. The majority of the system is underwater, of course.

Interviewer: That's impressive! I would have thought the largest mountain range was the Himalayas.

R. Vaughn: Yes, people only talk about what they can see. In fact, the oceans are rich with more than just marine life. In 1872, an English chemist discovered that microscopic fragments of gold are hidden in the water of all oceans. But even though the oceans hold nearly 18 million tons of gold, its concentration is only a few parts per trillion.
There is, however, undissolved gold in and on the seafloor. It's located at least a mile or two underwater and encased in rock. Mining for this gold may not be worthwhile. Currently there isn't a cost-effective way to mine or take out this gold. If all of the gold were extracted from the world's oceans, each person on earth could have four kilograms of the precious metal.

Interviewer: Oh really!

R. Vaughn: Well, there's more to marvel at: We have more detailed maps of Mars than we do of the ocean and we've only explored a miserly five per cent of the ocean floor. Two-thirds of all marine life remain unidentified. In fact, researchers recently found unique microbes down there. These do not require the sun to maintain their energy but get it from a chemical reaction instead. This life form is making scientists rethink where else they might find life in the solar system. Other recent discoveries have included a "ninja" shark with a dimly glowing head, in addition to a nesting ground where more than a thousand deep-sea octopuses huddled in the rocks with their eggs.

Interviewer: That's amazing!

R. Vaughn: Exactly! There are also sounds from the depths of the oceans that cannot be explained with any certainty. The legendary "Bloop" is one of the loudest ocean sounds ever recorded, and for a long time no one knew for sure what made it. It seemed to mimic oceanic animal noises.
However, the Bloop's volume was too great to be made by any sea creatures known to science. Today we know that it was caused by an underwater ice quake – large icebergs fracturing into pieces.

Interviewer: Fantastic, let's listen to a recording of the Bloop …

Adapted from: Vaughn, Aubrey. "15 Fun and Surprising Facts about the Earth's Oceans"
Hickok, Kimberly. "Ghostly Dumbo Octopus makes Rare Appearance in Dazzling Deep-Sea Video"
Deamer, Kacey. "7 Bizarre Facts about the Ocean" [all online available on: https://www.livescience.com]

Task 3: The Great Pacific Garbage Patch

(Audiotrack: QR-Code S. 96 / Aufgabe S. 49)

The Great Pacific Garbage Patch – or GPGP for short – is the largest of five huge offshore plastic accumulations **floating** in the world's oceans. It is located halfway between Hawaii and California.
The **amount** of the plastic in the GPGP is estimated to weigh approximately 80,000 tons. Experts suppose that a total of 1.8 trillion plastic pieces are drifting in the patch. This is equivalent to **250** pieces of rubbish for every human in the world – an enormous plastic count. Once plastic **finds** its way into the garbage patch, it falls apart into smaller micro-plastics under the effects of sun and waves.
The vast majority of plastics are made of **thick** or hard polyethylene or polypropylene, as well as destroyed fishing nets and ropes. In terms of object count, 94 per cent of the total is represented by microplastics smaller than 0.5 cm. Once they become this small, microplastics are very **tough** to remove. In addition they are often mistaken for food by marine animals.

Adapted from: The Ocean Cleanup. "The Great Pacific Garbage Patch" [online available on: https://www.theoceancleanup.com]

Task 4: Oceans' Health

(Audiotrack: QR-Code S. 96 / Aufgabe S. 50)

Reporter: The Oceans' health is in great danger and the oceanologist, Prof. Waters, is here with me now to tell us about the most urgent issues. Prof. Waters, let's start with the buzz word 'overfishing'.

Mrs Waters: Well, actually overfishing is having some serious impacts on our oceans. Firstly, it may wipe out a complete species. Other species depending on those fish for survival are affected as well. In other words, overfishing can cause marine animals to starve.

Reporter: Are there any species that are particularly affected by overfishing?

Mrs Waters: Yes, indeed. Overfishing is a serious issue with sharks. Sharks are killed in tens of millions each year, mainly for their fins. Shark-fin soup is an exclusive delicacy. It's a common practice to catch sharks, cut off their fins, and toss the fish back into the ocean where they are left to die.
This is horrendous.

Reporter: That's awful! Shark finning is a practice that needs to end. Now let's talk about the ocean itself.
What can you tell us about so-called 'dead zones'?

Mrs Waters: You know, ocean dead zones are everywhere, and growing. They're areas in the oceans where life is impossible, because there is not enough oxygen. The number of dead zones is increasing at an alarming rate, with over 400 known to exist, and the number is expected to rise.

Reporter: And what's the reason for this development?

Mrs Waters: It's believed that global warming is one prime aspect for what's behind the changes in ocean behaviour that causes dead zones.

Reporter: Prof. Waters, in how far does pollution affect the health of the oceans?

Mrs Waters: Well, pollution is really getting out of hand. One of the scariest pollutants is mercury – also known as quicksilver. It literally ends up on our dinner table.

Reporter: But where does the mercury come from?

Mrs Waters: According to the Environmental Protection Agency, coal-fired power plants are the largest industrial source of mercury pollution in the country. The mercury is absorbed by organisms at the bottom of the food chain and as bigger fish eat smaller fish, it works its way back up the food chain right to us, most notably in the form of tuna.

Reporter: And what exactly are the risks for us human beings?

Mrs Waters: Mercury has toxic effects on the nervous system. Internal organs such as lungs or kidneys may also be damaged.

Reporter: That's dramatic. Now let's talk about what can be done to save our oceans …

Adapted from: Heimbuch, Jaymi. "The Ocean has Issues" [online available on: https://www.treehugger.com]

Task 5: Saving the Seas

(Audiotrack: QR-Code S. 96 / Aufgabe S. 51)

Presenter: Welcome to our radio podcast 'Saving the Seas'. With me in the studio today are wildlife biologist Jean Wiener from Haiti, Sylvia Earle, who has spent more than 60 years researching marine life, and Pierce Brosnan, the famous James Bond actor and activist in saving our oceans.
Now, Mr. Brosnan, who can save our oceans if not James Bond? But seriously, what can our listeners do in their everyday lives to protect our oceans?

Mr Brosnan: Oceans cover more than 70 per cent of the Earth, and provide 50 to 85 per cent of the oxygen in the air we breathe. Put simply, if the oceans die, we die. That's why we – all of us – need to make some changes. Even small things can help. For example don't buy products with microplastics. Millions of these tiny pieces end up in our rivers, which eventually carry them out to the sea. There, fish and other sea life mistake them for food and devour them.

Mr Wiener: What I want to add: you could attend clean-up events or just pick up trash every time you go. It's a quick and simple way to get involved.

Presenter: Sounds like a good start, Mr. Wiener. What else do you suggest, Mrs. Earle?

Mrs Earle: It's a fact that certain types of fish are so popular they are dying out from overfishing. So a good idea is eating sustainable fish only. There are apps that can help you find markets.

Presenter: All of you have made personal contributions to preserving our oceans. What exactly did you do, Mr. Brosnan?

Mr Brosnan: My wife and I are passionate about efforts to protect our planet's great whales and their ocean habitat. Therefore, we joined the International Whaling Commission in their ongoing fight to protect these magnificent creatures. Many people think we saved the whales in the 1970s, but surprisingly, whales face more threats today than ever before.

Presenter: And what was your project about, Mr. Wiener?

Mr Wiener: In 1989 I returned to Haiti, where I was born. I started the Foundation for the Protection of Marine Biodiversity in 1992 when I fully realized how serious damage to the ecosystem was. Local fishermen had told me alarming stories about how much harder it was to find fish.

Presenter: Your project is called 'Mission Blue', Mrs. Earle, tell us more, please.

Mrs Earle: Mission Blue goes on expeditions and produces documentaries about vital oceanic ecosystems worldwide. This way we try to reach viewers all over the world. Our principal aim is to protect 30 per cent of the ocean by 2030. This may not sound much but with less than four per cent of the ocean currently protected in any way, we still have a lot of work to do.

Presenter: Could you recommend any literature for those listeners who would like to learn a bit more, Mr. Brosnan?

Mr Brosnan: I'd recommend Mrs. Earle's books 'The World Is Blue' and of course 'A Message of the Oceans'. They're both tremendous reading.

Mrs Earle: There is a good introduction to life in the oceans called 'Marine Biology' by Peter Castro. It stresses that the world's oceans are an integrated system.

Presenter: Thank you for this useful input. And thank you for coming!

All: It was a pleasure! Bye ...

Adapted from: Millennium Post. "Brosnan joins Save Whale Campaign" [online available on: https://www.pressreader.com]
The Goldman Environmental Prize. "Jean Wiener" [online available on: https://vvww.goldmanprize.org]
Mission Blue. Silvia Earle Alliance. "How to protect the Oceans" [online available on: https://mission-blue.org]

LCT 2020

Task 1: Tips for your Internship

(Audiotrack: QR-Code rechts / Aufgabe S. 60)

1. On your first day as an intern, picking out what to wear can be unnerving, especially if you're not familiar with the company dress code yet. Even if you find suits boring, you may want to think twice in order to create an appropriate impression.
2. Depending on the office culture, close employees and interns may go and have a snack together during their work-days. However, don't assume that this is an open invite but wait until they ask you to come along.
3. Your internship may take place in summer. This is the perfect time for outings or events which may include all sorts of beverages. Before ordering one for yourself, make sure you understand the company culture. It may be in your best interest to sip on some soda.
4. Sometimes you are the only intern in an office, or you may find yourself scheduled apart from the other interns. If you think you are isolated, it's comforting to stay calm and focused until you get to know some people.
5. If you think you can go on vacation with family or friends, you might be wrong. As an intern, you may have to miss out on a week of sun and sand. But finding out about your future job is certainly worth not having a break.

Adapted from: Goecke, Amanda. 5 Awquard Moments You Might Have at your Summer Internship (online available on:https://www.hercampus.com/money-career/5-awkward-moments-you-might-have-your-summer-internship-how-prepare) and Meneo, Kimberley. 10 Awkward Moments Every Intern Experiences (online available on: https://www.society19.com/10-awkward-moments-every-intern-experiences/)

Task 2: Young Businessman

(Audiotrack: QR-Code oben / Aufgabe S. 60)

Reporter: This is Kelly Smith from Radio 1. This time for an exclusive interview with Moziah Bridges, the 19-year-old teenpreneur and owner of the startup 'Mo's Bows'. Hi Mo, you've become a famous bow-tie designer. Tell us, what's a typical day for you?

Mo Bridges: For me it begins with a full day of school, homework, and mail packaging. After school I organize my orders to be shipped. Then I take time to write my clients a handwritten note to say "Thank you", to let them know how much I appreciate their support. After dinner, I may practice for an upcoming speech.

Reporter: Some kids know early on in life what they want to do, long-term. When did you know that going into the fashion business was something you really longed for?

Mo Bridges: That was at a young age. My dad was very into fashion, you know. He used to dress up with a tie, even if he wasn't going anywhere. Some celebrities on TV were also wearing bow ties. I wanted to do something fun, something that no one else was doing. I think I found that.

Reporter: Oh, I see! So why did you start out with bow ties? Why not neckties?

Mo Bridges: As a younger kid, I wore neckties every day with my school uniform. However, looking at the shops at the mall could see that bow ties were coming back into style. So I asked my granny how to sew. That's how the idea came to be. I decided to turn my passion into fashion and created my startup "Mo's Bows". I saw myself as a trendsetter. It wasn't about financial success at all.

Reporter: What have you learned as a successful teenpreneur?

Mo Bridges: I've learned to work hard and to have fun because both are important.

Reporter: And what will be the next thing we can look forward to?

Mo Bridges: We've just renewed our licensing contract with the NBA. This means we'll produce exclusive bow ties for each of the organization's professional basketball teams. Next, my team and I plan to create neckties with colorful graphic prints. And an idea close to my heart is showing people that we care. My dream is to found a charitable organization, but at this point I cannot really tell you more.

Reporter: What would be the one piece of advice you'd give to a teenager who is considering starting a business?

Mo Bridges: I would tell them to figure out exactly what they like doing and why.

Reporter: Thanks a lot, Mo, for being with us today!

Adapted from: Soetan, Rochelle. Moziah Bridges of Mo's Bows Talks About Building a Business (online available on: https://www.blackenterprise.com/teenpreneur-moziah-bridges-mos-bows/) and Mo's Bows. Our Founder (online available on: https://mosbowsmemphis.com/pages/store-categories)

Task 3: Unusual Jobs

(Audiotrack: QR-Code S. 99 / Aufgabe S. 61)

Bored with your office job? No need for that! Here are three jobs you will never believe exist.
Line stander: If you don't like queuing, just order a professional line stander. They queue up for hours to get you a concert ticket or a **sample** sales item. It's a hard job that can be well paid.
Fortune cookie writer: Did you know that your favorite Asian post-meal wisdom comes from a bunch of people writing Chinese fortune cookie **strips**? Approximately three billion fortune cookies are baked every year. As nobody wants to get the same words over and over again, **loads** of inspiring one-liners need to be written.
Bed tester: Getting paid to lie in a bed? You'd think this job would have an infinite waiting list of **crazy** applicants, but there's more to it than taking a nap. Your job is not as simple as that: you are to check on a variety of **factors**. For example, you must make sure that mattresses and pillows are up to standard for grand hotels. Well, would you want to switch to one of these jobs?

Adapted from: BrightSide. the 13 Most Unusual Jobs [online available on: https://brightside.me/wonder-curiosities/the-14-most-unusual-jobs-393960/

Task 4: At a Job Fair

(Audiotrack: QR-Code S. 99 / Aufgabe S. 62)

Fair assistant: Hello, can I assist you?
Student: Yes, please. On your poster it says it's possible to do an apprenticeship in banking and study at the same time ...
Fair assistant: Absolutely. Our so-called 'foundation apprenticeships' combine work and study.
Student: Well, I want to go into banking. But I thought I'd have to do my A-levels first.
Fair assistant: A completed foundation apprenticeship is equivalent to A-levels. This means it qualifies you to study at university level. The big advantage of this programme is that you are permitted to enter a permanent job at this early stage. And don't forget: You'll receive a reasonable salary all along the way.
Student: That sounds attractive. And could I do the apprenticeship in Leeds?
Fair assistant: We offer apprenticeships throughout the UK. If not in Leeds, there should certainly be an option nearby.
Student: Perfect. Oh, and is it possible to gather some work experience abroad?
Fair assistant: Well, I'm afraid not, as the apprenticeship only takes 18 months. In any case, there will be multiple options later on. We have more than 9,000 offices worldwide.
Student: Wow! How good do you think are my chances of getting an apprenticeship?
Fair assistant: You should definitely apply. We're looking for candidates who are enthusiastic about banking. You've already shown that.
Student: Oh, thank you. So, what should I include in my application?
Fair assistant: We expect a covering letter, a CV and copies of your school certificates.
Student: Alright. And ... I'll send my application by e-mail.
Fair assistant: Certainly, put together all your digital files in a single PDF-document. This has become standard in most companies. And make sure the size is no bigger than 3 MB.
Student: Sure, no problem. Who do I address my application to?
Fair assistant: That would be Ms Nilay Khatun. You can find her details on our website.
Student: Would you mind if I quickly noted down her name?
Fair assistant: Of course not, it's N-I-L-A-Y K-H-A-T-U-N.
Student: Thank you very much for all the details.
Fair assistant: Not at all. All the best for your future career in banking [fade out ...]

Adapted from: HSBC. UK Apprenticeships [online available on: https://www.hsbc.com/careers/students-and-graduates/student-opportunities/uk-apprenticeship

Task 5: Learning a Job – What it Takes

(Audiotrack: QR-Code S. 99 / Aufgabe S. 63)

Radio host: Welcome to our programme series 'Learning a Job – What it Takes'. With me in the studio are Ellie McCooper, chief recruiter for a software company and Courtney Rookie, an apprentice at a ship engineering company. Hello!

Both: Hello. / Hi there.

Radio host: Ms McCooper, what are the things employers look for during a job interview?

E. McCooper: I'd say they start by discovering what their applicants already know about the job and if they're familiar with the business itself. You know it happens that applicants even mix up the main products of different companies they are applying to.

Radio host: Oops, you don't want to do that! But let's assume you want to give an applicant the job, what is important to you, in addition to knowledge and technical skills, of course?

E. McCooper: Definitely the so-called soft skills which usually come from life experience. They help us to interact properly.

Radio host: As a recruiter, what do you regard as the most important soft skill?

E. McCooper: The one that most employers expect is a high ability to communicate. In other words, you provide information clearly and exactly. This may sound obvious, but it's tougher than that.

Radio host: Courtney, in what way have communication skills played a role in your job so far?

C. Rookie: You know, to design a ship you need to combine lots of specific things. At the beginning I was too shy to ask for help. So I got stuck and lost a great deal of time. Now I'd say: explain your problem.

Radio host: That's good. Ms McCooper, what else do employers demand?

E. McCooper: As tasks become more and more complex, we need people who can work in a team. In my view, good teamwork means that every single member of a team will know when to listen and when to lead.

C. Rookie: Yes, you're right, during my apprenticeship we removed a heavy engine from a huge motor yacht, and I was so glad to have an experienced worker right next to me.

E. McCooper: And even if sometimes employees might not like each other, it's crucial that all of the team members work together effectively.

Radio host: That sounds reasonable. Now, let's complete the top three soft skills for young apprentices, Ms McCooper.

E. McCooper: I think that time management is arguably among the most valuable soft skills you can have as a school leaver …

C. Rookie: Yes, my boss always says: "Time management is the art of simply being on time". For him this also includes delivering things before the deadline. At the beginning it was very hard for me to get up for work at six in the morning, as I was used to starting school at nine.

E. McCooper: Ah, yes, err ... What I wanted to say is: estimating how much time you need for a particular task can be tricky, particularly if a task is completely new. This is one of the most difficult things to learn.

Radio host: To sum it all up, communication, teamwork and time management, are the top soft skills every school leaver should be able to show. Thank you Ms McCooper and Courtney for being here.

Both: You're welcome. / Anytime.

Radio host: For more information on soft skills ... [fade out]

Adapted from: Apprenticeship Stories. Engineering. Courtney's Story [online available on: http://www.apprenticeshipstories.co.uk/courtney-story/]
Success al School. What Soft Skills Do Employers Look for in Job Applicants? [online available on: https://successatschool.org/advicedetails/554/Skill-Up:-What-Soft-Skills-do-Employers-Look-For-in-Job-Applicants%3F]

LCT 2021

1. Weather Apps

(Audiotrack: QR-Code rechts / Aufgabe S. 72)

1 The apps which are most frequently used simply present predictions made by computer models. Apps like mine rely on meteorologists to supervise and correct the data. These scientists provide extra knowledge. This is why I trust my app.
2 Some forecasters can access more observations than others. In addition to satellites and radar, my app relies on weather balloons, devices to measure river levels, and sensors on airplanes and ships. This is why this app is clearly my favourite.
3 My app features the most important information at a glance. I like the functional graphic interface and design. In case I need more specific data, I use the browser version, which also offers high-definition radar imaging.
4 Weather apps generally have a good reason to ask for your location. But here is a word of warning: various weather apps ask for permissions on the smartphone that they don't need and shouldn't have. I don't want to give away too much private information on social media or to weather apps, so I use one which is trustworthy.
5 Most apps work just fine in urban areas, but suddenly seem unsuitable when you visit remote places. They use the most common weather sensors only. I need an app with a high level of expertise in regional weather for my own protection when I go hiking in the mountains.

Adapted from: Koebler, Jason. Stop Using Third-Party Weather Apps [online available on: https://www.vice.com]
McGrath, Jenny. Your WeatherApp May Not Be As Reliable As You Thought. Here's Why [online available on: https://www.digitaltrends.com)
Fleming, Nic. Why Are All My Weather Apps Different? [online available on: https://www.theguardian.com]
Horovitz, Kate. Why Do Different Weather Apps Have Different Forecasts? [online available on: https://www.mentalfloss.com]

2. An Interview with a Weather Forecaster

(Audiotrack: QR-Code oben / Aufgabe S. 72)

Reporter: Hello everybody! With the tornado season in full swing, I thought it'd be fun to introduce you to the weather forecaster Janice Dean, whose nickname on her job is "The Weather Machine". Welcome, Janice!
Janice: Hello.
Reporter: Let me start by asking, did you always want to study meteorology?
Janice: To be honest, it's been a long way ... actually, when I was a kid I just accepted the weather as a given fact, the long Canadian winters, Indian summers and lovely springs. It was only later on that I got interested in climate phenomena.
Reporter: Ok.
Janice: Then, after college, I worked as a part time radio host, just to make a living. This included the local weather, of course. Back then, you could do the weather without having a background in meteorology. So I became a weather presenter by chance.
Reporter: M-hm.
Janice: But five years ago, I decided to go back to university because I'd been hired to be a TV daytime presenter but I felt I couldn't do the forecast without the scientific knowledge. So I took meteorology classes.
Reporter: Very interesting. So, what's the most exciting part about your job as a meteorologist?
Janice: Oh, there are so many different weather phenomena: Fog is stunning when you see it with a view over a big metropolis like New York. Thunder snow is awesome and rare to witness. It has the same dynamics as a thunderstorm with thunder and lightning except it happens in a snowstorm. Hurricanes are one of the most fascinating systems. At their strongest, they are incredible to look at on satellite. Of course they can be devastatingly dangerous, so I prefer to watch them moving over water and not making landfall, where they can cause immense destruction.
Reporter: Is there an experience you'll always remember?
Janice: Absolutely. I can remember a call-in by a desperate balloon pilot while I was doing the midday weather report. It was in the days when smartphones and weather apps where still far down the road.
Reporter: Oh, I remember.
Janice: Exactly. But he had his mobile and was able to call us during the news and urgently wanted to know if the towering clouds he was approaching would become dangerous for him. Together we could find out where he was, and I made a kind of specialized regional forecast. Luckily, the pilot was able to descend immediately. I had warned him that the wind would grow stronger in the next 30 minutes.
Reporter: Wow, crazy.
Janice: Yes.

Reporter: And what were the most touching experiences?
Janice: Well, some weather stories might bring sadness. But on the other hand, anytime there is a heavy storm, I see communities and neighbors coming together to help one another. Such extreme weather events affect all people equally whatever their nationality or their income. Weather unites us across the world, and when a storm has rushed through communities, a lot of times that's when we get to see the kindness of others.

Adapted from: Hunter-Frederick, Allison. Interview with Weather Forecaster Janice Dean [online available on: https://lincolnanimalambassadors.wordpress.com]

3. Weather Report

(Audiotrack: QR-Code S. 102 / Aufgabe S. 73)

Good afternoon! It's a largely rainy but quite warm day today. Temperatures have been on the up after a **rough** start to the week. It's been rather unsettled with showers affecting Britain most days of the week. This weekend won't see any serious change to this pattern. There'll be **mild** winds and again some rain almost everywhere throughout the country. We'll see a deep low pressure system moving across the north on **Sunday**. It will bring more winds to the areas it affects in the north. At the same time there will be less rain. As the low pressure system **shifts** eastwards, there'll be a spell of north-westerly winds developing. It'll become colder, and with the strength of the wind on Tuesday it'll feel chilly. Next, we'll see high pressure building to the south-west and then to the **west** of Britain. This will drift overhead on Wednesday, which should be dry and calm, but still rather cool. The end of the week looks **wetter**. And the outlook for next week: warmer temperatures can be expected.

Adapfed from: BBC Monthly Outlook. [online available on: https://www.bbc.com]

4. Calling the Weather Service

(Audiotrack: QR-Code S. 102 / Aufgabe S. 74)

Weather expert: This is the Australian Hikers' Hotline. How can I help you?
Joshua: Hello, this is Joshua Phillips. We're on a seven-day hiking trip on Fraser Island. I'm afraid we ran into a problem. We lost our internet connection, so our phones can't tell us the way anymore. We're thinking about continuing our hike a little longer, but we're not sure because the clouds have become very dark. Do you think it's a good idea to continue?
Weather expert: Oh, I see. Yes, the mobile internet connection broke down today because the main cell tower was damaged. Ok, let me check. Can you describe where you are?
Joshua: We are pretty well in the middle of the island. I can see the dock for the ferry to Little Woody Island right in front of us.
Weather expert: Oh, okay. So I've got your location. Now let me check the weather for you ... err ... on my radar I can see that there is a storm coming up which is predicted to be short but rather heavy. You'll get about seven millimeters of rain per hour. That's a lot! You might want to think about staying under cover during the storm. The closest accommodation is a place called Kingfisher Bay but I'm afraid it's too far away from you. If you have the right equipment, I'd suggest you rather stay where you are.
Joshua: I'm not sure if we have everything we need. What do you think is necessary?
Weather expert: You should have a waterproof tent for the rain. A bright torch would be good, too. Finally, you really ought to have a strong rope to tie your belongings together, so that nothing gets swept away by the storm.
Joshua: Okay, got it. I am going to ask my friends but I think we have all of that. So, what's the weather going to be like in the next few days?
Weather expert: Based on our data, you should be fine tomorrow. However, the day after tomorrow will be worse again.
Joshua: Okay, I see. We planned on arriving in Happy Valley tomorrow evening anyways. Can you give us the telephone number of a decent hotel there? You know, nothing too fancy.
Weather expert: (laughs) Well, I'm not a travel agent. But you're lucky! Actually I know a good place to stay there. It's called Lil's Place. It's on Yidney Drive. You won't miss it, it's the largest house on the street.
Joshua: Great! Would you mind spelling the street name for me?
Weather expert: Sure. That's Y-I-D-N-E-Y D-R-I-V-E.
Joshua: Thank you so much for your help. Have a good day!
Weather expert: You too. Safe travels and goodbye!

Adapted from: Fraser Tours. Weather on Fraser Island [online available on: https://www.fraser-tours.com]

5. Floods and Droughts

(Audiotrack: QR-Code S. 102 / Aufgabe S. 74)

Presenter:	Welcome to "Radio Now". Today we're going to discuss a topic that affects a lot of people nowadays: "Floods and Droughts". Our experts are Mr Adams and Mrs Banks, both renowned meteorologists. Good morning!
Both:	Good morning. / Good morning.
Presenter:	Let's start talking about floods. A flood occurs when water inundates land which is normally dry. What factors increase the risk of a flood?
Mrs Banks:	Well, there are plenty of reasons, of course, but the most serious one is climate change.
Mr Adams:	Absolutely. Studies show that the increase in temperatures due to global warming has hardly any effect on the number of hurricanes, but on their travel speed. It slows them down. Although a slower speed may seem like a good thing, it's actually just the opposite. It also affects the rainfall, which will become heavier, resulting in greater danger of flooding.
Presenter:	Sounds scary.
Mr Adams:	It is. You don't necessarily need a mass of water. Most vehicles will be carried away by only two feet of water, and just six inches of water can knock a person off their feet.
Presenter:	That's quite remarkable.
Mrs Banks:	Indeed. Floods are the second-most widespread natural disaster with tremendous impacts. Apart from the billions in damage, possible contamination poses a threat to our drinking water. This is caused by chemical substances, which can mix and react with the water, and by uncleaned wastewater, of course. Residents of flooded areas can be left without power and clean drinking water, leading to outbreaks of disease.
Presenter:	Is there anything that can be done?
Mrs Banks:	Well, you can't really stop floodwater.
Mr Adams:	I'd recommend: Be prepared in case you need to evacuate. Assemble a waterproof emergency kit that contains a small first aid kit, a portable radio set – it might be useful to stay up-to-date with local news on flooding – and supplies, of course, so that you can survive for three days. Don't forget to check expiry dates once a year and replace items as needed.
Presenter:	What about extremely dry periods like droughts?
Mrs Banks:	Today, water is one of the world's most precious resources, and many people across the world do not have guaranteed access to safe drinking water. As climate change takes its toll, it's time to do something about it. My best advice to prepare for a drought is to collect water.
Mr Adams:	Collecting water is important, but we shouldn't forget about the role our forests play. When there are droughts, forests provide clean water. And when there are floods, trees store huge amounts of water. It's high time to protect our forests; there are several steps that must be taken urgently.
Mrs Banks:	Absolutely, governments need to adopt new policies ...
Presenter:	I see. Can you give us an example of a useful drought-preparation project?
Mrs Banks:	Well, take Perth in Australia. In the past, the city has had huge problems during droughts because there weren't enough natural water resources. Next year, they expect their complete water supply to be climate independent. The water-recycling program they started four years ago will then be fully established. ·
Presenter:	Thank you for that. In our next episode we'll be ... [fade out]

Adapted from: National Geographic. Flood [online available on: https://kids.nationalgeographic.com]
Howard, Jenny. Flood Safety Tips [online available on: https://www.nationalgeographic.com]
Impakter. Water in Our World: Our Most Precious Resource [online available on: https://impakter.com]
Morgan, Ruth. Watering The West [online available on: https://www.foreground.com.au]
European Environment Agency. Forests Can Help Prevent Floods and Droughts [online available on: https://www.eea.europa.eu]

LCT 2022

1. Specialised Bike Shops

(Audiotrack: QR-Code rechts / Aufgabe S. 82)

1 Most of our customers live in the city but love a healthy day ride. They want to get away from the traffic and take in all roads including any rough street surface, gravel roads or even singletrack forest trails. Some also use their bikes to go touring on holiday.

2 Sharing the love and interest for classic road bikes, we specialise in high-end cycles in full original glory. We give our customers the opportunity to buy or restore their classic steel bikes and turn them into real beauties again to keep them going.

3 With caring staff on hand we give support to choose from tricycles, handcycles and more. We don't construct our own bikes, but we keep a wide range of cycles in stock to meet all kinds of special needs. And all our cycles can be customised using adaptions such as wheelchair racks or pedal-assist motors.

4 Our customers are looking for the ideal bike to commute. Depending on the conditions of the route between the rider's home and job destination, we'll find the perfect solution. This could be a superlight fold-up pedelec to take on a bus once the city has been reached, or a gravel bike to ride through parks right into the city centre.

5 We build bikes to our customers' unique specifications from the bottom up. From rickshaws and pedicabs for tourists to extraordinary cargo-bikes or tandems for families, whatever kind of cycle you imagine, anything is possible. Let's make your vision become reality, too!

Adapted from: Branquinho, Lance. Should I Buy a Gravel Bike? The Pros and Cons [online available on: https://www.cyclingnews.com]
CSB Classic Steel Bikes. About & Philosophy [online available on: https://www.classicsteelbikes.com]
Get Cycling. Specialist Cycles [online available on: https://www.getcycling.org]

2. An E-Bike Trip through California

(Audiotrack: QR-Code oben / Aufgabe S. 82)

Assistant: *(door bell)* Good morning, how can I help you?
Tourist: Hi, my friends and I are renting e-bikes from you. I need some more information for our trip through California.
Assistant: Sure. Here's a map with the locations of charging points, repair shops and other important facilities. We're here, at the e-bike rentals pick-up in Carson City.
Tourist: Fantastic. Today we want to tour around Carson City before we head west. Where's the nearest charging station on our way?
Assistant: Hm, that depends how long you want to spend here. The bikes are fully charged now. The closest possibility's right at Lake Tahoe, but it's accessible only from 8 am till 6 pm.
Tourist: Actually, we wanted to be independent of opening hours.
Assistant: No problem. There's a charging point halfway to Sacramento on highway 50 that's open day and night, all year round.
Tourist: That's useful. What if any technical problems come up?
Assistant: Since our e-bikes are highly reliable you shouldn't worry too much. But if you have minor problems with your bikes we have a repair shop partner who will come and help you right away. Or he'll pick you up in his van and take you to Yuba City where his garage is located.
Tourist: Ok, great, could you give me his phone number, just in case?
Assistant: Of course.
Tourist: And is there something similar on our way south to San Jose?
Assistant: Then you're also quite close to our other partner garage right in the center of San Jose. Oh, sorry, I forgot they're on vacation this week. But *Mike's Bikes* in Stockton will provide you with a new e-bike within 12 hours. So ... don't worry.
Tourist: Good to hear. Can you recommend any e-bike friendly accommodations down there?
Assistant: That depends on your route. There's a large e-bike motel close to highway 80 between Sacramento and San Francisco with a big pool and spa. But since you said you want to head south I have a secret tip for you: Ride down to the San Luis Reservoir on highway 5. The e-bike motel's located in the heart of the state recreation area and offers all kinds of comfort for tired bikers. In addition, it boasts an awesome landscape with wild mountains and forests.
Tourist: Thanks. That's exactly what we're looking for!
Assistant: Great. Have you made up your mind where you'd like to drop off your bikes after your trip?
Tourist: Hm, not really.

Assistant: Well, our drop-off stations are in Santa Rosa in the north and in Fresno in the south.
Tourist: Actually, we're definitely going to the San Luis Reservoir, so we'll give back our bikes in Fresno in five days time.
Assistant: Sounds good. I'll inform them that you're coming.
Tourist: Great, thanks so much.

Adapted from: The Mercury News. Your EV Trip to Tahoe Just Got Easier [online available on: https://www.mercurynews.com]

3. Who Invented the Bicycle?

(Audiotrack: QR-Code S. 105 / Aufgabe S. 83)

In 1815, global temperatures dropped because of a natural disaster; the most powerful volcanic eruption in modern history **shocked** present-day Indonesia. This reduced harvests world-wide and caused working animals like horses to starve. The German inventor Karl von Drais realized the need for a mode of transportation that did not need to be **fed** like animals, and started working on designs for a human-powered, two-wheeled device. Drais's **running** machine had no pedals and no brakes and was propelled by the biker's feet. Drais's **best** run was a 9-mile, one-hour ride. As people began heading out on "dandy horses", however, it turned out they started to use sidewalks for their rides. This endangered pedestrians and led to **expensive** consequences, such as bans and fines. It took another 40 years until people developed bikes further and the public really became interested.

Adapted from: Earls, Stephanie. A Global Disaster Gave Us The Bike [online available on: https://www.outtherecolorado.com]

4. Bike Rental

(Audiotrack: QR-Code S. 105 / Aufgabe S. 84)

Cycletta: Welcome to *BRS24*, your self-service bike rental terminal.
I am Cycletta, your personal computer assistant. You are in the main menu. If you want to rent a bike today, say "rent today". If you plan to rent a bike in the future, say "rent later". In case you need help from one of our bike specialists, say "expert". A team of specialists can help you find a suitable bike, which is essential for a comfortable journey that you'll fully enjoy. Our experts can also solve technical problems for you.
Customer: Rent today.
Cycletta: Okay, rent a bike today. You can now choose between three types of bikes: explorer, metro and volt bikes. If you would like to tour the city on one of our metro bikes, say "metro". Say "explorer" if you want to ride over bumpy ground and enjoy the great outdoors. Say "volt" if you prefer a cozy ride with one of our e-bikes.
Customer: Explorer.
Cycletta: Okay, rent an explorer bike. Before you start your ride, please make sure you don't have a flat tire. If that is the case, you can use the air pump provided in the frame to your left. Also, test the brake handles in case the brakes don't work properly. It is very unlikely as our bikes are maintained regularly, but we want you to be as safe as possible. Finally, check the lock, as it works electronically and might possibly be low on battery. In case any of those points apply to your bike, please call our service hotline. If everything is fine, say "Next". If not, say "problem".
Customer: Next.
Cycletta: Okay, thank you. Now open our mobile app on your phone. Type in the following verification code to activate your bike. The code is 22VH – 9ZUH – S511 *(click sounds)*. Thank you. To finalize your booking, present your credit card now ... *(swipe card)*.
Sorry, there has been an unexpected error. We are canceling your booking ... *(beep sound)* Welcome to *BRS24*, your self-service ... *(fade out)*
Customer: What ... ?

5. Go Cycle

(Audiotrack: QR-Code S. 105 / Aufgabe S. 84)

Presenter: Welcome to our podcast *Dream Green*. Over the last ten years the number of cyclists has been exploding. Our two guests today are both playing their parts in this development. Welcome Mrs Powell and Mr Withers.

Mr Withers: Good morning.

Mrs Powell: Pleasure to be here.

Presenter: Mr Withers, you are the father of three children aged two to six. Recently you bought a so-called cargo bike. Why a cargo bike?

Mr Withers: Well, we live in the suburbs. My wife started to work again. She needs the car to go to work. We considered buying a second car, but we couldn't really afford it. Also there's little parking space around, and bikes reduce our carbon footprint. So we decided to go for a cargo bike instead.

Presenter: What exactly is a cargo bike, Mr Withers?

Mr Withers: Basically, it's not a new invention. Just think of the old days when it was constructed specifically to deliver heavy or bulky loads, such as milk cans. Today, you can choose the perfect bike corresponding to your needs.

Presenter: What kind of bike did you get, Mr Withers?

Mr Withers: We opted for a compact double lane bike, with a wheel box in front. At the moment we mainly transport our children – seats and rain cover are included, you know – but later, when our children get bikes of their own, we want to adapt our present bike for the grocery tour or, when staying overnight, we'll transport the camping equipment we need.

Presenter: I see. Mrs Powell, your start-up *Sunny Bikes* tries to meet the needs of your clients every day.

Mrs Powell: Right, my team and I upgrade existing bikes individually to turn them into solar-powered electric bicycles.

Presenter: What gave you the idea to start *Sunny Bikes*?

Mrs Powell: Well, funnily enough, I was in a similar situation to Mr Withers. As a family, we opted for a cargo bike. But with my two children on board, I could hardly push the bike uphill. However, we didn't want to replace it with an electric bike. I tried to think creatively and found a DIY solution: a motor with a solar-power device. It worked!

Presenter: Wow, congratulations! Can you give us some more details about *Sunny Bikes*?

Mrs Powell: Being solar-powered, our *Sunny Bikes* might not be extremely fast compared to other e-bikes – actually the pedal assist stops at 15 miles per hour. But of course, its solar-powered engine is very useful when you start from a standstill. You can also cover more miles with less effort. And they're eco-friendly, that's obvious.

Presenter: Now, I'm curious: what do you do on rainy days?

Mrs Powell: You don't really want to go on bike trips on rainy days *(laughing)* … seriously, of course, we've thought about that. The capacity of the batteries is quite good. Once you've parked your *Sunny Bike* outside for about five hours, it is fully loaded and ready to run up to thirty-five miles. On very sunny days, it can load in half an hour.

Presenter: Mr Withers, would that be an option for you?

Mr Withers: Yes definitely, this absolutely fits our idea of reducing our carbon footprint.

Presenter: Perfect. Thank you both for being here.

Adapted from: Greiderer, Karen Rieke. The Renaissance of the Cargo Bike #2 [online available on: https://www.bikecitizens.net]
Schindler, Christian. Solar Cycle [online available on: https://www.ebike-news.de]

Notizen

Notizen

Schule – und dann?

Tipps und Infos zum Start in den Beruf

- Bewerbungsunterlagen
- Anschreiben
- Lebenslauf
- Einstellungstests + Lösungen
- Assessment-Center
- Online-Tipps
- Bildungswege

Bewerbungsunterlagen

Auch, wenn die klassische Bewerbung per Post von vielen Firmen noch akzeptiert wird, so bevorzugen die meisten Betriebe inzwischen eine Online-Bewerbung. Dabei bieten große Unternehmen oft eigene Bewerbungsportale auf ihren Firmenwebseiten, in denen die Bewerber/-innen ein Onlineformular ausfüllen und ihre Unterlagen (Lebenslauf, Zeugnisse, ggf. weitere Nachweise und Bewerbungsfoto) hochladen können. Hat die Firma kein Bewerbungsportal, so verschickt der/die Bewerber/-in seine/ihre Bewerbung per E-Mail mit entsprechendem Anhang. Dabei empfiehlt es sich, die oben genannten Unterlagen in ein einziges Dokument zu packen, damit der/die Personalzuständige nicht lange suchen und nur eine Datei öffnen muss. Wichtig bei einer Online-Bewerbung (egal ob Bewerberportal oder E-Mail) ist jedoch immer eine seriöse E-Mail-Adresse, die Qualität der eingescannten Dokumente, das richtige Format (meist PDF) und die Dateigröße (max. 2 – 3 MB).

Für die Onlinebewerbung gelten die gleichen Maßstäbe wie für die klassische Bewerbungsmappe. Insbesondere das Anschreiben sollte die herkömmlichen Kriterien erfüllen (Briefkopf, Betreffzeile mit der ausgeschriebenen Stelle, die persönliche Anrede, das direkte Eingehen auf den angestrebten Ausbildungsplatz, korrekte Rechtschreibung und Zeichensetzung sowie einheitliches Layout, Grußformel und Unterschrift etc.) und dabei eine DIN-A4-Seite nicht überschreiten. Wird das Anschreiben als Anhang versendet, so sollte eine Kurzversion im Textfenster der E-Mail enthalten sein. Das Anschreiben kann aber auch Teil der E-Mail selbst sein.

Die folgende Liste gibt Ihnen einen wichtigen Überblick über die Unterlagen, die Ihre Bewerbung enthalten sollte:

Deckblatt (optional)

- Titel: Bewerbung für (Ausildungsplatz/Stelle)
- Kontaktdaten (Name, Adresse, Telefonnummer, E-Mail)

Bewerbungsfoto

- professionelles Bewerbungsfoto (bei Papierfoto: Name und Adresse auf Rückseite schreiben)
- Standard: Foto oben rechts im Lebenslauf oder auf dem Deckblatt

Anschreiben

- persönliche Kontaktdaten im Briefkopf aktuell und richtig
- Name und Adresse des Ansprechpartners richtig schreiben
- korrekte Betreffzeile, z. B. Bewerbung für/als (Ausbildungsplatz)
- Grund für Bewerbung angeben
- Bezug zwischen Anforderungen und eigenen Fähigkeiten formulieren
- nicht länger als eine DIN-A4-Seite
- fehlerfreie Rechtschreibung und Zeichensetzung; einheitliches Layout
- Grußformel und Unterschrift

Lebenslauf

- persönliche Angaben (Name, Anschrift, Telefonnummer und E-Mail-Adresse, Geburtsdatum, Staatsangehörigkeit)
- Schulbildung (besuchte Schultypen) und voraussichtlicher Schulabschluss
- Berufserfahrung: Praktika, Aushilfs- oder Nebenjobs, etc.
- außerschulisches Engagement (z. B. Ehrenamt)
- besondere Kenntnisse oder Fähigkeiten
- nicht länger als zwei DIN-A4-Seiten
- lückenlos, korrekte Zeitangaben
- Unterschrift

Anlagen

- Kopien von Zeugnissen, Referenzen, Zertifikaten

Anschreiben

Bevor Sie sich bei einer Firma bewerben, sollten Sie sich bei der dortigen Personalabteilung nach dem Namen der zuständigen Person erkundigen. Das Anschreiben sollte, so weit möglich, immer eine personalisierte Anrede enthalten; Formulierungen wie „Sehr geehrte Damen und Herren" sollten vermieden werden. Es macht auch einen guten Eindruck, wenn Sie sich vorher schon einmal über das Berufsbild informiert haben und in Ihrem Anschreiben darstellen können, warum gerade Sie sich für diesen Beruf eignen.
Außerdem ist es wichtig, dass Sie sich über das Unternehmen informieren, bei dem Sie sich bewerben. Vermeiden Sie dabei Schreib- und Kommafehler und vergessen Sie Ihre Unterschrift nicht.

Beispiel für ein klassisches Anschreiben

Marc Schmidt
Bahnhofstraße 158
35889 Krielinghausen
Telefon 06456 445932
E-Mail marc.schmidt@mail.de

Bäckerei Herrlinger
Herrn Fritz Herrlinger
Backgasse 15
33886 Wieshain

Krielinghausen, 15. Oktober 2021

Bewerbung um einen Ausbildungsplatz zum Bäcker

Sehr geehrter Herr Herrlinger,

durch Ihre Mitarbeiterin, Frau Fischer, habe ich erfahren, dass Sie ab dem 1. September 2022 einen Ausbildungsplatz zum Bäcker anbieten. Dafür möchte ich mich bei Ihnen bewerben.

Der Beruf des Bäckers ist bereits seit Langem mein Traumberuf. Die handwerkliche Arbeit in einer Backstube und der Umgang mit Lebensmitteln haben mich schon immer interessiert. Als Kind habe ich mit meiner Mutter oft Kuchen und Plätzchen gebacken, inzwischen backe ich alleine und probiere auch gerne neue Rezepte aus. In einem örtlichen Gasthof habe ich bereits erste Erfahrungen gesammelt.

Im Juni beende ich die Schule mit dem Hauptschulabschluss. Danach würde ich gerne bei Ihnen ein Praktikum machen, damit Sie mich vorab besser kennenlernen können.

Über die Einladung zu einem Vorstellungsgespräch freue ich mich.

Mit freundlichen Grüßen

Marc Schmidt

Anlagen: Lebenslauf mit Foto, Zertifikat Praktikum, Schulzeugnis

Lebenslauf

Ein in Aufsatzform formulierter Lebenslauf ist heutzutage nicht mehr üblich. Arbeitgeber und Arbeitgeberinnen erwarten stattdessen einen Lebenslauf in Tabellenform – und zwar:

- chronologisch geordnet (die in Deutschland üblichere, traditionelle Variante)
- umgekehrt chronologisch geordnet mit den neuesten Daten am Anfang (die moderne internationale/EU-Variante)

Beispiel für einen chronologischen Lebenslauf

Lebenslauf
Marc Schmidt

Bahnhofstraße 158
35889 Krielinghausen
Telefon 06456 445932
E-Mail marc.schmidt@mail.de

Persönliche Daten

Geburtstag und -ort	23. April 2007 in Krielinghausen
Staatsangehörigkeit	deutsch

Schulischer Werdegang

09/2013 bis 07/2017	Grundschule Krielinghausen
09/2017 bis 06/2022	Gesamtschule Krielinghausen • voraussichtlicher Schulabschluss: Hauptschulabschluss • Lieblingsfächer: Mathematik, Werken Teilnahme an der Koch-AG

Betriebspraktikum

02/2021 bis 03/2021	Frischmarkt AG, Winterhain Dreiwöchiges Schülerpraktikum • Einräumen der angelieferten Waren • Mitarbeit an der Kasse • Mitarbeit an der Brottheke

Aushilfstätigkeiten

08/2021 bis 09/2021	Gasthof „Sonne“, Krielinghausen Vierwöchiger Ferienjob • Tätigkeit als Küchenhilfe • Mitarbeit im Service

Hobbys	Backen, Kochen, Musik
Seit 10/2017	Mitglied im Musikverein (Posaune)

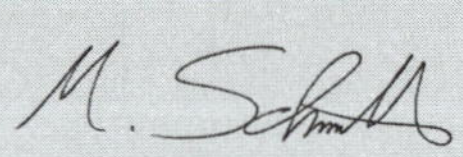

Krielinghausen, 15. Oktober 2021

Einstellungstests

Viele Schüler/-innen kennen die Angst vor Prüfungen. In der Schule hat man wenigstens den Vorteil, dass man ungefähr weiß, was drankommen kann. Berufseinstellungstests sind den meisten jedoch fremd und der Druck, sich gegen andere Bewerber/-innen durchzusetzen, verstärkt die Prüfungsangst meist noch.

Wir wollen Sie auf diese Situation vorbereiten und Ihnen die Angst vor dem Unbekannten nehmen. Dafür haben wir auf den nächsten Seiten einige Musteraufgaben zusammengestellt, wie sie in solchen Tests vorkommen können.

Es geht den Prüfer/-innen nicht nur darum, dass Sie alle Aufgaben korrekt lösen, sondern auch darum, wie Sie sich in einer solchen Situation verhalten und wo Ihre Stärken liegen.

Die Lösungen zu den Tests finden Sie auf Seite A14.

1. Logisches Denken

Zahlenreihen

Welche Zahl ergänzt die Zahlenreihe sinnvoll?

1. 2 6 12 20 30 ?

2. 16 23 28 38 49 62 ?

TIPP

Notieren Sie den Rechenschritt zur jeweils nächsten Zahl, dann kommen Sie meist schnell auf die Lösung.

Wortanalogien

1. Mehl verhält sich zu Kuchen wie Zement zu ...?

a) Bäcker b) Maurer
c) Haus d) Hefe

2. Schnecke verhält sich zu Ohr wie Knöchel zu ...?

a) Oberschenkel b) Fuß
c) Gartenhaus d) Pflanze

TIPP

Untersuchen Sie das vorgegebene Wortpaar und suchen Sie die bestehende Beziehung zwischen den Wörtern.

Beziehungen

1. Morgen ist Mittwoch. Welcher Tag war vorgestern?

a) Montag b) Dienstag c) Mittwoch d) Donnerstag
e) Freitag f) Samstag g) Sonntag

2. Es ist die Tochter deiner Großmutter, aber nicht deine Tante. Wer ist es?

a) Großmutter b) Nichte c) Cousine d) Tochter
e) Mutter f) Schwester g) Tante

Grafikanalogien

Bestimmen Sie aus den vier möglichen Grafiken diejenige, die die Bildgleichung sinnvoll ergänzt.

1.

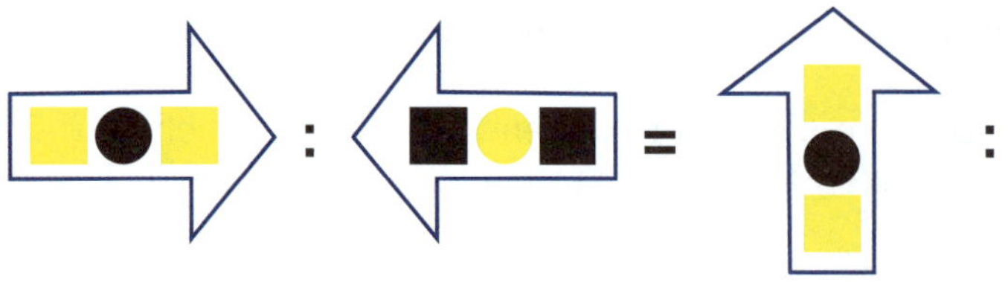

a) 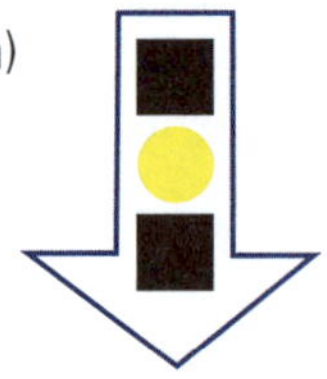

b) 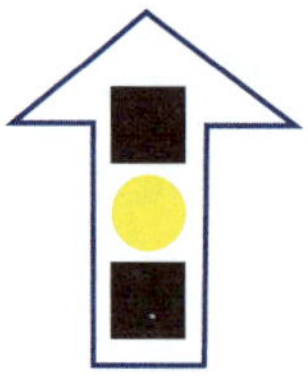

c) 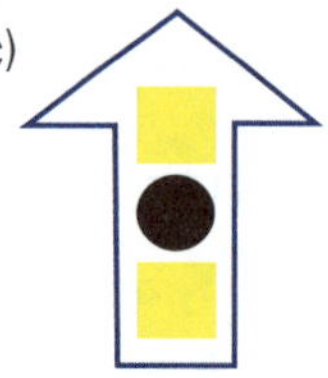

d) 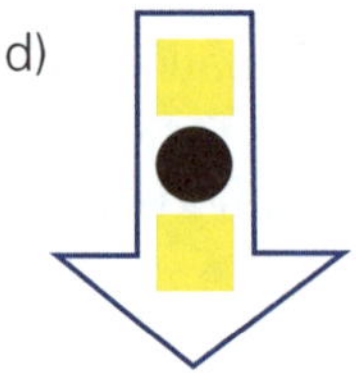

2.

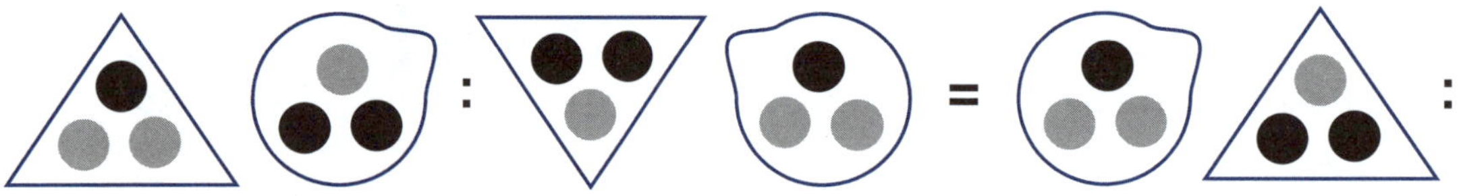

a) 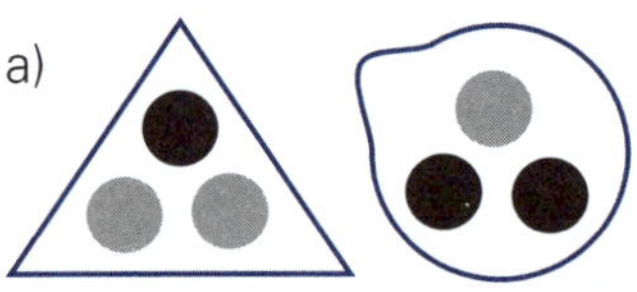

b) 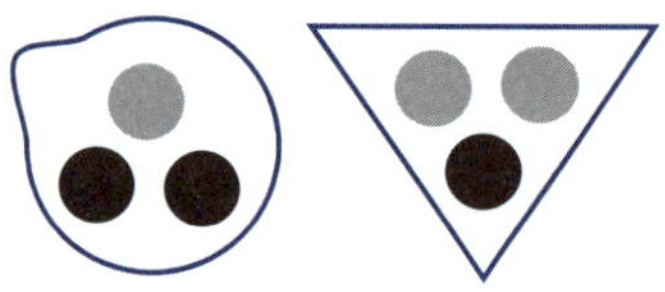

c) 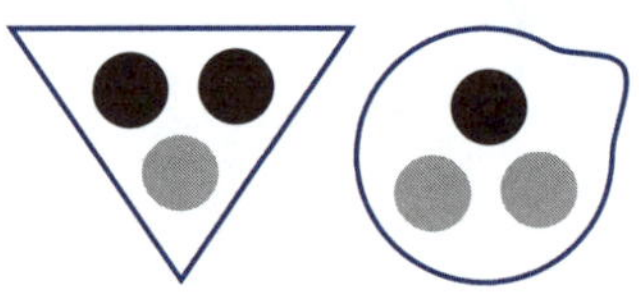

d) 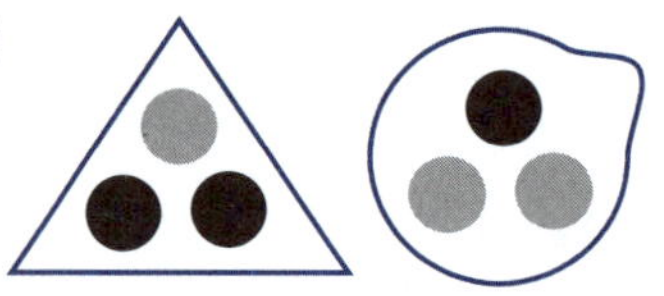

2. Konzentration

Die alphabetische Reihenfolge

Erkennen Sie die korrekten alphabetischen Buchstabenabfolgen von 3 bis 5 Buchstaben und unterstreichen Sie diese.

1. dhabanejdhenahjbekjabcdfgejndnansmjodnbdjwxyzjbdnrnmalmüppkdknshdkjklndhadnenduenduendopqr-
hzfunrucmchdtebnsmnaüskendhabezefghnmkelodhbezshynmnbabsebdnmeidjnantzbszxtgbsnxhzsstu-
vwb

2. hnsndnadhendnsjuvwxhdndnbdnmejdkalehijkdnmadnsomemaödefgnbdbanskjneksoxnaknbsjxonbshze-
baisbelmanslmnopzehbaisjbajsnenakmslxpklmhjdamsidjendhijdnsmalsneisxnmamsrstudbansmensuaylx-
vn

Kopfrechnen

Geben Sie das Ergebnis folgender Rechnung an. Rechnen Sie Schritt für Schritt, die Rechenregel „Punkt vor Strich" gilt hier nicht.

1. $6 + 6 - 3 + 7 - 5 \cdot 2 + 8 - 20 \cdot 2 + 7 =$

2. $81 : 9 + 7 + 5 + 3 : 2 + 13 \cdot 2 - 20 : 2 - 15 + 7 \cdot 2 - 6 \cdot 3 =$

Mosaik

1. In welchem Feld ist ein Mosaikbaustein falsch? Geben Sie an, ob A, B, C oder D richtig ist.

TIPP

Kreuzen Sie im Zweifelsfall die Antwort an, die Ihnen richtig erscheint.

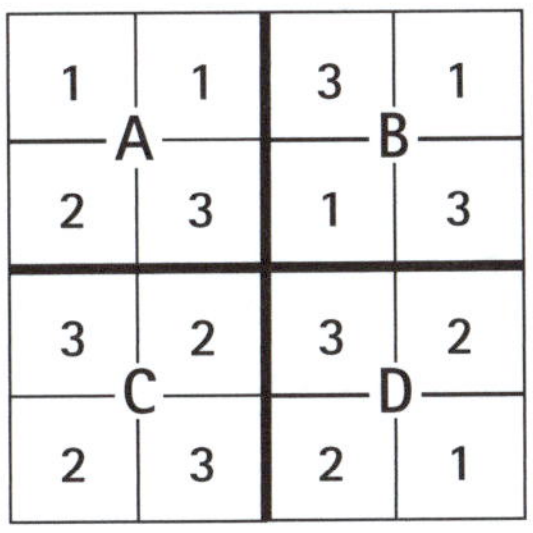

2. In welchem Feld ist ein Mosaikbaustein falsch? Geben Sie an, ob A, B, C, D oder E richtig ist.

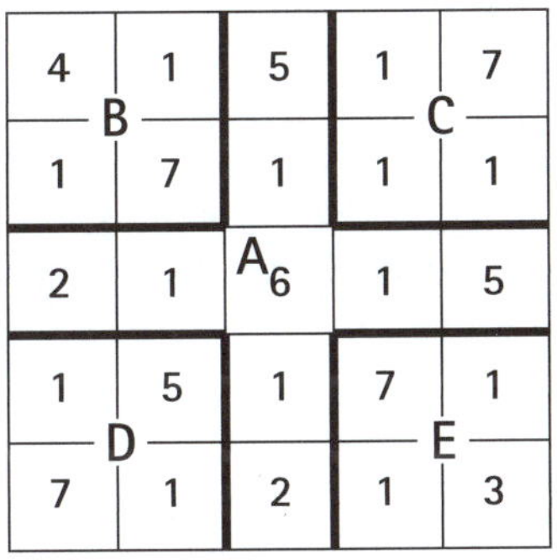

Additions-/Subtraktionsaufgaben

Rechnen Sie zuerst die obere und dann die untere Zeile aus. Ist das zweite Ergebnis kleiner als das erste, ziehen Sie es vom ersten ab und schreiben diese Differenz auf. Ist das Ergebnis der zweiten Zeile größer, müssen Sie beide Ergebnisse addieren.

1. 2 + 4 – 5
5 + 4 + 4

2. 7 + 8 – 3
4 + 5 – 2

3. 4 + 4 – 3
7 + 6 + 4

4. 4 + 5 + 4
9 – 8 + 7

5. 8 – 4 – 1
3 + 4 + 6

6. 3 + 8 – 3
4 + 3 + 2

7. 4 + 9 – 7
5 + 6 – 3

8. 9 – 2 + 7
3 + 2 + 4

9. 7 + 3 – 4
4 + 7 – 3

TIPP

Rechnen Sie jede Reihe für sich und schreiben Sie das Ergebnis auf. So verlieren Sie nicht die Übersicht.

3. Allgemeinwissen

TIPP

Wenn Sie sich nicht ganz sicher sind, gehen Sie nach dem Ausschlussverfahren vor und kreuzen Sie auf jeden Fall eine Antwort an.

1. Wie viel Liter Blut fließen durchschnittlich durch den menschlichen Körper?

a) 5 bis 6 Liter
b) 12 bis 14 Liter
c) 8 bis 10 Liter
d) 3 bis 4 Liter

2. Wie lautet das chemische Gegenstück zur Säure?

a) Salz
b) Oxid
c) Zucker
d) Base

3. Welche Einheit bezeichnet elektrischen Strom?

a) Hertz
b) Ampere
c) Watt
d) Pascal

4. Wie viele Seitenflächen hat ein Tetraeder?

a) 4
b) 6
c) 8
d) gar keine, es ist eine Kugel

5. Wie nennt man in der Informatik die kleinste Informationseinheit?

a) Chip
b) Unix
c) Link
d) Bit

6. Welches Wirtschaftssystem hat Deutschland?

a) Zentrale Marktwirtschaft
b) Soziale Marktwirtschaft
c) Kapitalistische Marktwirtschaft
d) Sozialistische Marktwirtschaft

7. An wie viele Länder grenzt Deutschland?

a) 6
b) 7
c) 8
d) 9

8. Wessen Interessen werden in der Kommunalpolitik vertreten?

a) Bundesländer
b) Bund
c) Landkreis und Gemeinde
d) Europäische Gemeinschaft

9. Wer war der erste Bundeskanzler der Bundesrepublik Deutschland?

a) Gerhard Schröder
b) Konrad Adenauer
c) Helmut Kohl
d) Ludwig Erhard

10. Unter welchem Namen schrieb der erste römische Kaiser Octavian Geschichte?

a) Caesar
b) Augustus
c) Romulus
d) Herkules

11. In welchem Drama Goethes wird die „Gretchenfrage“ gestellt?

a) Götz von Berlichingen
b) Faust I
c) Torquato Tasso
d) Egmont

12. Wer schrieb das Stück „Die Räuber“?

a) Johann Wolfgang von Goethe
b) Friedrich Schiller
c) Gotthold Ephraim Lessing
d) Wilhelm Hauff

13. Welcher Künstler malte die „Mona Lisa“?

a) Pablo Picasso
b) Michelangelo Buonarroti
c) Salvador Dali
d) Leonardo da Vinci

14. Wie heißen die Stimmlagen der Männerstimmen, absteigend nach der Höhe sortiert?

a) Sopran, Bass, Tenor
b) Tenor, Bariton, Bass
c) Bariton, Tenor, Bass
d) Alt, Tenor, Bass

15. Woraus besteht eine Nordische Kombination?

a) Skisprung und Skilanglauf
b) Skilanglauf und Schießen
c) Slalom und Abfahrt
d) Skiflug und Slalom

4. Sprachgefühl

Abkürzungen

Wofür stehen folgende Abkürzungen? Kreuzen Sie alle richtigen Antworten an.

1. a) Mofa = Montagefabrik
b) ABS = Autobahnschnee
c) FAZ = Frankfurter Allgemeine Zeitung
d) DIN = Deutsches Institut für Normung

2. a) IHK = Industrie- und Handelskammer
b) AGB = Angestelltengesetzbuch
c) USA = United States of America
d) EU = Europäische Universität

3. a) BASF = Badische Anilin- und Soda-Fabrik
b) PS = Pendelstrom
c) BVerfG = Bundesverfassungsgericht
d) VW = Volkswagen

Wortbedeutungen

Welches der vier Wörter passt nicht zu den anderen?

1.	2.	3.
a) Deutsch	a) Fußball	a) Buchstabe
b) Französisch	b) Tennis	b) Zahl
c) Schwäbisch	c) Basketball	c) Vokal
d) Englisch	d) Schwimmen	d) Konsonant

Fremdwörter

1. Was bedeutet das Fremdwort „heterogen"?

a) fremd
b) ungleichartig
c) stark erhitzt
d) keimfrei

2. Was bedeutet das Fremdwort „relativ"?

a) verhältnismäßig
b) sehr klein
c) sehr groß
d) verändert

Satzergänzungen

1. Das menschliche Verhalten wird von der … untersucht.

a) Biologie
b) Zoologie
c) Chemie
d) Psychologie

2. Im Straßenverkehr muss man besonders … sein?

a) aggressiv
b) mutig
c) schnell
d) aufmerksam

TIPP

Führen Sie zuerst die Aufgaben und Antworten zusammen, bei denen Sie sich sicher sind.

3. Der Stundenzeiger einer Uhr ist immer … als der Minutenzeiger.

a) länger
b) kürzer
c) dicker
d) dünner

Sinnverwandte Sprichwörter

Welches Sprichwort hat eine ähnliche Bedeutung wie das vorgegebene?

1. „Jeder kehre vor seiner eigenen Türe."

a) Wer anderen eine Grube gräbt, fällt selbst hinein.
b) Wer im Glashaus sitzt, soll nicht mit Steinen werfen.
c) Der Lauscher an der Wand hört seine eigene Schand.
d) Reden ist Silber, Schweigen ist Gold.

2. „Das Glück ist mit den Dummen."

a) Die dümmsten Bauern haben die größten Kartoffeln.
b) Den Tüchtigen hilft das Glück.
c) Scherben bringen Glück.
d) Wer nicht wagt, der nicht gewinnt.

Groß- und Kleinschreibung

Welcher Satz ist richtig geschrieben?

1. a) Aber heute Früh habe ich wieder einen Arzttermin.
b) Aber Heute früh habe ich wieder einen Arzttermin.
c) Aber heute früh habe ich wieder einen Arzttermin.

2. a) Sie hatte fünf einsen im Zeugnis und war zweite im Weitsprung.
b) Sie hatte fünf einsen im Zeugnis und war Zweite im Weitsprung.
c) Sie hatte fünf Einsen im Zeugnis und war zweite im Weitsprung.
d) Sie hatte fünf Einsen im Zeugnis und war Zweite im Weitsprung.

3. a) Als die englische Königin abends in ihr Schloss kam, war das Licht schon aus.
b) Als die Englische Königin abends in ihr Schloss kam, war das Licht schon aus.
c) Als die Englische Königin Abends in ihr Schloss kam, war das Licht schon aus.
d) Als die englische Königin Abends in ihr Schloss kam, war das Licht schon aus.

Rechtschreibung

Welches Wort ist richtig geschrieben?

1. a) Dampflockomotive
b) Dampflockomotife
c) Dampflokomottife
d) Damflockomotive
e) Dampflokomotive

2. a) Renaissanse
b) Renaissance
c) Rennaissance
d) Rennaisance
e) Renaisance

TIPP

Stellen Sie sich die Wörter ausgesprochen vor und überlegen Sie, welches richtig klingt.

Bilden Sie den Plural folgender Wörter.

3. Visum
4. Globus
5. Pizza

5. Mathematisches Denken

Dreisatz

1. Ein Motorrad benötigt für eine 125 km lange Strecke 22,50 Liter Benzin. Welchen Verbrauch hat das Motorrad auf 100 km?

2. In einem Betrieb kommen 60 % der Männer und 50 % der Frauen mit dem Auto zur Arbeit. Wie viel Prozent kommen insgesamt mit dem Auto, wenn dort 60 % Männer arbeiten?

3. Vier Personen haben ein durchschnittliches Gewicht von 69 kg. Die erste Person wiegt 76 kg, die zweite 61 kg, die dritte 65 kg. Wie viel wiegt die vierte Person?

Maßeinheiten

1. Wie viele Stunden und Minuten sind 7200 Sekunden?

a) 120 Stunden
b) 2 Stunden
c) 5 Stunden
d) 1 Stunde 20 Minuten

2. Wie viele Hektar sind 55 000 Quadratmeter?

a) 5,5
b) 550
c) 55
d) 5550

3. Wie viele Kubikmeter sind 300 Liter?

a) 0,3
b) 30
c) 3
d) 300

Prozent- und Zinsrechnung

1. Die Mehrwertsteuer (19 %) beim Kauf eines Fahrrads beträgt 57 Euro. Wie teuer ist das Fahrrad inklusive Mehrwertsteuer?

a) 243 Euro
b) 357 Euro
c) 300 Euro
d) 414 Euro

2. Nach welcher Zeit sind 15 000 Euro auf 20 000 Euro angewachsen, bei einer jährlichen Verzinsung von 5 %?

a) 6 Jahre und 216 Tage
b) 6 Jahre und 260 Tage
c) 6 Jahre und 220 Tage
d) 6 Jahre und 8 Monate

Gleichungen

Ergänzen Sie die fehlenden Rechenzeichen bei den Gleichungen, um auf die vorgegebene Lösung zu kommen. Die Rechenregel „Punkt vor Strich" gilt hier.

1. 8 … 4 … 1 = 31
2. 2 … 60 … 12 = -3
3. 11 … 20 … 5 … 12 = 99

6. Räumliche Vorstellung

Drehungen im Raum

In welcher Position befindet sich der Buchstabe nach der Drehung, wie es die Pfeile der Reihe nach vorgeben? Die Drehungen sind jeweils 90 Grad um die Raumachsen.

a) ☐ 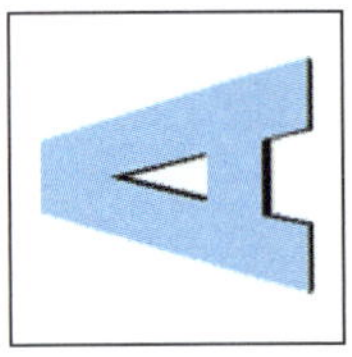

b) ☐ 

c) ☐ 

d) ☐ 

e) ☐ 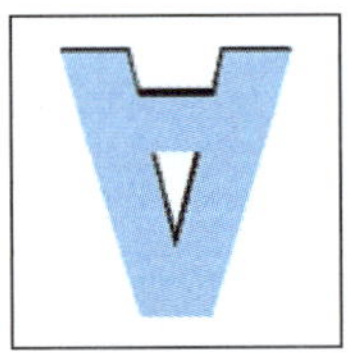

Flächen eines Körpers

Bestimmen Sie die Gesamtzahl an Flächen der vorgegebenen Körper.

1. 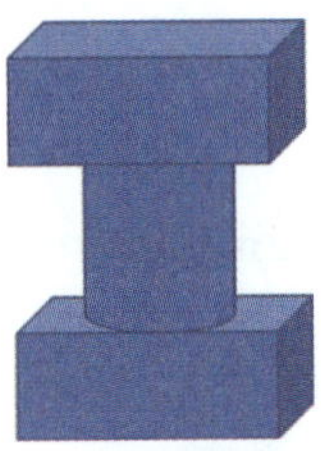

a) 15 b) 12 c) 14 d) 17

2. 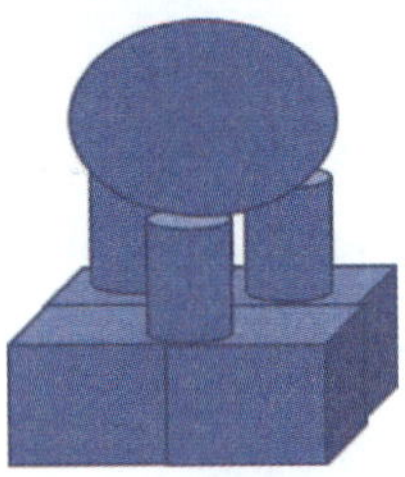

a) 32 b) 33 c) 34 d) 30

3. 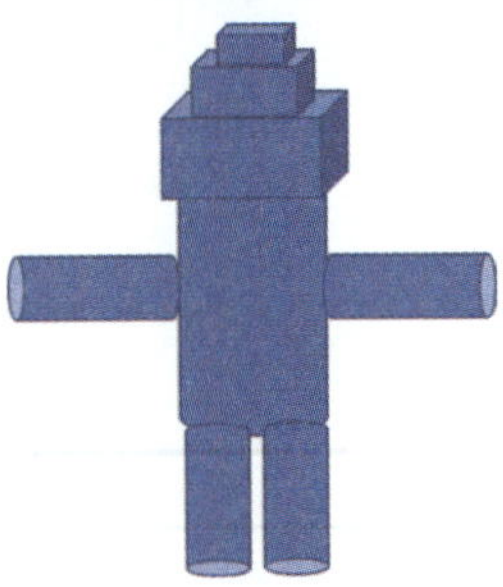

a) 31 b) 30 c) 29 d) 32

Spiegelbilder

Welche Figur passt nicht zu den anderen?

1. a) ☐  b) ☐  c) ☐ 

d) ☐  e) ☐  f) ☐ 

2. a) ☐  b) ☐  c) ☐ 

d) ☐  e) ☐  f) ☐ 

Würfelfaltung

1. Welcher Würfel lässt sich aus dieser Vorlage falten?

a) ☐  b) ☐  c) ☐  d) ☐ 

2. Aus welcher Faltvorlage lässt sich dieser Würfel falten?

a) ☐ 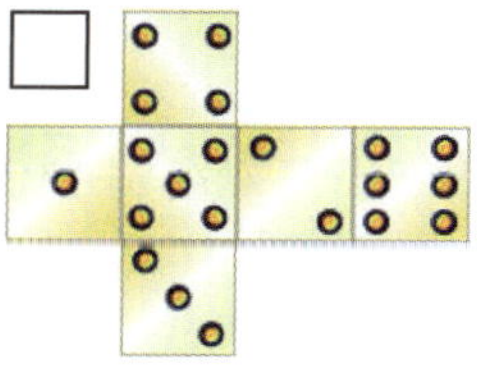 b) ☐ 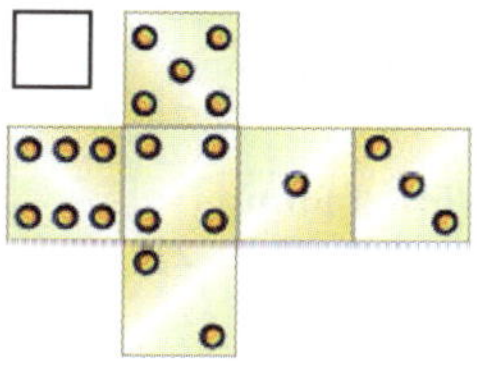 c) ☐ 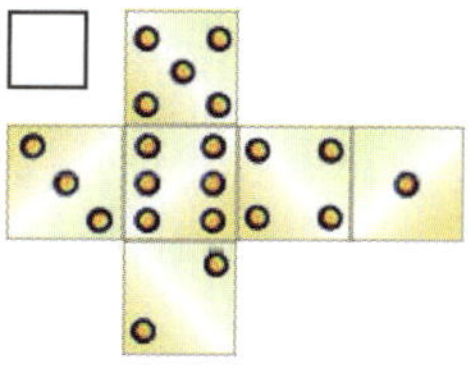 d) ☐ 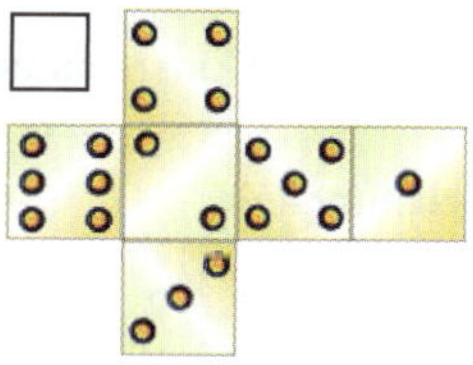

Lösungen Einstellungstests

1. Logisches Denken

Zahlenreihen

1. $2 \;^{+4}\; 6 \;^{+6}\; 12 \;^{+8}\; 20 \;^{+10}\; 30 \;^{+12}\; \mathbf{42}$
2. $16 \;^{+7}\; 23 \;^{+5}\; 28 \;^{+10}\; 38 \;^{+11}\; 49 \;^{+13}\; 62 \;^{+8}\; \mathbf{70}$
(Quersumme addieren)

Wortanalogien

1. c) Haus **2.** b) Fuß

Beziehungen

1. g) Sonntag **2.** a) Mutter

Grafikanalogien

1. a)  **2.** b) 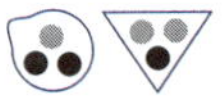

2. Konzentration

Alphabetische Reihenfolge

1. dhabanejdhenahjbekjabcdfgejndnansmjodnbdjwxyzjbdnrnmalmüppkdknshdkjklndhadnenduenduendopqrhzfunrucmchdtebnsmnaüskendhabezefghnmkelodhbezshynmnbabsebdnmeidjnantzbszxtgbsnxhzsstuvwb
2. hnsndnadhendnsjuvwxhdndnbdnmejdkalehijkdnmadnsomemaödefgnbdbanskjneksoxnaknbsjxonbshzebaisbelmanslmnopzehbaisjbajsnenakmslxpklmhjdamsidjendhijdnsmalsneisxnmamsrstudbansmensuaylxvn

Kopfrechnen

1. 27 **2.** 24

Mosaik

1. D **2.** C

Additions-/Subtraktionsaufgaben

1. 14 **2.** 5 **3.** 22
4. 5 **5.** 16 **6.** 17
7. 14 **8.** 5 **9.** 14

3. Allgemeinwissen

1. a) 5 bis 6 Liter
2. d) Base
3. b) Ampere
4. a) 4
5. d) Bit
6. b) Soziale Marktwirtschaft
7. d) 9
8. c) Landkreis und Gemeinde
9. b) Konrad Adenauer
10. b) Augustus
11. b) Faust I
12. b) Friedrich Schiller
13. d) Leonardo da Vinci
14. b) Tenor, Bariton, Bass
15. a) Skisprung und Skilanglauf

4. Sprachgefühl

Abkürzungen

1. c) FAZ = Frankfurter Allgemeine Zeitung
d) DIN = Deutsches Institut für Normung
2. a) IHK = Industrie- und Handelskammer
c) USA = United States of America
3. a) BASF = Badische Anilin- und Soda-Fabrik
c) BVerfG = Bundesverfassungsgericht
d) VW = Volkswagen

Wortbedeutungen

1. c) Schwäbisch **2.** d) Schwimmen **3.** c) Zahl

Fremdwörter

1. b) ungleichartig **2.** a) verhältnismäßig

Satzergänzungen

1. d) Psychologie **2.** d) aufmerksam **3.** b) kürzer

Sinnverwandte Sprichwörter

1. b) Wer im Glashaus sitzt, soll nicht mit Steinen werfen.
2. a) Die dümmsten Bauern haben die größten Kartoffeln.

Groß- und Kleinschreibung

1. c) Aber heute früh habe ich wieder einen Arzttermin.
2. d) Sie hatte fünf Einsen im Zeugnis und war Zweite im Weitsprung.
3. a) Als die englische Königin abends in ihr Schloss kam, war das Licht schon aus.

Rechtschreibung

1. e) Dampflokomotive **2.** b) Renaissance
3. Visa oder Visen **4.** Globen oder Globusse **5.** Pizzas oder Pizzen

5. Mathematisches Denken

Dreisatz

1. 18 Liter **2.** 56 Prozent **3.** 74 kg

Maßeinheiten

1. b) 2 Stunden **2.** a) 5,5 **3.** a) 0,3

Prozent- und Zinsrechnung

1. b) 357 Euro **2.** d) 6 Jahre und 8 Monate

Gleichungen

1. 8 x 4 – 1 = 31
2. 2 – 60 : 12 = -3
3. 11 + 20 x 5 – 12 = 99

6. Räumliche Vorstellung

Drehungen im Raum

1. c)

Flächen eines Körpers

1. a) 15 **2.** c) 34 **3.** b) 31

Spiegelbilder

1. a) **2.** c)

Würfelfaltung

1. a) **2.** b)

Assessment-Center (AC)

Ein weiterer gängiger Test für die Auswahl von Azubis ist das sogenannte Assessment-Center (AC). Der Begriff kommt aus dem Englischen („to assess“ = bewerten, beurteilen). Grundidee ist es, die Kandidaten und Kandidatinnen in vorgegebenen Situationen zu beobachten, welche den künftigen Aufgaben entsprechen. Hierbei zählt eher die persönliche Eignung als die fachliche Qualifikation.

Bestandteile eines Assessment-Centers sind in der Regel Rollenspiele, Planspiele, Gruppendiskussionen, Einzelvorträge, Fallstudien und psychologische Testverfahren. Üblich sind diese AC mittlerweile bei Großunternehmen wie Banken und Versicherungen, aber auch bei der Polizei oder im öffentlichen Dienst.

Tipps für ein AC-Auswahlverfahren

- ▶ freundlich und offen sein
- ▶ Blickkontakt mit den Gesprächspartnern halten
- ▶ Interesse zeigen und Fragen stellen
- ▶ seine eigene Meinung selbstbewusst vertreten
- ▶ die Meinung anderer respektieren
- ▶ sich aktiv an Diskussionen beteiligen
- ▶ ehrlich sein, kein falsches Wissen vorgeben
- ▶ kühlen Kopf und Ruhe bewahren

Onlinetipps

Es gibt im Internet viele Möglichkeiten, Eignungstests zu machen und so noch intensiver zu üben. Auch zum Thema Bewerbung kann man im Internet hilfreiche Tipps finden. Hier einige Links:

- ▶ www.planet-beruf.de
- ▶ www.azubiworld.com
- ▶ www.ausbildung.info
- ▶ www.ausbildungspark.com
- ▶ www.bewerbung.de
- ▶ www.bewerbungsdschungel.com
- ▶ www.berufswahl-tipps.de
- ▶ www.azubi-azubine.de
- ▶ www.jobinspektor.com
- ▶ www.azubot.de
- ▶ www.stuzubi.de
- ▶ www.azubiyo.de

Für die Inhalte der aufgeführten Websites übernehmen wir keine Haftung. Das gilt auch für alle auf diesen Websites angebrachten Links.

Anmerkungen:

Schematisierte Darstellung des Bildungswesens. Die Verteilung der Schülerzahlen in der Jahrgangsstufe 8 für das Jahr 2016 stellt sich im Bundesdurchschnitt wie folgt dar: Hauptschule 10,8 %, Realschule 18,9 %, Gymnasium 36,2 %, integrierte Gesamtschule 16,8 %, Schularten mit mehreren Bildungsgängen 12,2 %, sonderpädagogische Bildungseinrichtungen 4,2 %.

Die Durchlässigkeit zwischen den Schularten und die Anerkennung der Schulabschlüsse sind bei Erfüllung der zwischen den Ländern vereinbarten Voraussetzungen gewährleistet.

Die Dauer der Vollzeitschulpflicht (allgemeine Schulpflicht) beträgt neun Jahre, in fünf Ländern zehn Jahre, und die anschließende Teilzeitschulpflicht (Berufsschulpflicht) drei Jahre.

1 In einigen Ländern bestehen besondere Formen des Übergangs von der Kindertagesstätte oder der Kindertagespflege in die Grundschule (Vorklassen, Schulkindergärten). In Berlin und Brandenburg umfasst die Grundschule sechs Jahrgangsstufen.

2 Beschulung von Schülerinnen und Schülern mit sonderpädagogischem Förderbedarf in inklusivem Unterricht an allgemeinen Schulen oder an sonderpädagogischen Bildungseinrichtungen mit entsprechenden Förderschwerpunkten. Schulbezeichnung nach Landesrecht unterschiedlich. Sonderpädagogische Bildungseinrichtungen mit dem Förderschwerpunkt „Lernen“ und sonderpädagogische Bildungseinrichtungen mit dem Förderschwerpunkt „Geistige Entwicklung“ haben schulspezifische Abschlüsse.

3 Die Jahrgangsstufen 5 und 6 bilden eine Phase besonderer Förderung, Beobachtung und Orientierung über den weiteren Bildungsgang mit seinen fachlichen Schwerpunkten.

4 Haupt- und Realschulen existieren in nennenswerter Zahl nur noch in fünf Ländern (Baden-Württemberg, Bayern, Hessen, Niedersachsen, Nordrhein-Westfalen). In Bayern trägt die mit der Hauptschule vergleichbare Schulart die Bezeichnung Mittelschule. Die Bildungsgänge der Hauptschule und der Realschule werden auch an Schularten mit mehreren Bildungsgängen mit nach Ländern unterschiedlichen Bezeichnungen angeboten.

5 Die folgenden Schularten mit zwei Bildungsgängen fassen die Bildungsgänge der Haupt- und der Realschule pädagogisch und organisatorisch zusammen: Regelschule (Thüringen), Sekundarschule (Bremen, Sachsen-Anhalt), Verbundene Haupt- und Realschule (Hessen), Regionale Schule (Mecklenburg-Vorpommern), Realschule plus (Rheinland-Pfalz), Regionalschule (Schleswig-Holstein), Oberschule (Brandenburg, Sachsen), Mittelstufenschule (Hessen). Der Bildungsgang des Gymnasiums wird auch an Schularten mit drei Bildungsgängen angeboten. Die folgenden Schularten umfassen die drei Bildungsgänge der Hauptschule, der Realschule und des Gymnasiums: Integrierte Gesamtschule, Kooperative Gesamtschule, Integrierte Sekundarschule (Berlin), Oberschule (Bremen, Niedersachsen), Stadtteilschule (Hamburg), Gemeinschaftsschule (Baden-Württemberg, Saarland, Sachsen-Anhalt, Schleswig-Holstein, Thüringen), Sekundarschule (Nordrhein-Westfalen).

6 Die allgemeinbildenden Schulabschlüsse nach Jahrgangsstufe 9 und 10 tragen in einzelnen Ländern besondere Bezeichnungen. Der nachträgliche Erwerb dieser Abschlüsse an Schulen des zweiten Bildungsweges und beruflichen Schulen oder durch eine Externenprüfung ist möglich.

7 Zugangsvoraussetzung ist die formelle Berechtigung zum Besuch der gymnasialen Oberstufe, die nach Jahrgangsstufe 9 oder 10 erworben wird. Der Erwerb der Allgemeinen Hochschulreife erfolgt seit 2012 in der Mehrzahl der Länder nach Jahrgangsstufe 12 (achtjähriges Gymnasium). An Schularten mit drei Bildungsgängen wird der gymnasiale Bildungsgang in der Regel nicht auf acht Jahre verkürzt.

8 Die Berufsoberschule besteht bisher nur in einigen Ländern und bietet Absolventen mit Mittlerem Schulabschluss und abgeschlossener Berufsausbildung bzw. fünfjähriger Berufstätigkeit die Möglichkeit zum Erwerb der Fachgebundenen Hochschulreife. Bei Nachweis von Kenntnissen in einer zweiten Fremdsprache ist der Erwerb der Allgemeinen Hochschulreife möglich.

9 Die Fachoberschule ist eine zweijährige Schulart, die aufbauend auf dem Mittleren Schulabschluss mit Jahrgangsstufe 11 und 12 zur Fachhochschulreife führt. Für Absolventen mit Mittlerem Schulabschluss und einer beruflichen Erstausbildung ist in den meisten Ländern der unmittelbare Eintritt in Jahrgangsstufe 12 der Fachoberschule möglich. Die Länder können auch eine Jahrgangsstufe 13 einrichten. Der Besuch der Jahrgangsstufe 13 führt zur Fachgebundenen Hochschulreife und unter bestimmten Voraussetzungen zur Allgemeinen Hochschulreife.

10 Berufsfachschulen sind berufliche Vollzeitschulen verschiedener Ausprägung im Hinblick auf Zugangsvoraussetzungen, Dauer und Abschlüsse. In ein- oder zweijährigen Bildungsgängen wird eine berufliche Grundausbildung, in zwei- oder dreijährigen Bildungsgängen eine Berufsausbildung vermittelt. In Verbindung mit dem Abschluss eines mindestens zweijährigen Bildungsgangs kann unter bestimmten Voraussetzungen die Fachhochschulreife erworben werden.

11 Zusätzlich zum berufsqualifizierenden Abschluss ggf. Erwerb des Hauptschulabschlusses oder des Mittleren Schulabschlusses. Unter bestimmten Voraussetzungen ist zusätzlich der Erwerb der Fachhochschulreife möglich.

12 Fachschulen dienen der beruflichen Weiterbildung (Dauer 1–3 Jahre) und setzen grundsätzlich den Abschluss einer einschlägigen Berufsausbildung in einem anerkannten Ausbildungsberuf und eine entsprechende Berufstätigkeit voraus. Unter bestimmten Voraussetzungen ist zusätzlich der Erwerb der Fachhochschulreife möglich.

13 Einschließlich Hochschulen mit einzelnen universitären Studiengängen (z. B. Theologie, Philosophie, Medizin, Verwaltungswissenschaften, Sport).

14 An Pädagogischen Hochschulen (nur in Baden Württemberg) wird für verschiedene Lehrämter ausgebildet. Im Einzelfall ist auch ein Studium für Berufe im außerschulischen Bildungs- und Erziehungsbereich möglich.

15 Die Berufsakademie ist eine Einrichtung des tertiären Bereichs in einigen Ländern, die eine wissenschaftsbezogene und zugleich praxisorientierte berufliche Bildung durch die Ausbildung an einer Studienakademie und in einem Betrieb im Sinne des dualen Systems vermittelt.

16 Die Studienstrukturreform mit der Umstellung auf Bachelor- und Masterabschlüsse an deutschen Hochschulen ist weitgehend abgeschlossen. Nur eine geringe Zahl von Studiengängen führt zu einem Diplomabschluss.

Stand: Juni 2018

Grundstruktur des Bildungswesens in der Bundesrepublik Deutschland

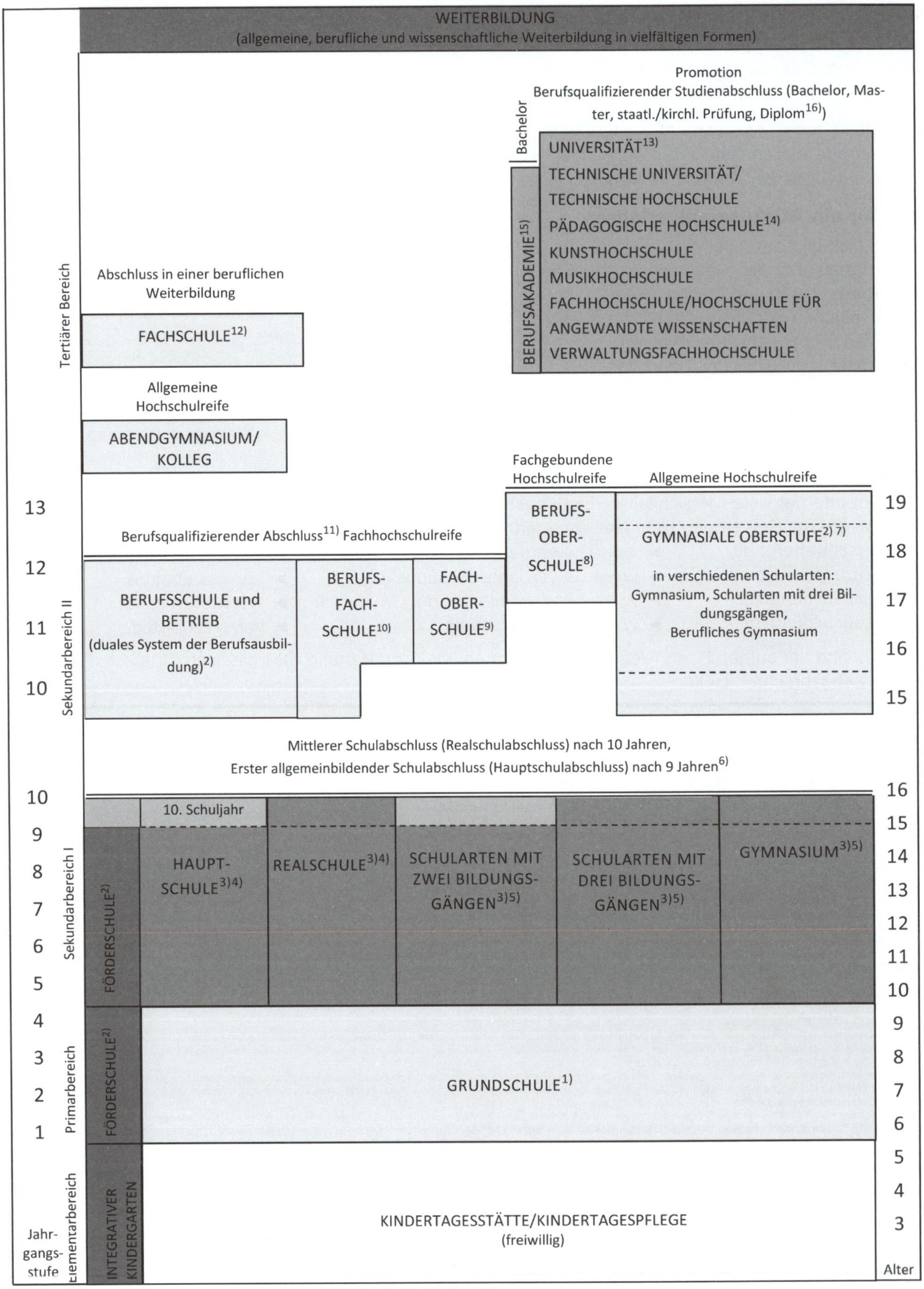

Herausgeber: Sekretariat der Ständigen Konferenz der Kultusminister der Länder in der Bundesrepublik Deutschland, Deutsche EURYDICE-Informationsstelle der Länder, Taubenstr. 10, 10117 Berlin, Tel. 030 25418-499. © KMK 2018

Inhaltsverzeichnis

Training

A. Listening Test ... 6

B. Written Test

Part I: Reading ... 7

Part II: Use of English ... 8

Part III: Guided Writing ... 10

Prüfungen

Prüfung 2018 ... 12

Prüfung 2019 ... 15

Prüfung 2020 ... 18

Prüfung 2021 ... 21

Prüfung 2022 ... 24

Die Lösungsvorschläge im Teil *Written Test Part III: Guided Writing* sind als Orientierungshilfen gedacht. Andere Lösungen werden dadurch keinesfalls ausgeschlossen.

A. Listening Test

Task 1

A – B 4 C – D – E – F 1 G 2 H 3

Task 2

1. D **2.** C **3.** B **4.** C

Task 3

Finally = Unfortunately
closed = open
midnight = noon
skin = dental
before = after

Task 4

Name	What they do
Betty	has contact with young adults between 18 and 25 years.
Catherine	*gives* advice to people about products.
Tom	advises people on their holidays.
Holly	cares for ill people, brings food, medicine.
Jack	▶ *collects information* ▶ writes articles
Bill	works with people between 10 and 16 by teaching them things.

Task 5

1. … (three day) school trip to Cape town.
2. … was imprisoned for 27 years.
3. … they did a (hop-on hop-off) bus tour around the city.
4. … the huge fish tanks.
5. … it looks like a table from the distance.
6. … cable car stopped suddenly.
7. … that she was afraid of heights.
8. … the view (from above) was breathtaking.

B. Written Test

Part I: Reading

Text 1

Task 1

	true	false	not in the text
1.		✓	
2.	✓		
3.			✓
4.	✓		
5.	✓		
6.			✓
7.		✓	
8.	✓		

Task 2

1. a) ☑ **2.** a) ☑ **3.** b) ☑ **4.** b) ☑

Task 3

1. Tausende junge Mädchen waren gekommen und die Polizei verlor die Kontrolle. Das Event musste abgesagt werden.
2. Die YouTuber machten Filme zu Gesundheitsfragen für das Portal der Kampagne.
3. Da ihre Fans ihnen vertrauen. Wenn sie in ihren Filmen von einem Produkt begeistert sind, wird das als Kaufempfehlung betrachtet.
4. Sie war zunächst nur bei einer einzigen Drogeriemarktkette erhältlich. Die Produkte waren zeitweise bereits am ersten Tag ausverkauft.

Text 2

1	2	3	4	5	6
D	A	B	C	D	B

Text 3

A	B	C	D	E	F
3	6	1	4	2	5

Text 4

Task 1

	true	false
1.	✓	
2.		✓
3.		✓
4.	✓	
5.	✓	
6.		✓
7.		✓
8.	✓	

Task 2

1. Sie entdeckten, dass bereits aus jedem teilnehmenden Land Landsleute in London lebten.
2. ▶ Erbaut wurde es 1741 als hugenottische Kirche.
   ▶ Die meiste Zeit des 19. Jahrhunderts war es eine baptistische Kapelle.
   ▶ 1893 wurde es eine Synagoge
   ▶ und im späten 20. Jahrhundert dann eine Moschee.
3. ▶ Das Schiff Empire Windrush landete mit 492 Passagieren.
   ▶ Diese wurden in ungenutzten Bombenschutzräumen unter Clapham Common untergebracht
   ▶ und an die Arbeitsvermittlung in Brixton verwiesen.
4. Die Iren bauten Hafenanlagen, die Kanalisation und das Schienennetz.

Text 5

Task 1

(1) have	**(2)** am	**(3)** have	**(4)** How	**(5)** you
(6) when	**(7)** much	**(8)** years	**(9)** looked	**(10)** experience

Task 2

(1) Thank	**(2)** are	**(3)** to	**(4)** pick	**(5)** need
(6) time	**(7)** have/need	**(8)** get/receive	**(9)** Before	**(10)** call/ring

Part II: Use of English

Task 1

A	B	C	D	E	F
2	4	1	6	5	3

Task 2

1. celebrity	**2.** huge	**3.** prominent
4. frequently	**5.** necessary	**6.** accepted

Task 3

a) works b) have been c) am reading d) snows e) am going to repair f) met

Task 4

renting – to expect – transportation – are advertised – generally – available – recommend – to uphold – move

Task 5

A	B	C	D	E	F
3	7	2	4	1	5

Task 6

1. annual **2.** initiated **3.** sometimes **4.** incorporates **5.** aim

Task 7

1. numerous **2.** behaving **3.** explanation **4.** entrance
5. angry **6.** necessary **7.** excitement

Task 8

a) better b) worst c) highest d) more expensive e) greater f) the most exciting

Task 9

a) who b) whose c) which d) who e) which f) which

Task 10

A	B	C	D	E	F
5	1	2	6	3	4

Task 11

a) made – come
b) are supposed to
c) had – done
d) am used to
e) let – know

Task 12

a) will learn b) had c) had told
d) doesn't learn e) knew f) would be cycling

Task 13

different – During – source – estate – tiny – flat – Shortly

Task 14

morning – cold – first – join – survive – toddler

Task 15

1. have an increase in **2.** lot of practice **3.** is too loud **4.** never even heard of him

Task 16

on/in – with – at – in – below – into – from – towards – between – for

Task 17

1. raining
2. decided
3. badly
4. obviously
5. saved

Task 18

1. are (very/quite) diverse
2. usually consists of
3. we will travel to
4. In order to enter

Part III: Guided Writing

Task 1

A letter

Dear Jason

Thanks very much for your last letter, which I received today. Since I've already wanted to tell you about my holidays, I sat down right away to write back to you.
My friend Tobias and I went to Ireland – we had saved a long time for this trip and it was really worth it.
One day we decided to rent two scooters to drive around the countryside. The first thing that really bothered us, was that we had to drive on the wrong side of the streets – it took us quite some time to get used to it. But once we were, it was super fun.
We drove along these narrow roads, with turns one after the other. Then suddenly, behind one bend, there was an enormous flock of sheep – we nearly weren't able to break in time. Then we had to wait till they were shepherded to the other side of the road until we could drive on. We found places which were so deserted that they looked like being from another century. It was really great and so much fun that we immediately decided we would definitely do that again next year.
Looking forward to hearing from you again soon.

Yours
Stefan

Task 2

Letter of application

Markus Bader
Steinweg 10
89360 Allendorf
Germany

London Office Inc.
Ms Clare McWilliams
24-144 Royal Avenue
London BT1 1EB
Great Britain

23rd August 2022

Dear Ms McWilliams

With reference to your advertisement in the London Telegraph of August 21st, I would like to apply for the position of a general office clerk.
I am 17 years old and have just finished school successfully. I am well-skilled in the use of standard office application software, such as MS Word, Excel and Powerpoint. My mother tongue is German, but I also have a very good command of English. I learnt English at school and last year I spent three months in Brighton, England, to do an internship at a consulting firm. During my internship I have gained general office experience and also improved my communication skills.
I am particularly interested in this job as I would like very much to gather further work experience abroad. I enclose my curriculum vitae. Please do not hesitate to contact me if you should require further information.

Yours sincerely
Markus Bader

Task 3

Entry to a survey

According to the chart there are two major ways for young people to get the money they need for things like eating out with friends, buying fancy clothes or a new gadget. In both instances they ultimately get their money from their parents: either as regular pocket money or they do chores around the house and get paid for it. Followed by that is babysitting, paper rounds, dog walking and other non-specified jobs.
I think the advantage of part-time jobs is that most of these jobs aren't regular ones, so young people are rather independent and can organize their work around school.
Typical part-time jobs for my friends are paper rounds, working at fast-food restaurants, mowing the lawn of neighbours or walking their dogs.
In addition to my pocket money I earn some more at the café right across my street. They had a sign out one day, which said they were looking for part-time jobbers who have good people skills. I introduced myself to the owner, we sat down and talked and afterwards she said she would give it a try with me. That was two years ago and I have worked there since. It is great fun and I meet a lot of nice elderly people who give good tips. This way I don't have to ask my parents for further money and can buy myself all the things I like to have.

Task 4

A story about our last school outing

... "No I haven't seen him."
"Nor have I," I answered.
Nervously we looked around and remembered our teacher's rule: never wander off alone. What should we do? We called for him, we looked in the shops – we searched everywhere, but he was nowhere to be found. Where could he have gone? Had he been kidnapped?
Oh God, we started thinking in worst-case scenarios and really panicked, after another half an hour had gone by and he was still missing. Deciding that it was no good to search any longer on our own, we walked back preparing ourselves to tell our teacher what had happened.
But when we came up to our tents a freshly showered Peter walked towards us, a big grin on his face, "Where have you been so long? I thought you got lost. When I couldn't find you anymore I turned around and came back here. After all, our teacher did tell us not to wander off alone, didn't he?" Although we were glad that nothing had happened to him we were also really angry with him for scaring us so much – so we walked past him without a word. He had a lot of apologising to do until we were friends again.

Task 5

Your letter to the hostel for more information

Stefanie Groß
Messerstraße 5
87463 Markdorf
Germany

Backpackers' Paradise Hostel
Mr Ian McGowen
107 High St
Edinburgh EH1 1S6
Scotland

Dear Mr McGowen

I have read your advert in Youth Magazine and am very interested in the job you offer. Nevertheless there are some things I would like to know in advance.
What would the working hours per day be? Do we have some free-time or are we supposed to work all day? As I am partial to computers I would love to work in the office, I have good people skills, too, so I could even answer the phone. If that isn't possible what would my other options be? And what can I expect in terms of payment?
Another thing that I'd like to know is whether you provide vegetarian food, as I have been a vegetarian since grade school. Do we as staff have to share bedrooms – and if so with how many?
One more minor detail: you say applicants have to be 16 or older – I'll be 16 on 15th July, would it be possible for me to start at the beginning of July or would I actually have to wait until the 15th?
I am looking forward to hearing from you.

Best regards
Stefanie Groß

Task 6

E-Mail to a friend

From: numaz@yahoo.net
To: musti@mail.de
Betreff: Hollywood

Hi, Musti,

Yesterday my guest family drove to Hollywood with me – it's not too far from here, so we only had to drive for about two hours. I could hardly wait to get there.
The first thing we did, was walk down Sunset Boulevard, where I saw a lot of movie stars we normally only see in the magazines in Germany.
But to tell you the truth: sometimes I was a bit concerned, because whenever there was a star in sight there were quite a lot of people who wanted to get an autograph or a picture.
I could understand their excitement of meeting their favourite star – I was excited, too – and maybe get the chance to talk to them. But I felt sorry, too, for the stars. It must be really horrible if people recognize you wherever you go and will not even let you eat in peace. Of course they earn a lot of money, but they are also regarded as public property and they can never be just themselves, except at home.
And don't get me started on the paparazzi – those are really crazy. They would do just about anything to get a good picture.
We saw a lot more that day, but I'm running short of time and will tell you some more in my next e-mail.

Take care,
Numaz

Prüfung 2018

Listening Test

Task 1

A – B 1 C – D 4 E 3 F 5 G – H 2

Task 2

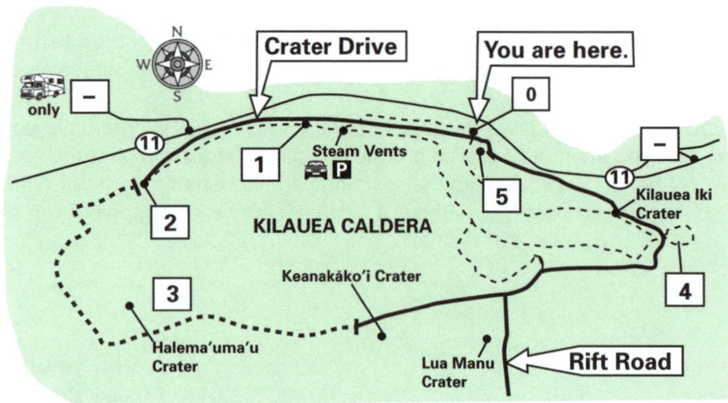

Task 3

<u>sights</u> = rights
<u>hauled</u> = called
<u>choice</u> = voice
<u>vision</u> = mission
<u>shown</u> = flown

Task 4

1. rock-like structures
2. almost half (of them)
3. ▶ rising sea level / melting polar ice / water rises faster than corals grow
   ▶ warming of the sea/water
   ▶ algae / tiny plants start producing poison / turn toxic
4. they don't get enough oxygen
5. ▶ like a vacuum cleaner
   ▶ it collects the sea plants
6. ARECCAWI

Task 5

1. … fire is over.
2. … was forbidden at school(s).
3. … (traditional) language is part of (her) everyday life.
4. … less than 1,000 speakers.
5. … (the) language of a larger group of people / (the surrounding) larger language(s).
6. … get their catch/fish to the shore.
7. … understand the (words/phrases of the) song.
8. … "See you later!"

Written Test

Part I: Reading

Task 1

No.	T	F	N
1	✓		
2		✓	
3			✓
4			✓
5	✓		
6		✓	
7	✓		
8	✓		

Task 2

A	B	C	D	E	F
3	7	1	6	2	5

Task 3

1	2	3	4	5	6
D	B	C	A	D	B

Task 4

1. ▶ weil er zum Duke of Buckingham ernannt worden war / wegen seines neuen Titels
2. ▶ King George III kaufte das Haus.
▶ Das Haus wurde stark erweitert.
▶ Victoria erklärte es zu ihrem offiziellen Aufenthaltsort / zu ihrer offiziellen Residenz.
3. ▶ Glocken in den Räumen der Angestellten nicht hörbar
▶ Lüften der Badezimmer fast unmöglich
4. ▶ keine zufriedenstellende/ausreichende Heizung in den Kinderzimmern
▶ nicht genug geeigneter Platz für Übernachtungsgäste
5. ▶ wenn die königliche Familie im Sommer abwesend ist
▶ bei königlichen Empfängen
6. ▶ dass die Queen nicht in ihrer Residenz / zu Hause / anwesend ist

Part II: Use of English

Task 1

1. watchful
2. (to) restore
3. rarely
4. (to) recover
5. incredible

Task 2

A	B	C	D	E	F
0	6	4	5	1	3

Task 3

1. connected
2. include/included
3. popularity
4. strongly
5. (had) received

Task 4

1. Unless they came from / Unless coming from
2. were able to invest
3. Instead of (wearing) light dresses
4. succeed in curing patients
5. how they celebrated Christmas / how Christmas was celebrated

Task 5

1. whose / her
2. expected / were expected
3. by
4. hard
5. doing
6. enormously
7. having
8. had not been / hadn't been
9. than
10. have influenced / have been influencing

Part III: Guided Writing

Task A – E-Mail

Dear Sir or Madam,

Yesterday I saw your advertisement and I'd like to apply for the job as a café assistant in your Museum Garden Café.
Before reading your ad I had thought about working during my summer holidays. So, this job is a good opportunity for me to earn some money. As I have always liked the friendly atmosphere of a museum and a café, I would be happy to work there. Being a very sociable person, I enjoy talking to people and serving guests.
That's why I worked as a waitress in a local restaurant last year. While I was doing this job, I gained basic knowledge of hygiene and food safety regulations. One of my tasks was to serve up dinner. Some years ago, I occasionally assisted the cook at our school canteen, where I helped to prepare the meals and to do the washing-up.
If you don't mind, I have some questions about the job. First, could you tell me how many hours per week I would have to work? I'd also like to know the duration of this job. Last but not least, are there any special clothes required? Some cafés are much stricter than others. Therefore, I would be very glad if you informed me about that.
Regarding your youth garden party, I would recommend to start a web campaign to attract more young people. I am aware that history is not very popular with the younger generation but maybe it would be fun for the guests to dress up in clothes of the Victorian era. And if some specialties of the 19th century were served, it would give the guests a good impression of what life was like at that time.
Please let me know if you like my ideas and if you consider me for the job. I'm looking forward to hearing from you soon.

Yours faithfully,
Mary Smith

Task B – Personal text

Dear Sir or Madam,

Recently, I heard of your online project and I'd like to participate in it.
The first thing to say about my social life at present is that I have many friends who I meet at school. In my spare time I am very influenced by social media. Although I often check my smartphone for messages from friends, I spend much time with my family talking to them and doing things together. Last but not least, I would like to mention our local soccer club, where I play soccer twice a week.
An important event in my personal past was my first day at school. There I met some boys who are my best friends now. In the afternoon my relatives came and we had a big garden party. I felt very important. Looking back, I must say that this day changed my life because I started becoming an independent person.
Since that time, I have had many wishes for the future, for example, I wish to travel to many countries with my friends. After that, when I have grown a bit older, I would like to have a good job and to settle down to family life. But my greatest hope is that my people stay healthy.
Writing a blog or keeping a diary is important. You can express your feelings and take down what you have experienced. This might be helpful in many situations. Later you can read everything and look back to all the events in your life. If you want to keep your personal details private, you should decide to keep a diary, but if you prefer other people to take part in your life, you'd better write a blog. Then readers can learn from your experiences or they can respond, especially if you seek advice.
I hope you like my text and publish it in your project.

Yours faithfully,
Tom Miller

Listening Test

Task 1

A –   B 4   C 1   D –   E 3   F –   G 5   H 2

Task 2

1 B   2 C   3 D   4 D

Task 3

flowing = floating
account = amount
215 = 250
winds = finds
slick = thick
rough = tough

Task 4

1. ▶ may wipe out a (complete) species
   ▶ other species are affected as well / can cause marine animals to starve
2. ▶ for their fins are cut off
   ▶ for shark-fin soup / for an exclusive delicacy
3. ▶ not enough oxygen
   ▶ global warming
4. *source:* (coal-fired) power plants
   health dangers: ▶ ends up on our dinner table / works its way up the food chain
   ▶ toxic effects on (the) nervous system
   ▶ (internal) organs/lungs/kidneys may be damaged

Task 5

	Brosnan	Wiener	Earle
Ideas to save our seas:	don't buy products with microplastics	▶ attend clean-up events ▶ pick up trash every time you go	▶ eat sustainable fish ▶ use apps to find markets for sustainable fish
Projects and initiatives:	▶ (face) more threats (than ever before) ▶ need protection	▶ realized (serious) damage to the eco-system ▶ alarming stories from local fishermen / about how much harder it was to find fish	protect 30 per cent by 2030
Further reading:	'A message of the Oceans'		(world's) oceans are an integrated system

Written Test

Part I: Reading

Task 1

A	B	C	D	E	F
5	6	**0**	4	7	2

Task 2

No.	T	F	N
1		✓	
2			✓
3		✓	
4	✓		
5			✓
6	✓		
7			✓
8		✓	
9			✓
10		✓	

Task 3

1	2	3	4	5	6	7
E	C	A	G	**B**	F	D

Task 4

1. Besuch der Häftlinge durch Familien und Anwälte
2. ▶ das Atmen war schwierig
   ▶ eine Art Schneeblindheit
3. oft grausam, manchmal überraschenderweise freundlich
4. ▶ man musste sich gut benehmen, um eine Zeitung lesen zu dürfen
   ▶ die Zeitung wurde (vorher) zensiert
   ▶ politische Beiträge wurden herausgeschnitten / man erhielt eine Zeitung mit Löchern
5. Körper berührte beim Hinlegen gegenüberliegende Wände
6. ▶ war spärlich eingerichtet
   ▶ Glühbirne/Licht brannte Tag und Nacht

Part II: Use of English

Task 1

1. (to) possess / possessed
2. (to) assume / assumed
3. (to) govern / governed
4. (to) reflect
5. (to) ascend / ascending

Task 2

A	B	C	D	E	F
6	3	**0**	5	2	1

Task 3

1. social
2. equality
3. responsibility
4. contribute
5. improvement(s)

Task 4

1. Instead of letting
2. If Mandela had not become/been
3. July 18 was formally declared
4. in order to transform
5. It is not important how

Task 5

1. have fought / have been fighting
2. are protected
3. ourselves
4. as
5. to be
6. better
7. ruled
8. in
9. respectfully
10. would / might (have to) pay

Part III: Guided Writing

Task A – E-Mail

I suppose you have already heard about the Giant Pacific Garbage Patch, which consists of approximately 80,000 tons of plastics. It covers an area of about 1.6 million square kilometres. As it is still growing, the situation will become even worse for the marine creatures and seabirds.
We can't watch this tragedy any longer and so I made up my mind to do something against it. First of all, I'll try to avoid buying products wrapped in plastics. Besides that, I decided to use glass bottles instead of plastic ones. But most important is to inform the public and therefore I want to print flyers, which I'll hand out to people in town.
However, I am a single person and I need the help of other people to bring about a change in our lifestyle. Maybe you can help me and blog some information on Instagram. It would be really marvellous if our teacher promoted us too. He could organize a campaign with us at school. And last but not least, I want to ask all my friends to support my project.
Hopefully, lots of people can be convinced by these actions so that in the future much more will be done to save our planet. Demonstrations might also attract the attention of politicians. Maybe then they will pass more laws against pollution.
Finally, I'd like to invite people from other countries to take part in our movement because it's a global problem which we have to face together.
Please tell me what you think about my ideas.

See you soon,
Julian

Task B – A Letter of Application

Dear Sir or Madam,

After reading about your exchange programme for students from Germany and South Africa I'd like to apply for it.
As I am fond of travelling, this would be a good chance to see a new continent which I haven't visited before. Besides that, I'm very interested in learning about the language and culture of this country. Another reason for applying is that I would like to meet and make friends with people who live in a completely different part of our world.
Surely my good knowledge of English and French will be useful for the communication with our exchange partners and their families. Last year, I stayed in our twin town in France for two weeks. There I could gather valuable experience in the field of a student exchange. It was rather easy to find new friends because I am a very communicative and friendly person. I'm helpful and reliable as well. That's why I was a great help for my host family with their little son.
But there are still some details I'd like to know about the stay. First of all, can you tell me which town or area I will go to and are the exchange students expected to stay with a family or in a hostel? Furthermore, it is important for me to get some information about the costs and necessary previous vaccinations.
When my exchange partner visits me, I will go to Munich with him. It is one of the biggest cities in Germany and there is a museum called Deutsches Museum. This is an attraction for tourists who are interested in science and technology. However, Munich has many more sights to offer. Maybe we are lucky to be there at the time of the Oktoberfest, where you come to know traditional Bavarian outfits, typical food and brass music.
I hope you take me into consideration and I'm looking forward to your answer.

Yours faithfully,
Martin Wagner

Prüfung 2020

Listening Test

Task 1

A 5 B – C – D 1 E 3 F 4 G – H 2

Task 2

1 A 2 B 3 C 4 B

Task 3

simple = sample
quips = strips
lots = loads
lazy = crazy
sectors = factors

Task 4

1. ▶ qualifies to study at university level
   ▶ (permission to enter a) permanent job (at an early stage)
   ▶ salary all along the way
2. everywhere in the UK/Leeds or nearby
3. 18 months
4. covering letter
5. ▶ (all files in) one document / PDF
   ▶ (size) no bigger than 3 MB
6. Nilay Khatun

Task 5

1. … what they know about this job. / … if they´re familiar with the business (itself)/with the main products (of the company).
2. …life experience.
3. … clearly and exactly.
4. … ask for help. / … explain your problem.
5. ▶ … know when to listen and when to lead.
   ▶ … work together effectively. / … work together even if they don´t like each other.
6. … (simply) being on time. /… delivering things before (the) deadline.
7. … the task / it is completely new.

Written Test

Part I: Reading

Task 1

No.	T	F	N
1	✓		
2		✓	
3	✓		
4	✓		
5		✓	
6			✓
7	✓		
8		✓	
9		✓	
10			✓

Task 2

A	B	C	D	E
4	7	1	5	3

Task 3

1	2	3	4	5	6
C	D	B	B	D	A

Task 4

1. zur Verbesserung der Lebens- und Reisebedingungen in London
2. a) TfL war bisher hauptsächlich auf manuelle Verkehrszählungen angewiesen.
   b) Sie werden nur an begrenzten Orten durchgeführt.
   Sie können nur einen Überblick über die Straßennutzung an einem bestimmten Tag zu einer bestimmten Zeit geben.
3. a) Es hat sich gezeigt, dass sie bis zu 98 % genau sind.
   b) Daten können rund um die Uhr erfasst werden und so ein deutlich detaillierteres Bild der Straßennutzung liefern.
   c) Die Videos werden innerhalb von Sekunden ausgewertet und verworfen, sodass keine persönlichen Daten gespeichert werden.
4. Sie sind ein wesentlicher Bestandteil der Planung neuer Radwege in London / um herauszufinden, wo Investitionen in neue Infrastrukturen am besten zum Ziel führen.
5. Er möchte die giftige Luft, den schlechten Gesundheitszustand und den Klimanotstand in London bekämpfen. / Bis 2041 sollen 80 Prozent der Fahrten in London zu Fuß, mit dem Fahrrad oder mit öffentlichen Verkehrsmitteln gemacht werden.

Part II: Use of English

Task 1

1. purpose(s)
2. inconvenience
3. embarrassed
4. obvious
5. (to) expand

Task 2

A	B	C	D	E	F
6	2	4	3	7	**0**

Task 3

1. essential
2. examine
3. exhausted
4. identify
5. valuable/valued

Task 4

1. In order to get images or videos which look deceptively real, you **can alter people's faces** with the aid of Artificial Intelligence (AI).
2. Deepfakes **are said** to often have serious consequences for the individuals abused in them.
3. You **might not have heard** about how deepfakes are technically created.
4. An alternative Christmas speech of the Queen **was published by** a British television network in 2020.
5. **Unless the technology** to detect deepfakes is not improved, deepfakes might cause serious harm to individuals or even societies.

Task 5

1. hadn't/had not met
2. to finance
3. was produced/had been produced
4. is regarded
5. immensely
6. most progressive
7. employing
8. has affected/has been affecting
9. significant
10. remembering

Part III: Guided Writing

Task A – Review about the TV XY 5000

As I moved into a new flat, I decided to buy a new TV set. My old one was outdated and I couldn't go online with it. Furthermore, the image was frequently blurred. So, it was the right time for a change.
Unfortunately, there was some trouble which I hadn't expected. It all started immediately after the TV had arrived. When I wanted to test it, I noticed that the attached cable was only 20 centimetres long which made it impossible to plug it in. The second problem occurred while watching a programme because the maximal volume of the loudspeakers was very low. Then I needed a special code to connect the TV to the Internet but I couldn't find it.
Of course, I looked for it everywhere but without success. That's why I asked my dad for help. He suggested to contact the hotline. The lady on the phone explained to me that it was on a sticker at the bottom left corner of the screen. The problem of the short cable could be solved by using a simple extension cord whereas the sound system didn't satisfy me at all. Turning it up and down again didn't make a change.
All in all, I have to say the product isn't worth the money. For this reason, I returned the TV set. If you are looking for a perfect TV, I would recommend you to go to a local shop where you can inspect the device before buying it. I'd also advise you to test the TV in the shop, because then you can find a fault at once. You should keep the certificate of warranty even if you are perfectly pleased with your purchase since there might be something wrong at a later time.
I hope this review is helpful and you can make a better choice.

Task B – E-mail to invite participants

Hello young inventors,

Starting a network of young inventors, I want to invite you to take part in this project.
In my opinion it is a great idea to have such a network because everybody who is interested in inventing new things can join us. It is a platform where young people can easily exchange opinions or discuss topics. In addition, we can learn from each other or ask others for advice.
Now I give you some organisational details for the first meeting. My suggestion is to meet on 1st August at 7 p.m. Every participant should have a laptop or a tablet and an internet access so that we can easily communicate online. It would be even better if all of us had a webcam so that we are able to make a video conference.
In August we'll discuss some basic topics. On the one hand, it is important to find out how often and at which time we want to meet regularly. On the other hand, we have to find out the likes of the members and consequently what will be most interesting for all of us. Last but not least we simply come to know one another.
In order to promote our project, we could design our own website. Besides that, each of us can invite friends to join us. Furthermore, posters that we put up in our town or flyers are also good possibilities to inform more young people and to attract their attention.
If you want to know more, please send me an e-mail. Then you get further information about my plan and the first meeting.
I'm looking forward to your answer.

Yours,
Jacky

Listening Test

Task 1

A –   B 3   C 4   D 5   E –   F 1   G –   H 2

Task 2

1 D   2 D   3 C   4 B

Task 3

tough → rough
wild → mild
Monday → Sunday
drifts → shifts
rest → west
better → wetter

Task 4

1. (because) the (main) cell tower was damaged
2. seven millimeters / 7 mm of rain per hour
3. Kingfisher Bay
4. ▸ waterproof tent
   ▸ bright torch
   ▸ strong rope
5. Yidney Drive

Task 5

1. … heavier rainfall.
   … greater danger of flooding.
2. … (only) two feet of water.
3. … chemical substances / substances which mix and react with the water
   … uncleaned wastewater.
4. … a (portable) radio (set)
   … supplies for three days / to survive.
5. … collect/store water.
   … (take several steps to) protect (our) forests.
6. … a water-recycling program.

Written Test

Part I: Reading

Task 1

No.	T	F	N
1		✓	
2			✓
3	✓		
4	✓		
5		✓	
6		✓	
7	✓		
8	✓		
9			✓
10		✓	

Task 2

A	B	C	D	E
3	5	7	2	1

Task 3

1	2	3	4	5	6	7
A	C	B	C	A	D	B

Task 4

1. bestehende Diktaturen durch demokratische Regierungen (zu) ersetzen, (die ihrem Volk dienen)
2. ▶ die Regierung versuchte ständig, sie mit einschüchternden Anrufen zu entmutigen
   ▶ verurteilte sie mehrfach zu Gefängnisstrafen
3. ▶ schult Reporter/-innen in Mediennutzung
   ▶ veröffentlicht jährliche Berichte zur Pressefreiheit im Jemen
4. die (legale) Errichtung eines unabhängigen Radiosenders für Journalistinnen
5. ▶ gewalttätige Herrscher vor Gericht (zu) bringen
   ▶ eine moderne Demokratie (mit allen notwendigen Institutionen) (zu) errichten

Part II: Use of English

Task 1

1. (to) admit / admitted
2. (to) impress / impressed
3. (to) pause / paused
4. (to) guess
5. (to) inspire / inspired

Task 2

A	B	C	D	E	F
6	7	3	5	**0**	2

Task 3

1. health
2. scientific
3. powerful
4. life
5. improve

Task 4

1. **If we want to understand** Tharpe's success, we must look at the musical styles in her songs.
2. She sang **gospel songs as well as** big band swing jazz.
3. **Rosetta Tharpe used to play** only in the US, before she toured Europe in 1964 as part of the Blues & Gospel Caravan.
4. Legends such as Johnny Cash and Little Richard **were inspired by Tharpe**.
5. Scorsese's documentary "The Blues" **is definitely worth watching** for Rosetta Tharpe fans.

Task 5

1. do not / don't need
2. were
3. in
4. setting
5. truly
6. was founded
7. are designing
8. of
9. be downloaded
10. collaborating

Part III: Guided Writing

Task A – Letter to the headmaster

Dear Mr Smith,

Again and again I have realized that many fellow students are not really interested in politics. Therefore I came up with the idea to start a democracy club at our school to prove that politics is anything but boring.
In my opinion young people should be politically active, because often their interests are not adequately represented by politicians. And politics always has to do with our future. For this reason all of us should participate in current discussions. However, the most important aspect is to inform every student about how governments work and to make everybody aware how each of them plays a decisive part in a democracy.
I'd like to suggest several projects that might be interesting. Maybe we can make a political day and representatives of different parties could come to our school and discuss with us. Secondly, we could go to the town hall and meet the mayor and other members of the city council. Nevertheless, the best thing would be to visit our parliament and attend a conference there.
The club should be organized by some reliable students and a teacher, who supports them. As most pupils leave school at 1 p.m., it is surely possible to find a suitable room for our meetings where we could meet two hours a week in the afternoon. For a start I intend to ask some of my classmates if they like to join the club. Then we can work together and make flyers, which we hand out in the breaks. Another possibility would be to make an announcement over the school PA system[1].
I have already talked to some of our teachers and they say it's a good idea. So, I hope you also agree.

Sincerely,
Peter White

[1]PA system – Lautsprecheranlage

Task B – E-mail to the radio channel

Dear Sir or Madam,

While listening to your radio channel I heard that you intend to award a prize to an extraordinary woman. As I greatly admire Michelle Obama, I would like to suggest her.
When Barack Obama became president of the US in 2009 she became the first African-American First Lady. She herself grew up in humble circumstances and worked very hard to go to top universities and become a successful lawyer. But then she gave up her job and supported her husband and his work.
Once I saw a TV programme about the Obamas, which made me realize that the president's wife is a very remarkable person. Soon afterwards I started looking for more information on the Internet. There I came across some articles about her as a politically very active person who stood up for the rights of socially deprived people and for example started campaigns encouraging African-American girls to get a good education.
Therefore, she deserves being considered and it would be great if she won the award of your radio channel. Besides that a monetary prize could surely find a use in one of her projects. Last but not least her commitment should be appreciated as well in an excellent portrait to make her better known.
This is important because the world needs role models. Many people want to have someone to look up to. You can get inspired to do the same or similar things and especially young people, who are looking for life goals, need the motivation of a trustworthy person.
I'd really hope that Michelle Obama is chosen and look forward to hearing about her in the radio programme.

Yours faithfully
Jenny Miller

Prüfung 2022

Listening Test

Task 1

A 3 B 4 C 2 D – E – F 5 G – H 1

Task 2

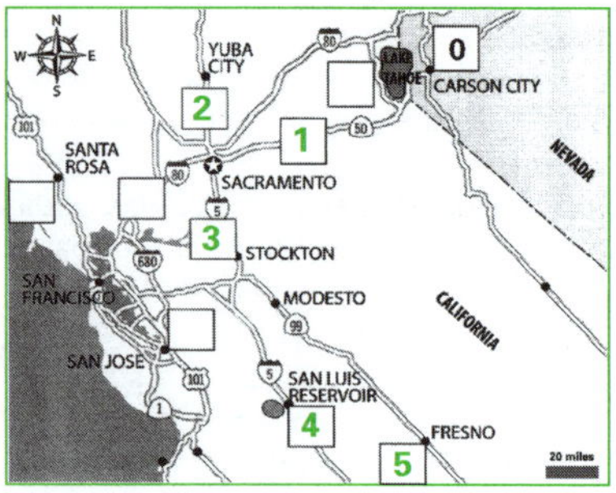

Task 3

rocked → shocked
bred → fed
stunning → running
test → best
extensive → expensive

Task 4

1. ▶ help find a perfect bike, the best bike (for you)
   ▶ solve technical problems
   ▶ experts for technical problems
   ▶ specialists for choosing the suitable bike
2. ▶ ride over bumpy ground
   ▶ enjoy the (great) outdoors
3. ▶ flat tire / tire lacks air
   ▶ brakes don't work (properly)
   ▶ (electronic) lock low on battery
4. 22VH – 9ZUH – S511

Task 5

1. ... there is little parking space
   ... bikes reduce our/the/their carbon footprint
2. ... deliver heavy loads/bulky loads/milk cans
   ... deliver heavy things
3. ... transporting children
   ... the grocery tour
   ... transporting camping equipment
4. … could hardly push the bike uphill
   ... didn't want (to replace her bike with/to get) an e-bike/electric bike
   … could hardly go up the hill
5. ... start from a standstill
   ... cover more miles / cover miles with less effort
   ... be/they are eco-friendly
   ... to reduce the carbon footprint
6. ... capacity of the battery/batteries is (quite) good
   ... fully loaded bike runs up to thirty-five/35 miles

Written Test

Part I: Reading

Task 1

No.	T	F	N
1		✓	
2		✓	
3			✓
4	✓		
5	✓		
6	✓		
7			✓
8	✓		
9		✓	

Task 2

A	B	C	D	E
6	4	1	3	5

Task 3

1	2	3	4	5	6	7	8	9
C	B	A	D	C	D	B	C	A

Task 4

1. ▶ weil sie langsamer/weniger schnell wachsen
   ▶ Sie wachsen langsamer, und deshalb ist die Wahrscheinlichkeit beschädigt zu werden geringer.
2. ▶ Baum/Bäume ohne Schädlinge / unerwünschte Insekten oder Krankheiten
   ▶ dass die Bäume keine ungewollten Schädlinge oder Krankheiten mitbringen
3. ▶ Wer zuerst kommt, mahlt zuerst/wird zuerst bedient.
   ▶ Diejenigen, die zuerst kommen, werden zuerst bedient / bekommen zuerst etwas.
4. ▶ es reduziert den/weniger Wettbewerb um Mineralstoffe/Nährstoffe und Wasser
   ▶ Der Kampf/Wettstreit um das Wasser und die Mineralien/Nährstoffe wird dadurch verkleinert.
5. ▶ zweimal (so groß wie) der Wurzelballen
   ▶ Das Pflanzloch soll doppelt so groß sein wie der Wurzelballen.
6. ▶ Versehentliches Abmähen / Abschneiden wird vermieden.
   ▶ Tiere werden vom Fressen der Zweige abgehalten, Verbiss wird verhindert.
   ▶ um zu verhindern, dass der Baum/das Bäumchen aus Versehen abgemäht wird
   ▶ um zu verhindern, dass die Zweige/Äste/Triebe von Tieren gefressen werden

Part II: Use of English

Task 1

1. (to) appear
2. (to) regard
3. (to) focus/focuses
4. (to) switch/switches
5. impact

Task 2

A	B	C	D	E	F
6	7	**0**	5	2	4

Task 3

1. essential
2. famous
3. challenging
4. reflection
5. freedom

Task 4

1. We know that European paper before the 18th century was handmade, **although its/the exact composition** is still a mystery.
2. Studies suggest that in early times, paper **was made by craftsmen** from hemp or linen, in particular old rags.
3. The methods of making handmade paper today **are the same as those / are still the same as** used in the middle ages.
4. The production of paper by hand **includes mixing / the mixing of** soaked recycled paper or cooked plant fibre in a kitchen blender.
5. Online you can find **both tutorials and images** of handmade paper.

Task 5

1. secretly / can secretly
2. whose
3. than
4. found
5. has been called
6. known
7. healthier
8. were not / weren't
9. are
10. spreading

Part III: Guided Writing

Task A – Letter of application

Dear Sir or Madam,

After reading about your summer youth program, I decided to apply for it.
At the beginning I'll tell you why I came to this decision. Since I am very interested in nature and like to be outside, I think it is a good idea to work in a national park. Besides that it is an opportunity to visit the US, which has been my dream for a long time. Last but not least, being paid for the work makes it easier for me to afford the stay in America.
As I mentioned before, I'm concerned with nature. Therefore I'd choose to protect species. I like animals and want to learn more about their lives and habitats. Even more important seems to me the preservation of plants. It's highly important for our ecosystem to protect endangered species. If more of them die out, further problems will arise for our environment.
In the last years I spent my holidays on my grandfather's farm where I looked after the cows and helped in the fields. So, hard physical work or bad weather shouldn't be a problem for me. There I also found out that I can handle animals pretty well. On the farm and at school I have always worked independently. I grasped new tasks rather quickly.
Finally I want to tell you I'd rather stay with a family, because it's my first stay in the US. Maybe the family could help me if I had any questions. Moreover this would give me the chance to come to know their customs and lifestyle and to make friends with Americans.
I hope to be considered for the project and I'm looking forward to your answer.

Yours faithfully
Simon Bauer

Task B – Blog entry

Hey guys, here's a little catch-up about what happened to us lately. Let's start at the beginning …

… when my friend Paul and I decided to go hiking in Yosemite National Park.
Our backpacking tour had led us to San Francisco and after some days in the big city we were longing for an adventure in nature. Paul suggested to visit Yosemite National Park, which was not too far away. Just going around in a bus with a group of tourists was not our style. So we went on a hiking tour. Both of us are keen on sports and this was the challenge we were looking for.
At the entrance of the park we saw an advert for a hotel about twenty miles away. Although it was quite far, we booked a room there. In the evening we were tired but happy to reach the place. We had a delicious meal and slept peacefully in our beds. Not knowing how far we would get on the next day we didn't look for a hotel in time. When it got dark we arrived

at a log cabin. There were no windows or doors. We simply sat down inside and ate our last sandwiches. Soon afterwards we fell asleep.
In the middle of the night we were woken by the barking of a dog and a voice. Someone was walking his pet at night. The dog lead must have been very long. Otherwise the dog couldn't have been able to enter the log cabin. Its wet nose sniffed our faces. We kept still. Nobody should find us in our hideaway. Luckily the man called off his dog and it obediently left without giving his secret away.
Not surprisingly I'd recommend future travellers to plan their trips more carefully. If you don't want to take your tent with you, find a hotel in time. Besides that, it is helpful to know where you can buy food and drinks. Then you needn't carry your heavy backpack over long distances. Finally, wear suitable clothes and good walking boots. Such a tour can become extremely exhausting.
All in all it was really exciting and a special experience.
Bye for now,
Peter

Notizen

Notizen

www.pauker.de

Auf der Suche nach mehr Übungsmaterial?

- ✔ Arbeitsheft mit 17 Texten und Audiotracks
- ✔ inklusive Lösungen
- ✔ alle Hördateien zum Download oder per QR-Code abrufbar
- ✔ zum selbstständigen Training des Hörverstehens
- ✔ vielfältige Aufgabenformate und alltagsnahe Themen

Hier geht es direkt zum Buch auf unserer Website.

9 783889 978677

hutt lernhilfen